Phenomenal Praise for
ANDREW M. GREELEY

continued . . .

ALSO BY ANDREW M. GREELEY

HAPPY
ARE THE
MERCIFUL

A BLACKIE
RYAN
NOVEL

ANDREW M. GREELEY

JOVE BOOKS, NEW YORK

HAPPY ARE THE MERCIFUL

A Jove Book / published by arrangement with
the author

PRINTING HISTORY
Jove edition / March 1992

Map by Heidi Hornaday.

ISBN: 0-515-10726-3

Jove Books are published by The Berkley Publishing Group,
200 Madison Avenue, New York, New York 10016.
The name "JOVE" and the "J" logo
are trademarks belonging to Jove Publications, Inc.

PRINTED IN THE UNITED STATES OF AMERICA

10 9 8 7 6 5

**For Jim Mahoney
—who knows all about Blackie**

The Beatitudes

THIS SERIES OF STORIES, featuring the Most Reverend (as he must now be called) John Blackwood Ryan, S.T.L., Ph.D., D.D. *(honoris causa)* is orchestrated around the Beatitudes from Jesus' Sermon on the Mount. A variant form is found in Luke's so-called Sermon on the Plain, which is accompanied by parallel Woes. I chose Matthew's version, which is probably later and derivative, because it is so much better known.

The Sermon on the Mount is not, according to the scripture scholars, an actual sermon Jesus preached but rather a compendium of His sayings and teachings, edited by the author of St. Matthew's Gospel, almost certainly from a pre-existing source compendium.

The Beatitudes represent, if not in exact words, an important component of the teaching of Jesus, but they should not be interpreted as a new list of Rules. Jesus taught that rules are of little use in our relationship with God. We do not constrain God's love by keeping rules, since that love is a freely given starting point in our relationship (a passionate love affair) with God. We keep rules because all communities need rules to stay together and because as ethical beings we should behave ethically, but that, according to Jesus, is a minor part of our relationship with God.

The Beatitudes are descriptive, not normative. They are a portrait of the Christian life as it becomes possible for those who believe in the Love of God as disclosed by Jesus. If we trust in God, we are then able to take the risks, the Beatitudes imply, never living them perfectly, of course, but growing and developing in their radiant goodness and experiencing the happiness of life that comes from such goodness.

From *Who's Who*

RYAN, JOHN BLACKWOOD. Priest; philosopher; born Evergreen Park, Il., September 17, 1945; s.R.Ad. Edward Patrick Ryan, USNR(ret.) and Kate Collins; A.B., St. Mary of the Lake Seminary, 1966; S.T.L., St. Mary of the Lake Seminary, 1970; Ph.D., Seabury Western Theological Seminary, 1980. Ordained Priest, Roman Catholic Church, 1970; Ass't Pastor, St. Fintan's Church, Chicago, 1970–1978; Instructor, classics, Quigley Seminary, 1970–1978; Rector, Holy Name Cathedral, 1978– ; created Domestic Prelate (Monsignor) 1983; ordained Bishop 1990; Author: *Salvation in Process: Catholicism and the Philosophy of Alfred North Whitehead*, 1980; *Truth in William James: An Irishman's Best Guess*, 1985; *Transcendental Empiricist: The Achievement of David Tracy*, 1989. Mem.Am. Philos. Asc., Soc.Sci. Stud.Rel., Chicago Yacht Club, Nat. Conf. Cath. Bshps. Address: Holy Name Cathedral Rectory, 732 North Wabash, Chicago, Il. 60611.

More's the pity, Sean Cronin is like no present or past Cardinal Archbishop of Chicago. John Blackwood Ryan is like no present or past auxiliary bishop of Chicago. All other characters are fictional, even those who are not fictional.

Using artistic license, I have changed for the purpose of this story two statutes of Illinois law. In God's Illinois, as opposed to mine in this story, a jury must decide on the death penalty. Moreover, after such a sentence there is an immediate mandatory appeal to the State Supreme Court.

Terry Goggin and Richard Daley provided technical information on the functioning of the Circuit Court of Cook County, but neither are responsible for any modifications or mistakes I have made. I must also apologize to Kelly Welch, the Corporation Counsel of the City of Chicago in God's world, for replacing him with Patrick T. "Packy" Ryan in my world; both are admirable and effective men in their respective worlds.

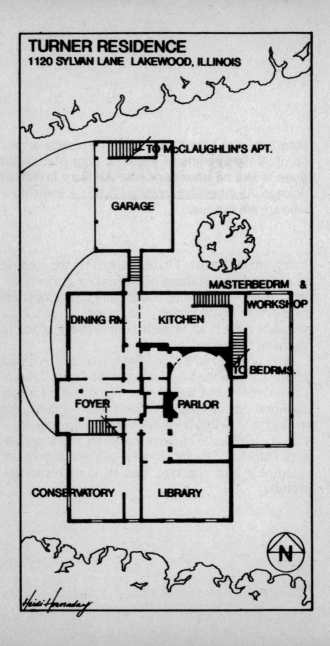

PROLOGUE

1

"IF SHE DIES, FATHER, IT WILL BE MY FAULT." THE YOUNG
man's handsome face was grim. "And now I'm convinced that she's innocent."

One felt that he looked familiar, the kind of man one had
seen somewhere in a painting or perhaps in a film. He might
have been a Florentine painter in the time of Lorenzo the
Magnificent. Or a courtier in the service of Cesare Borgia.
Or a decadent modern Roman in a Fellini film. Or a mob
lawyer in one of the multitudinous Godfather films.

Not much above medium height, thick, wavy hair parted
in the middle, perfect teeth, sallow skin, finely chiseled face,
troubled brown eyes, a quick and friendly smile, his impec-
cable three-piece black double-breasted suit with a hint of
chalk thread and his blue shirt with white collar also hinted
that he might be a model who would appear in a Ralph
Lauren advertisement in *GQ*.

In fact he was an assistant state's attorney for the County
of Cook, one of the more than half a thousand law school
graduates who were charged with the impossible task of protecting law and order in said county; and his name was
Terrence Guido Scanlan—his good looks and his middle

name from his maternal grandfather and his first and last name from his paternal grandfather.

He was from the West Side of Chicago (River Forest actually) and had attended Holy Cross College, two attributes which did not necessarily prove that he was an inferior species of human but which did raise some doubts in my South Side/Notre Dame mind.

"Indeed," I observed judiciously, not wanting to appear as fascinated as I was at the prospect of solving another problem for my Lord Cardinal, Sean Cronin, by the Grace of God and long-suffering patience of the Apostolic See, Archbishop of Chicago.

"Blackwood." That latter worthy, clad in crimson cape and cummerbund over a black cassock with crimson buttons, had stormed into my rooms at Holy Name Cathedral bearing two large dishes of chocolate chocolate chip ice cream. "I need a favor."

The ice cream was proof that he needed something. In my Lord Cronin's vocabulary the word "favor" implies something that he wanted you to do yesterday.

"Indeed," I said, looking up from the VGA screen on my Compaq 386/20 computer, on which I had been investigating the peculiarities of the Mandelbrot Set.

"There's a kid coming in who wants to talk to you about a problem, kid named Terry Scanlan. Assistant state's attorney."

He moved a stack of books from the least burdened chair in my office—about which my sibling Nancy (who writes science fiction stories for children) had said that it would make one of Charles Dickens's cluttered offices look neat—and collapsed into it.

As the years pass, Sean Cronin looks ever more like the wild Irish gallowglass warrior that he would have been in an earlier incarnation—lean, haggard, handsome, long blond hair turning gray, and normally hooded blue eyes. When the hoods recede and those eyes glow like fires on the peat bog, one thinks that Cardinal Cronin is either half-saint or half-mad.

Arguably both.

"Ah," I observed, turning off my Chaos program.

The Cardinal was devouring his share of ice cream, which I strongly suspected was larger than mine, beneath the poster of Baltimore Colt John Unitas that decorated my wall along with the other two Johns of my adolescence, Pope and President.

"Turner case."

"Indeed." I peered at him through my thick glasses.

"You know to whom the money reverts, if she is executed?"

"That fact has escaped me."

"The Catholic Bishop of Chicago, a Corporation Sole."

"How unseemly."

"Precisely . . . with all the troubles we have now the last thing the Church in this city needs is to be tied up in a murder scandal."

"Phone calls from your brother in Christ Herr Kardinal Josef Ratzinger asking why you were permitting the simple faithful to be scandalized in this fashion?"

He winced at the thought and muttered an obscenity of the sort one does not expect to hear from a prince of the Church.

"Thinks she didn't do it."

"Interesting. Is he married?"

"Of course not."

"Hormones?"

He waved a spoonful of chocolate delight at me. "Sure. She's a pretty kid. And he's an unmarried young male. But that's not the point."

"The point is?"

"I don't think she did it either."

"Hormones."

His eyes shone manically. "As you would say, arguably."

"You know her then?"

"She's on one of my boards."

"Indeed."

"But that's not really the point." He polished off the ice cream and jumped to his feet, the hint of battle pumping adrenaline through his circulatory system. "The point is that the Archdiocese ought not to be mixed up in a murder case."

"There was the case of one of your predecessors of happy memory."

"Which one?" He turned at the door to glare at me.

"The one who is reliably believed to have been killed by one of his priests for cheating at poker on a Palm Sunday evening in the last century."

"I don't play poker." He spun to leave.

"Not with cards."

"Oh yes," he grinned wildly, "it seems to be a locked room case, two locked rooms, I'm told."

He was well aware of my fatal weakness for locked room phenomena.

"Indeed!"

"See to it, Blackwood!" He stormed down the corridor, crimson robes trailing behind him.

Later that day, trying not to rub my hands together in satisfaction, I said to young Terry Scanlan, "I've read about the case of course—who in this city has not?—and heard summaries, doubtless inaccurate, on television. But why don't you refresh my aging memory?"

"I prosecuted the case, Father, excuse me, Bishop, and now I'm convinced that she didn't do it . . . but I can't prove it."

His brown eyes glistened with the moisture that precedes tears.

TERRY SCANLAN'S STORY

2

MY BATTERED 1987 CHEVY CELEBRITY CRUNCHED SLOWLY down the newly plowed road on a frigid Saturday morning in January. The sun had just appeared above the horizon to wash the frozen slate that was Lake Michigan with a rose glow. A crystal blue sky had chased away the shades of night. Fifteen below zero, the weather report had said. The wind had died so with the wind chill factor it was only twenty below. The high today would be minus two. Tomorrow it would be warmer, with a chance of more snow, possible accumulation six to eight more inches. Chicago would barely have dug out from one blizzard when it would be assaulted with another.

Thirty-six hours before, the same forecasters had warned of a possibility of one to two inches accumulation. They had missed by six inches, most of it delivered between the hours of ten last night and four this morning.

Why, I asked myself as I had many times during the brutal winter, was I not practicing law in Dade County or San Diego County or Alemeda County or Pima County? Why was I poking along a side street in the North Shore suburb of Lakewood, looking for a mansion in which a double murder was alleged?

Always careful—alleged. Innocent till proven guilty.

In theory.

You have to understand up front that a state's attorney in the county of Cook becomes bloodthirsty pretty early in his career. In almost all cases we get, the identity of the criminal is obvious. Our only questions are about whether we can find enough proof to obtain conviction. Questions of guilt or innocence rarely arise. Once we make a decision to seek an indictment, we assume guilt and set out to prove it.

Innocence is a matter for the jury to decide.

There isn't any other way to do it.

"A winner this time, Terry," Dan Hills, the first assistant state's attorney, had trumpeted into my phone when he woke me from my monastic sleep. "Double murder. Lakewood. Prominent people. Turner. 1120 Sylvan. Lots of publicity. Get up there and take care of it."

"No."

I hung up.

He rang again. "What the hell's wrong with you?"

"I've resigned. I'm going into private practice."

I hung up again.

And got out of bed and answered the phone for the third time.

"I quit," I told my boss. "I'm going over to City Hall to work for Rich."

I hung up yet again.

Not a bad idea, and not an idea that I hadn't considered often in the last several weeks.

The phone rang. Dan Hills was persistent.

"Are you kidding?"

"Yes."

I hung up for the fourth time.

Lakewood is not familiar territory for me. It took me a long time, even when the light of dawn finally appeared, to find Sylvan Lane. I thought that I'd at least give these rich North Shore suburbs credit for one thing: they were efficient at plowing their streets after snowstorms.

Not that my own home suburb, River Forest, was any less efficient. We weren't quite so affluent however.

The road, or lane as I supposed it should be called, took a gentle curve toward the lake. I didn't have to look for a house number to know that I was at 1120 Sylvan Lane. The house that loomed up in front of me looked like it had been taken from a Christmas card—big, sprawling Georgian with a vast snow-covered lawn, evergreen trees all around, curving drive up to the immense portico, not so much an English country house as an American architect's fantasy of an English country house, a Disney World English country house—with maybe Sir Winston up from Westminster for a weekend of drinking.

Today it glittered with icicles and snowdrifts against the splendid blue background of the sky and back light from a rising sun. Good opening for a film.

The vehicles crowded in front of the house suggested that I had been beaten by Channel 2 and Channel 5, the State Police, the County Police, the Lakewood Town Police, and the Cook County medical examiner. The van of the last-named pulled out just as I turned into the drive.

"Where you think you're going, Mister?" a red-faced Lakewood cop, bundled in a big down jacket and a thick fur hat shouted at me.

A car like mine wouldn't under ordinary circumstances be permitted to stop in Lakewood.

I rolled down my window and flashed my ID.

"Scanlan. State's attorney."

He inspected my card suspiciously and then, as if it were against his better judgment, waved me on.

I don't like suburban cops. They are more honest, better

educated, more articulate, and create the illusion of being more professional than Chicago cops. In fact, compared to their colleagues in the city, they know from nothing about what crime really is because there are so few crimes committed in their jurisdictions.

How many murders are there in Lakewood in a year? Even in a decade?

They would be, nonetheless, arrogant and supercilious to the seemingly young and inexperienced assistant state's attorney.

I didn't care. I was the one who would decide whether there would be an indictment.

"Cold enough for you, Terry?" a TV cameraperson asked me.

"Refreshing, Lynn. How are the kids?"

Always be nice to the TV crews, Dan Hills tells me. He claims he learned it from Cook County's former state's attorney and now Chicago's mayor.

"Who the fuck are you?" demanded yet another Lakewood cop at the door.

"State's attorney," I snapped at him, not bothering with the card this time. "Who's in charge of this disgrace?"

"Chief Stewart." He was taken aback by my anger.

"Yeah. Fucking amateur."

"He's in the parlor."

The "parlor" was a room large enough for the junior prom. Gray and royal blue, First Empire furnishing, a big rural canvas over the fireplace. All tasteful and expensive— and trite.

The Chief, in a uniform appropriate for *The Student Prince*, stood in the middle of the room, surrounded by various Lakewood dicks, uniformed and not, some crime lab people, and other assorted hangers-on. They all were wearing overcoats or parkas or down jackets and one variety or another of fur hat, although they were inside a house. Their boots had left trails of slush on the Persian carpet, whose value could keep an inner-city Catholic school going for a couple of years.

The Chief was a movie cop, tall, handsome, solid, full head of black hair. Bet he worked out every morning before breakfast. The thought of it made me remember how tired I was. His light blue uniform with four stars on his collar was, I thought, pretty.

"Who the fuck are you?" he demanded.

Not much imagination in their vocabulary.

"Scanlan. State's attorney. What are you running here? A fucking TV program? Clear out that driveway. Do you want a defense attorney to argue before a sympathetic jury that we intimidated witnesses and suspects because we permitted TV cameras at the door of a murder site?"

I've never heard a defense attorney use that argument. But if you want to establish that you're in charge, you come in and act high-handed and unreasonable.

A Chicago cop would have laughed in my face. But this was not a Chicago cop.

"Yes, sir. Right away." He turned to rush toward the door and then paused and stuck out his big hand. "Good to know you."

"Likewise." I shook hands with him and flashed my Robert Kennedy grin (as my mother calls it). From that point on I owned Chief Stewart.

"Bodies gone?" I said to one of the other cops.

"Meat wagon carried them away."

"Mode of death?"

"Throats cut. Sharp instrument. Medical examiner thought it might be a medical scalpel."

"Medical examiner take away the bodies?"

"Just left."

"Yeah." I sounded skeptical because I was still wearing my skeptic's mask.

"Time of death?"

"Early last night. Not before seven-thirty. One of them talked to a friend on the phone at that time. Friend tried to call back all night."

"Yeah." This time I almost sneered.

Look, if you're the state's attorney from Chicago, it's a role you gotta play. The problem is not that I'm good at it. The problem is that I was good at it the first time I tried.

"Alleged perpetrator in custody?"

"Daughter. Only kid. Kind of a looker. Medical school."

I rolled my eyes. The media would love this one. Sex and gore. Can't beat it.

"She confess yet?"

He shrugged. "Chief read her Miranda. She called her lawyer. He's upstairs with her now."

"She do it?"

"Who else? She inherits it all."

"On coke?"

"Can't tell. Wouldn't be surprised. Seems all spaced out."

"Yeah."

I started to remove the ski parka that served as my coat in the winter—my coat when I was playing state's attorney. I shivered. Damn cold, even inside. I put the coat back on.

"Anything stolen?"

"An empty safe. Jewelry. Cleaned out."

I whistled.

Chief Stewart returned with the self-satisfied air of a man who had done what he'd been wanting to do all along.

Now I played diffident. "Sorry to be late, Chief. You folks clean up your streets real good, but where I come from they don't run in circles and curves."

Poor little kid from Taylor Street, see?

"No problem," he said genially, "no problem at all."

"Can you brief me someplace quiet before you talk to the alleged perpetrator, if the man lets her talk?"

"Sure. Let's go into the library. Men, I'll be in the library when Mr. Parks comes down."

"Chandler Parks?" I asked the Chief.

"He's a neighbor, Mr. Scanlan . . ."

"Terry . . . Chandler Parks, *Senior*?"

"Yessir. Of Rollins, Parks, McBride, and Jonathan."

We walked into the oak-paneled library, which would have served nicely for a medium-sized city. The couches and chairs were smooth maroon leather and the rug on the polished hardwood floor was a red-and-cream oriental. The books didn't look like they had been worn out from reading. The library was for smoking cigars and drinking cognac, behavior in which I suspected the Turners did not indulge.

"Where do they get their money?"

"Electronics . . . Is Mr. Parks a good attorney?"

"Asshole."

I would not want my life hanging on his advice. However, he might find a good trial lawyer for a client because he could have the sense to ask his junior partners for a suggestion.

We sat on either side of a desk that was either a Sheraton or a good imitation. My sister Beth would have been able to tell at a glance.

"Let's have it." I sighed.

"I think she did it," he began, "though right now it all looks circumstantial."

He'd seen too many cop movies.

"My boss, Dan Hills, will make that decision. He doesn't believe in wasting taxpayers' money on cases you can't win. He also thinks it's embarrassing to lose."

The son of a bitch knew this would be a big one. That's

why he woke me the day before I was supposed to leave on a vacation. Keep the disillusioned young man in the office by hooking him on a big one.

"There are a few interesting little quirks, like the locked door."

"Let's have it, Chief."

It was interesting all right. The locked door especially. And the undisturbed snow.

3

_____

THE DECEASED WERE JOHN AND MARY TURNER, CAUCA-
sian, in their middle sixties. They had died in bed, their
carotid arteries severed by a very sharp instrument. Their
bedroom was in a large two-storey suite that had been added
at the rear of the house, facing the lake. Access to the suite
was obtained by climbing to the second floor of the main
house and then walking down a staircase to the entrance of
the addition. A second set of stairs from the addition went
down to the garage. Entrance to the addition itself was
through a single large oak door. The door had an elaborate
lock, manufactured in Switzerland, which could only be
opened or closed when the door was shut.

"What's that all about?" I demanded. Already the case
was beginning to look very messy.

"They wanted privacy. Mr. Turner was an engineer. Mrs.
Turner was his assistant. Their money came from designs
he developed. He was afraid of thieves I guess. Whenever
he was in a creative mood, they locked themselves in
there. Wait till you see it."

"Yeah."

Mrs. Turner had phoned her friend and neighbor Mrs.
Rodney Kincaid the previous evening about seven-thirty.

17

She said that they were working on a new invention which would revolutionize automotive engineering and that therefore she could not participate in a protest scheduled for Monday. There was a separate phone in the addition the number of which the Turners had given to only a few people. Mrs. Kincaid knew that the Turners did not watch television or listen to the radio when they were at work in the addition or workshop as they called it. When she heard the sudden winter storm warnings at eight o'clock, she called them to urge them to prepare for it by turning up the heat in their suite. There was no answer. She called repeatedly for the next several hours and still received no answer. She went to bed but was unable to sleep because she knew they were both in relatively poor health, the husband with a weak heart and the wife with diabetes. Finally, at three in the morning, she got out of bed and peered through the snow and the trees at the Turner house. The workshop, mostly glass, was lit up, she later reported, like there was a party inside. She called them again on the private number and still there was no answer.

Even though her husband thought she was foolish to worry about the Turners—he said they were strange people anyway—she then called the number of the main house and awakened Clare Turner from bed.

Clare Turner, a fourth year student at Loyola Medical School, had returned about five after an exam and after picking up her dog at a vet's. The housekeeper, Mrs. Dermot McLaughlin, told her that her parents were at work in the workshop. Miss Turner, accustomed to such behavior, drank a bowl of soup and ate a ham and cheese sandwich, read a novel by Margaret Atwood, and went to bed.

When she was awakened by the phone call from Mrs. Kincaid, Miss Turner went to the door of the workshop and pounded on it for some time. Then she awakened the McLaughlins, who lived in a four-room apartment over the garage, on the intercom. Dermot McLaughlin, the chauffeur, tried to batter the door down. Unable to do that, he had to drill a hole in the door and cut out a panel with a saw. Miss Turner then was able to reach inside the door and open the lock. They rushed in and saw that the floor of the bedroom was covered with blood. Miss Turner, despite being very sick, rushed to the phone and called the police.

The murder weapon had not yet been recovered.

"Why couldn't they have opened the door from the outside?" I asked, liking this case less and less.

"There is only one key and it was inside the workshop."

"What the hell does that mean?"

"You've got to go to Switzerland to get a copy made and they won't make it unless you sign all documents."

"So they had a copy?"

"Miss Turner denies it."

"How did the perpetrator get in?"

Chief Stewart shrugged. "I told you there were some interesting aspects of the case. I think she did it. Who else? What did the McLaughlins have to gain? They had a gold mine here. There was no else in the house. But, like I say, it's an odd one. Then there's the snow."

"The snow?"

"Yeah. When we got here this morning we were right behind the snowplow. There weren't any tracks ahead of us and no trace of footprints anywhere around the house. It's hard to see how anyone coming up to the house after eight last night and before four this morning could have got in and got out without leaving some traces."

"And if they did get in, they wouldn't be able to get into the annex without the key which was already inside?"

"You got it."

Yeah, I had it all right.

"Why don't you go upstairs and see if Miss Turner will have a few words with us?"

A smart lawyer would say no way. Even a mediocre lawyer would want to think about it. But Chandler Parks was an asshole. Maybe he'd let her talk and we'd get something.

Otherwise we'd have no case at all.

4

"**M**R. PARKS," THE CHIEF SMILED GENIALLY, "THIS IS Terry Scanlan from the State's Attorney's Office."

Chandler Parks was your compleat North Shore WASP lawyer, tall, trim, handsome, elegantly dressed in a dark gray three-piece—worth at least a thousand—even at this hour on a frozen Saturday morning. His silver hair was carefully combed, his mustache neatly trimmed, and his Harvard tie impeccably knotted. He was clearly an important man—until you noticed that his eyes were a little vague.

A real asshole.

"Obviously not your real name." He turned away from my outstretched hand.

Score a point for him.

"Miss Turner, this is Mr. Scanlan."

The young woman nodded.

At first I thought she was a teenager, jeans, a white Loyola sweatshirt, navy blue down jacket, sneakers, hair tied in a ponytail, no makeup—she could have been one of my sisters routed out of bed early in the morning. Rumpled and frumpy, I thought, hardly the looker that the cop had promised.

"I see no reason," Parks cleared his throat so as to warn us that he was going to say something important, "why my cli-

21

ent cannot answer your questions. I must note, Chief, that I see no grounds for going so far as to give her a Miranda warning at this point."

"Her parents have been murdered in their bed, Mr. Parks," I said briskly. "She is, I believe, their major heir. I'm sure that a lawyer as sophisticated as yourself understands that's enough reason to give her the option of having a lawyer present."

Point and counterpoint. The Chief departed to find a note taker.

The suspect's facial expression had not changed when I hinted that she might be suspected of killing her parents. Only as the conversation continued did I realize that my first impression was wrong. Clare Turner was an archduchess, albeit an icy one. She was as tall as I am, slender and supple with naturally graceful movements and firmly sculpted breasts. Her auburn hair, round face, and high cheekbones suggested something almost Slavic. She was totally composed, no sign of grief or fear or any other emotion. Behind rimless glasses her gray eyes seemed empty.

I had seen those empty eyes before; they belonged almost always to the psychopathic criminal, a person devoid of conscience.

I disliked her instantly. She's a spoiled rich kid, I told myself, who slit her parents' throats for the money to sustain her drug habit.

Now I ask myself whether even then I was hiding a subliminal sexual reaction that had hit me in the gut—among other places.

"We have only a few questions, Miss Turner," the Chief said as we arranged ourselves around a coffee table in the library and a woman patrol officer set up a tape recorder and opened a notebook.

"Excuse me, Chief," I interrupted, "I wonder, Ms. Turner, if I might open the drapes? It's pretty dark in here."

She shrugged indifferently.

The drapes were maroon and heavy, matching the plush carpet. When I pulled the drawstring, frigid sunlight flooded the room. Everyone squinted. That was the idea. The sun would be behind my head and in Clare Turner's eyes.

"Well, then, I guess we're ready."

"With your permission," the young woman's mouth seemed barely to move, "I'll ask Moire to make us some coffee. It's a very cold morning."

She didn't wait for permission, but rose, walked across the room, and spoke into the house phone. When she returned she sat in another chair, her face out of the sunlight. If she realized that she had scored a point against me her blank face and stoic eyes did not reveal it.

Or was there a sudden quick glint in those lifeless brown swamps?

A smart one, I thought. Her parents are dead and she's thinking about how to arrange the scene.

Finally we let the Chief begin.

"You returned to this house at what time last night, Miss Turner?"

"About five, I believe. I had finished an exam earlier in the afternoon, picked up my dog at the vet's and drove up here."

"You don't live with your parents, Ms. Turner," I interrupted her.

"No."

"Why not?"

"I attend Loyola Medical School in Maywood. It's much too long a drive from here especially in the rush hours. I come home on weekends. With Fiona."

I had no right to ask that question. Probably I would not

even have the right to ask it on the witness stand in a trial. Chandler Parks let me get away with it. This case would be like taking candy away from a little kid. I couldn't believe my good luck.

The luck would continue all the way through.

"Fiona?"

"My dog. I live in an apartment on South Harlem in Oak Park. Alone. The dog is for protection."

How long would it take on the I-90 to go around the city and get up here? Half hour when there was no traffic. I filed that for reference.

"Did your family approve of you living away from home?"

"I think they would have preferred that I lived here."

"Well, now." The Chief was, I think, disturbed by how much I was getting away with. "What did you do when you came home?"

"The first thing was to run with Fiona. She doesn't get much exercise during the week. Neither do I."

"Then?"

"Moire—Ms. McLaughlin, our housekeeper—told me that my parents were in the workshop. I know they don't like to be bothered in there. So I ate a sandwich and a bowl of soup, took a shower and then curled up in my study with a book. I was tired from the test and from the long drive home and from the exercise. I went to bed about nine-thirty."

She spoke quietly and impassively as if she were reading a paper at an academic meeting.

"Did you get along well with your parents?" I cut in again.

Again Parks was silent.

"As well as most unmarried women my age do. We had our differences. We loved one another."

Her eyes seemed to be somewhere in another universe.

"What kind of differences?"

"They were much older than I am. They wanted to live to see grandchildren. They wanted me to be a socialite. I wanted to be a doctor."

"What specialty?"

"Psychiatry."

"You went to sleep promptly, Miss Turner?" the Chief continued doggedly.

"I was very tired."

"And you did not wake until you received Mrs. Kincaid's phone call?"

"That is correct."

"What was your reaction?"

"April Kincaid is a bit of a pest and a bit of bore. This time she was right. I told her I would check the workshop. My parents could become so involved in their work that they would not notice the change of weather or the time of day."

"The weather was important?"

"They kept the temperature in the workshop low to help them remain awake while they were working. It's mostly glass, you see. My father liked to have a sense of spaciousness while he hunched over his computer. They would be unaware of a snowstorm or a sudden drop in temperature."

"I see. What did you do after the call?"

"Excuse me for a moment. Thank you very much, Ms. McLaughlin. Sugar, Chief? Mr. Scanlan? Chandler? Very well, after the call, I pounded on the door for some minutes. It's a thick door, but they should have been able to hear my pounding and my shouts."

"You're welcome, dear." Ms. McLaughlin, a handsome, motherly woman in her middle fifties, patted Clare Turner on the shoulder.

"Were you concerned?" I asked.

She did not look at me. Or at anyone.

"Certainly. My parents were both in poor health."

"Then what did you do?"

"I called the McLaughlins' apartment and told Dermot what was happening. He came over in a couple of minutes. He was unable to break the door down or to remove the hinges. He had to saw a hole through the door."

"Why didn't you use a key, Ms. Turner?" I asked.

"There is only one key, Mr. Scanlan."

"Surely that can't be the case."

A normal human would have been furious at my harassment. Clare Turner didn't seem to give a damn.

"It is the case, however. My father loved gadgets. The lock was a very special Swiss gadget. It also provided a security that he felt he needed for his inventions . . ."

"But no security system in the house?" I interrupted her.

"No."

"Why not?"

"There used to be one. It kept going off when he crossed a barrier accidently. So he had it torn out."

"Wasn't that a little eccentric?"

"Was it?"

"I'm asking you."

Sparks were leaping back and forth between us, a current that was carrying many different messages—dislike, antagonism, desire, attraction.

"He did not like distractions. The security system for the house distracted him. I don't think it was eccentric to remove it."

"I see."

"He was, you see, much more an inventor than an administrator. He retired recently as president of Turner Electronics, so he could concentrate on inventions."

She was opening up a little.

"But only one key?"

"The lock makers would provide others, but only if you

sent them the owner's certificate with several signatures. I'm sure the certificate is somewhere in the workshop."

"What did you do when the hole was cut in the door?" Stewart continued.

"I opened it and rushed in."

"And saw?"

"My parents on their beds, their carotid arteries cut."

Her voice did not waver, her expression did not change. A jury would eat her alive.

"And you felt?" I interjected.

"Sick."

"No grief?"

"My parents are very private people, Mr. Scanlan. So am I a very private person."

"Then what did you do?"

"I called the Lakewood Police, Chief. And Dr. Cline. And St. John's Rectory."

"Are you not almost a doctor yourself, Ms. Turner?"

"Almost isn't good enough, Mr. Scanlan, not under these circumstances, not when it's your family, not ever really."

"At that time did you think your parents were dead?"

"I had not the slightest doubt about that."

"Then what did you do after you made the calls?"

"I waited in the parlor for the people I had called to come. The police came first. With the snowplow. Father Mike was right behind them. I took him to the workshop."

"Was anything missing?"

"My mother kept her jewelry in the safe where Dad had his designs. When I brought the priest into the room, the safe was open. I glanced in it because I was worried about the designs. I noticed that his papers seemed to be there but Mother's jewelry was missing."

"All of it?"

"All of it."

"How much was it worth, Ms. Turner?" I asked.

"It's difficult to say, Mr. Scanlan. I assume that our insurance agent has a list, is that not so, Chandler?"

The asshole nodded. "I believe that the valuation would be in excess of a hundred thousand dollars."

"You're sure that you did not see your parents until you discovered their bodies?" Stewart asked gently.

"Quite sure."

"How do you think the killer entered and escaped?"

She hesitated. "I don't know. He would have had to come in the front door of the house, ring the front doorbell unless he had a key. Then he would have had to come up the stairs to the second floor and then down the back stairs to the workshop. He would have had to persuade my parents to let him in. Perhaps it was someone they knew."

"How would the murderer have escaped?" I demanded.

"It would have been impossible for him to have escaped," she said flatly. "The door was locked from the inside."

"There was no one in the room when you and Mr. McLaughlin burst in?"

"That is correct, Mr. Scanlan."

"But they're dead, Ms. Turner. And the killer is gone."

"I am aware of both facts, Mr. Scanlan."

The coffee was excellent, but I am not Special Agent Dale Cooper.

And she was not Lara Flynn Boyle. More mysterious. Perhaps more voluptuous too for that matter.

"How do you explain them?"

"I have no idea."

"Do you use narcotics, Ms. Turner?"

The woman patrol officer lifted her pen from her notebook: she knew my question was thoroughly outrageous.

"You mean illegal narcotics?" She glanced at her cup of coffee.

"Yes."

"I smoked marijuana a couple of times when I was in high school and snorted coke three times when I was in college. No more and nothing since then."

"Why not?"

"I did not like the loss of control."

"A few more details and we'll be finished, Miss Turner." The Chief was obviously angry at me. "Where did you attend high school and college?"

"Lakewood High and Barat."

"Lived at home?" I snapped.

"Yes."

"And when were you born?"

She paused and glanced at Parks. He didn't give her any hints, the idiot.

"I don't know."

"You don't know?" I blurted.

"No, Mr. Scanlan, I don't know. I was adopted you see. Not as a neonate, but as an infant. In 1968. I'm not sure how old I was. Perhaps about two. I do have some memories of a time before I was part of this family. I assume that I am twenty-three or twenty-four."

"Have you made any attempts to find out about your life before adoption?"

She did not reply for a couple of moments. Then she said in almost a whisper, "Yes."

"And you learned?"

"Nothing."

"Nothing."

"That's right, Mr. Scanlan, nothing . . . Will you investigate that subject?"

"Perhaps."

"If you learn any more than I did, I hope it would not be unethical for you to tell me."

For just that second or two she seemed vulnerable. I admit my heart action increased.

"If we can, we will. Of course."

An adopted daughter who had murdered her parents for the money to sustain a drug habit! Great case!

But damn little evidence other than circumstantial.

A young male patrol officer appeared at the door and beckoned the Chief out of the library. Moire came and removed the coffee cups and saucers.

"Would you like a roll, Mr. Scanlan?" The archduchess being gracious to a serf.

"No, thank you, Ms Turner."

Looking back on that moment, I suppose that's when my hormones began to work—and I began to overcompensate for them.

You see, I've always been a romantic. I dream about archduchesses. Moreover my search for a wife had been monumentally unsuccessful. I was lonely and hungry.

Actually she had not told us anything incriminating. I'd have to check all the facts out anyway. She'd saved me some trouble.

Maybe she knew that and didn't care.

The Chief signaled me into the corridor.

"Look at this!" He held up a plastic case inside of which there was an olive-drab shoulder pack of the sort that college students use. "We found it in her Porsche in the garage."

"What's in it?"

He tilted the bag so I could see. "A scalpel covered with blood, plastic gloves of the sort doctors use, and a whole lot of diamonds and rubies and pearls."

"Wow!"

"It's your call." He looked at me evenly. "Should we confront her?"

"Nothing to lose. Asshole in there won't stop us."

"If you say so."

"Do you recognize this bag, Ms. Turner?" I asked when we reentered the library.

"It looks like one of my book bags."

"Did you use it yesterday?"

"No, I did not."

She seemed utterly unperturbed by the question.

"Your car is the Porsche?"

"It is."

The woman patrol officer with the tape recorder glared at me. Sisterhood is powerful even if you're a cop.

"Would it surprise you to know that this bag was found in the front seat of your car?"

"It would. I didn't put it there."

"Would you care to tell me what's inside it?"

She stood up and walked over to where the Chief was holding the bag in the plastic bag. "Tilt it a little, Mr. Stewart, so I can see."

I scurried around to get a look at her face.

"What do you see, Ms. Turner?"

She did not bat an eye.

"I see a scalpel with blood on it, medical gloves and some of my mother's jewels."

"How do you explain their presence in your book bag in your car?"

"I have no explanation."

"Is it your scalpel, Ms. Turner?"

"I don't own a scalpel, Mr. Scanlan. Doctors do not carry them like they would a stethoscope. I want to be a psychiatrist not a surgeon."

"And the gloves?"

"I don't use those kind of gloves. I never bring the ones I do use home."

"And the jewels?"

"Mr. Scanlan." She did not sound angry or offended or even exasperated and I thought I saw the glint in her eyes again. "Those would be at the most only a tiny fraction of my mother's precious stones."

5

"**S**HOULD I TAKE HER IN AND BOOK HER?" CHIEF STEWART asked me when Clare Turner and her lawyer, against whom she had grounds for a malpractice suit, had left the library.

I thought about it. The snow and the cold would preempt all other news over the weekend. We'd get better coverage if we waited till Monday. We also might have more evidence. I'd be able to consult with Dan Hills.

I'm ashamed now of the thoughts about TV. They showed how jaded I had become. Not much idealism left.

"Not now. She's not going anywhere. Let's see if her prints are on the scalpel."

Clare Turner left with her lawyer "for a friend's house," still showing no signs of grief or fear.

"Let's talk to the McLaughlins," I said to the Chief. "I want to see what kind of witnesses they're going to make."

As it turned out they would make very good witnesses indeed—an Irish immigrant couple in their late middle years, attractive, articulate, respectful, with just a touch of wit lurking behind their words. Dermot McLaughlin might have been a stevedore, instead of a chauffeur; bald with a thick mustache, he was a giant barrel of a man with arms like

33

pine trees and fists like pile drivers. He was a few pounds overweight, but even his paunch seemed more muscle than fat.

His wife was a wisp of a woman, hardly more than five feet tall with flashing blue eyes, a long thin nose, and a grimly determined jaw, a character from one of Sean O'Casey's plays. She was clearly in charge and did almost all the talking in a high-pitched voice that was hard to turn off.

"Sure, isn't it a terrible thing to happen to such lovely people and themselves giving us a chance at this wonderful job after they met us when we were tending to the castle they rented in Ireland? And the poor thing herself, isn't it a terrible shame to be so cruel to your parents, and herself spending all that time at the doctor's? Sure, isn't the poor child sick in the head and not to blame for what she does?"

"Miss Turner sees a psychiatrist?"

"Doesn't she see your head doctor, and herself a woman too, four days a week? And weren't her parents thinking that was an awful waste of money?"

"She had to ask her parents for the money for the psychiatrist?"

"Weren't they the most generous ma and da in the world and themselves giving her whatever she wanted, even paying for her medical school tuition? Wasn't all she had to do was ask them?"

"They gave her whatever money she needed as soon as she asked?"

"Weren't they good parents now? And like all good parents, didn't they keep her waiting for a few days or weeks, just so she could learn the meaning of not having everything she wanted as soon as she wanted it?"

"I see."

"And haven't I been saying all along, Dermot, haven't I

been saying no good would come from sending one like that to medical school?"

"Medical school."

Dermot was apparently one of those Irish men who assented to whatever their wives said, by repeating the last two words of her sentences.

"Now didn't I say, Dermot, didn't I say that she's too spoiled and lazy to be a doctor? Didn't I say, if I said it once I said it a thousand times, didn't I say that doctors work hard and that one has never worked an honest day in her whole life?"

"Whole life."

"Mind you," Moire McLaughlin veered off on another track, "she's always been nice to us. 'Please' and 'thank you' and 'Mr. McLaughlin' and 'Mrs. McLaughlin,' just as nice as you please, poor dear."

"Poor dear."

"You feel sympathy for her?"

A good defense attorney would try to trip Moire up as she raced ahead, make her look like a babbling woman. He'd have his work cut out for him.

"Ah, don't I feel terrible sorry for her? I said to my Dermot, didn't I now, Dermot, with all that money why study to be a doctor? Wouldn't she have been much better off married to a nice young man, and weren't there lots of them around too and herself a bit on the large side if you take my meaning?"

"She had many suitors?"

"Scads of them. And weren't they nice boys, every single one of them?"

She turned to her husband for confirmation.

"One of them." This time it took three words for him to confirm his wife's statement.

"Just the kind of boys her parents were hoping for. Ah,

Mr. Scanlan, they so wanted to be able to live to see their grandchildren. 'Twas all they could talk about. And herself just laughing like it was a grand joke." She began to sniffle. "Poor dear people."

"Does Clare have many friends?"

"Sure, does she have any friends at all except that brute of a dog?"

"Fiona?"

"A terrible big and noisy and mean animal, if you ask me. Wasn't I saying to herself, ah, God be good to her, that I'd not have that beast in my house?"

"Is the dog still around, Chief?"

"Miss Turner took her along, Terry. She is the biggest dog I have ever seen."

"Doesn't she talk about her friends at the medical school all the time?" Moire McLaughlin raced on. "But, haven't I been saying all along, haven't I now, Dermot, haven't I been saying all along, that it's a grand strange thing that we never see any of them up here and this such a super house for entertaining?"

"For entertaining," Dermot agreed.

"Were her arguments with her parents violent?"

"Now what would you mean by violent?" Moire's shrewd blue eyes considered me carefully. "Would she ever shout at them or they at her? Weren't they all quiet people? Wouldn't it have been better altogether if they did shout some of the time and the weekends when she was home so tense like that you'd want to scream at them and not a word being spoken at dinner from the beginning to the end?"

"I see."

"And them taking her off the streets when she was a mere orphan waif."

"Literally?"

"Ah, no," she winked at me, "only in a manner of speaking."

"I understand."

"They wouldn't have lived many more years anyway, and both of them, the poor dears, God be good to them, in such bad health. And weren't they working on this new invention of himself just so there would be plenty of money for that ungrateful child for the rest of her life?"

"A tragedy."

"She's a cold one, isn't she now, Dermot? Polite and respectful, like I say, but no emotions at all, at all, like a sphinx, in a manner of speaking."

"Cold, is she?" I had slipped over into Irishspeak.

"Haven't I said that? And hasn't that Dr. Murphy made her even worse? Cold and contentious, isn't she, Dermot? Isn't it Dr. Murphy this and Dr. Murphy that, Dr. Murphy all the time?"

"All the time."

"Dr. Murphy is Ms. Turner's psychiatrist?"

"Haven't I said so? And, if you ask me, isn't that the woman that put the idea into her head to become such a doctor herself? I ask you now, Mr. Scanlan, is that any kind of a job for a woman?"

A woman psychiatrist named Murphy. Could it be Mary Kathleen Murphy? I would want no part of her on the witness stand arguing diminished responsibility. One of my ambitious colleagues, convinced that he could twist any psychiatrist into knots on the stand, especially a woman psychiatrist, had blown a trial when he tried to take on that woman.

Would they plead diminished responsibility? Maybe we could plea bargain on those grounds, a nice neat solution. Guilty but mentally ill. Twenty years. Or not guilty by reason of insanity. Indefinite time in a mental institution but a review every ninety days. It would depend on more evidence—her prints on the scalpel for example. That was a long shot unless Clare Turner was clumsy.

She didn't seem to be a clumsy young woman; quite the contrary, she seemed almost neurotically self-possessed. Yet the crime looked like a clumsy one.

"Might I ask," I pretended to hesitate, "whether the Turners were generous employers?"

"Generous, is it?" Tears formed in Moire's eyes. "Generous is it?" Her voice rose. "Would you call it generous if people paid us together a salary in six figures and room and board?"

"Six figures is it?" I was getting good at Irishspeak.

"Haven't I said so? Weren't they the most generous people in all the world?"

"Weren't they now?" I agreed.

No reason to kill a golden-egg-laying goose like that, was there now?

"And isn't it all over now?" She began to sob. Her husband led her gently out of the library.

"Is that kind of salary out of line for servants up here?" I asked the Chief.

"Somewhat," he agreed, "but the good ones who are few and far between I'm told do all right for themselves. And the chauffeur was probably paid by the firm as part of Mr. Turner's retirement package. The housekeeper probably dusted the workshop which made her partially a business expense too."

"We may be in the wrong professions, Chief."

"I've often thought that." He sighed heavily.

"They don't seem to have any solid motive for murder," I observed. "Even if the jewels are worth a hundred big ones, they'd get less than a third of that from a fence. They'd make that in a couple of months here."

"That was my line of thought too."

"What's the world coming too, Chief," I sighed this time, "when servants use bankers' language. Six figures indeed."

"This is Lakewood, Ter," he replied.

I checked the chronology the McLaughlins had given Chief Stewart. John and Mary Turner had withdrawn into the workshop at the beginning of the week. Moire tried to bring meals in to them on a fairly regular basis, but the "poor things" didn't know day from night. She had brought supper in about five o'clock the night before. She had to knock several times on the door to gain their attention. Finally Mrs. Turner opened the door. Mr. Turner was hunched over a computer monitor; his wife returned to reading "one of them big stacks of paper that come from the machine."

Moire laid out the table for them, "nice warm soup," and some roast beef sandwiches—they never ate more than sandwiches when they were at work. She poured coffee for them from the coffeemaker in the workshop and urged them to eat. Mr. Turner never said a word; he was staring at the screen as if lost in thought. Moire then gathered up the remnants from lunch and prepared to depart—they did not want her coming back for the dishes from one meal until she brought the next one. Mrs. Turner thanked Moire and accompanied her to the door. After Moire had left, Mrs. Turner closed the door and locked it; Moire was absolutely sure she had heard the key click in the lock.

"Didn't they want to be left alone and untroubled when they were working, poor dear things?"

"Were the sandwiches eaten, Chief?"

"Nope. They were still on the table, untouched, when we arrived."

"They were like that," Moire insisted. "They'd let perfectly good food go to waste because they didn't even realize that it was there."

She had washed up the dishes and straightened out the kitchen. There was nothing else to do before breakfast the next morning, so she and Dermot had retired to their apartment above the garage—and a "nice snug place it is"—and watched TV, thankful for their nice snug place as the blizzard hit them, the winds howling off the lake and the snowflakes beating against the window.

"We didn't think we heard any unusual noises," Moire continued, "though didn't I say once to you, Dermot, that the wind sounded like the cries of damned souls?"

"Damned souls."

They were awakened by Clare Turner about three in the morning, the wind still howling and the snow still pelting the windows. She sounded upset—"not much mind you but she's not a great one for emotion." Mrs. Kincaid—that "nasty busybody" in the next house—had called to say that her parents were not answering the private phone in the workshop. Clare had been pounding on the door for ten minutes. Would Dermot come and see if he could rouse them?

"Wasn't I saying to Dermot that it was a terrible mistake to give that daft woman the private number and it wouldn't be private any longer if she had it. And then didn't Dermot—"

"I'd like to hear his description of it, Mrs. McLaughlin."

Her mouth closed like a trap. It would not, I thought, stay shut for long.

"Well, the lass was pounding the door and shouting. She did seem a mite upset. So I pounded and shouted, myself being able to make more noise than she was."

He stopped, as though his recitation was over.

"And then?"

"Didn't she tell Dermot to break down the door?"

"Please, Mrs. McLaughlin." I raised a hand in plea for silence from her. She seemed quite upset.

"She asked me if I thought I could break down the door . . . and meself kind of strong. Well, the hinges were on the inside . . ."

"The door opened in?"

"Didn't he say that very thing?"

"So then what did you do, Mr. McLaughlin?"

"Well, I banged into it pretty hard."

"Then?"

"Didn't she tell him to get tools?"

"Mrs. McLaughlin, I must hear his description. If there is a trial you won't be able to answer for him on the witness stand. I will ask you now and for the last time to be silent while your husband is telling the story. If you are not, I'll have to ask the Chief to remove you from the library."

"Well, I never . . ."

"Will there be a trial, Mr. Scanlan?" Dermot McLaughlin was kneading his hands uneasily.

"I hope so. If we can find the killer we will certainly put him or her on trial, unless there is a guilty plea . . . Now what did you do?"

"Well, I went back to my tool shop in the back of the garage and brought back a power saw and a power drill."

"And then?" One had to pry every sentence out of him with a question.

"Then I drilled four holes in the door near the lock—hard going, solid oak."

"Then?"

"I cut out the square I'd made with the holes and took it out."

"Why didn't you use the spare key?"

He looked at me as if I had asked an astonishing question. "There wasn't any spare key, Mr. Scanlan."

"Are you sure?"

His wife opened her mouth and shut it again when I raised my hand.

"If there were one, I never seen it."

"Very well, then what happened?"

"Then Miss Clare reached in and turned the key from the inside."

"The key was in the lock?"

"Yessir. It was always in the lock."

"Could it have been turned from the outside?"

"No sir. You'd have to see the lock, sir."

"All right. Then what happened?"

"Well, Miss Clare runs down the stairs and pulls open the drapes around the part of the workshop they used as a bed-room."

"And?"

"And she screams like and then turns around and vomits."

"You stood watching her?"

"No, sir. I ran down the stairs and catches her as she like collapses."

"Uh-huh?"

He would make a good witness, slow and easy so the jury could get the picture without any effort. Better than his wife by far.

"Well, she gets control of herself pretty quick and says something like she has to call the priest and the doctor and the police."

"Are you sure of the order?"

He frowned, trying to concentrate.

"I think so, sir."

"How upset did she seem?"

"More upset than I had ever seen her, sir, but still that's not very upset compared to most people."

"What did you do then?"

"Well, I like peeked in at the beds."

"You saw?"

Suddenly his tongue was untied. "The worst thing I ever saw, sir. Blood all over, more blood than I thought I'd ever see. On the sheets and the blankets and the drapes and the floor and the windows and the two of them lying there on their beds like they were grinning at me but with an open neck instead of an open mouth. I was almost sick too. I got out of there in a hurry, let me tell you. And I wouldn't let Moire," comforting arm around his wife, "go look, not for all the money in the world."

"So to the best of your knowledge, Mr. and Mrs. Turner were alive at five-thirty and dead about three-thirty the next morning?"

They both nodded solemnly.

"Someone had entered their workshop and slit their throats during those ten hours?"

They nodded solemnly again.

"Someone who would have had to come into the house through one of the other entrances, climb up the stairs to the second floor, walk down the special staircase to the door of the workshop, enter it, kill them, and escape the same way?"

"Or," Chief Stewart intervened, "someone would have had to come through the garage and up the stairs to the entrance of the workshop. There were two entrances to the garage you see, one from the kitchen and the other from the workshop."

"And a third entrance from the McLaughlins' apartment?"

"Isn't that the way my poor Dermot got to the door that night? Down from our apartment, across the garage, then up to the workshop?"

"What was in the garage?"

"Wasn't there just two cars—the Lincoln town car the poor dears used and herself's German sports car?"

"I see."

In principle, then, either the McLaughlins or Clare Turner could have slipped into the room and committed the crimes. What motives might the former have? Their berth here was "snug" all right. They were doubtless very well paid, lived comfortably, and did very little work. The lure of the diamonds arguably could have been too much for them. We would have to check them out, lest a smart defense attorney do the same thing. If I were defending Clare Turner, I'd try to put the blame on this twosome.

"Would you have heard anyone sneaking through the garage?"

They looked at each other.

"Wasn't there too much noise from the wind that night?" Dermot said.

"Was there?"

"Didn't I just say so?"

"On an ordinary night?"

Dermot nodded grimly. "I'm a light sleeper, sir. I would have heard them."

"The garage door was locked?"

"Wasn't every door in the house locked? Wasn't I supposed to check them every night? Weren't they mortal scared that someone would steal one of his inventions?"

"Were there any doors from the outside to the workshop?"

"The windows, sir, of course the windows."

"Windows?" I glanced at Chief Stewart.

"As you'll see when I take you through the workshop, Terry, the top half of the workshop is mostly window, thick, Thermopane glass. During the spring and summer, John Turner liked the sense that they were working outdoors. He had an electric mechanism which opened the windows—

lifted them up and out. Of course if they had been opened last night the two rooms in the workshop would have been covered with snow."

"Not if they were only opened for a moment or two . . . Dermot, where are the controls for the windows?"

"Aren't they inside the workshop," his wife cut him off, "right next to Mr. Turner's computer thing?"

"So the killer had to have a key to either the garage or the house and also one to the workshop? If the killer came from the inside, he'd still need a key to the workshop?"

Again the solemn nods of the two heads.

"So there has to be a spare key somewhere?"

"Not that I've ever seen," Dermot said slowly.

"Wasn't I after herself all the time to get one? Didn't I say what would we do if you were both sick inside there at the same time?"

"And she said?"

"She said yes, they'd have to write to Switzerland and get another one, but they never did."

"One last thing, Mrs. McLaughlin." The Chief smiled benignly. "Who came to the house after twelve noon yesterday?"

"Wasn't it a quiet day because of the weather? Weren't the only people I saw all afternoon the plumbing repair men who came along about three-thirty to fix the drain in me sink?"

"They left?"

"Wasn't it about four-fifteen?"

"I see."

The extra key could ruin a case, at least against a smart defense attorney. We could show that Clare Turner had the motive for killing her parents, but, unless we could explain how she had gained access to her parents' workshop, we would not be able to show opportunity.

"We're going to have to check them out, Chief, but they seem honest enough."

"They do that, though the woman talks a lot."

"Goes with the ethnic culture."

"We also have to find out how she got into the workshop. There has to be an extra key. I want to know all the details, especially about the documentation required for a second key, if it's true that's what's needed."

"It's hard to believe that a lock can have only one key, isn't it?"

"It sure is."

"But there are other people in Lakewood who have similar locks, even the Kincaids next door. They showed it to me when I checked their security system."

Damn. I'd forgotten that.

"A security system in this house?"

He shook his head placidly, knowing that I'd forgotten something.

"No, sir. Mr. Turner didn't believe in them."

"An odd man."

"No one ever denied that."

"OK, let's have a look at the laboratory or workshop or whatever they call it."

"One question, Terry."

"And that is?"

"What if there isn't another key?"

"There has to be. She's hid it somewhere. We'll find it."

I was less confident than I sounded.

6

"THIS IS KIND OF WEIRD." THE CHIEF LUMBERED UP THE broad staircase to the second floor of the Turner mansion.

"A huge place," I agreed, thinking that a visit from a jury to a place like this, allegedly to visit the scene of the crime, would make them even more resentful against a woman who had lived in such luxury for all her life.

"That's not what I mean."

"What did you mean?" I looked down the hallway on the second floor—three bedrooms on either side, a veritable hotel.

"You'll see in a minute . . . That's Ms. Turner's room at the far end. Do you want to look inside?"

"Why not?"

The room was as bland as the woman, neat and dull, not particularly feminine and no hint of character or personality—blue drapes and bedspread, bed already made, an Apple Macintosh computer on an antique desk, a wall of library shelves with medical books, an emphasis on psychiatry and fiction. Next to her bed one of the Barcester books by Trollope. There were no decorations on the wall, neither painting nor poster.

"Bed made already?" I asked.

"She made it while she was waiting for us."

My mother would have done the same thing if there were a murder in our house. But from her it would have been tolerable. From Clare Turner, whom I was trying to dislike intensely, it was intolerable.

I say that now; I didn't think it then. I was tired and discouraged and agonized about life. I had made the mistake Dan Hills always warned against: I had permitted personal animosity to intervene in front of professional adversarial animosity. I can be honest about it now. Even then it was either hate Clare Turner or, in my state of celibate loneliness and frustration, fall in love with her.

"Where's the dog?" I asked.

"She took it with her when she went to the Murrays' house over on Gleneagles Lane."

"Yes, you told me that. As much a brute as Mrs. McLaughlin would have us believe?"

"Big mutt. Biggest I've ever seen. Friendly unless she thinks you're a threat to Clare."

"Notice the brown belt?" The Chief gestured toward the top of the dresser.

"Hmm," I responded. The young woman would not be someone with whom to mess. Though it might be interesting to mess with her—in a constructive and respectful fashion, I added piously.

What would Clare be like in bed?

That was an utterly irrelevant question.

I looked out the window on the front lawn, trying to control the anger that was surging inside of me. The TV trucks were inching toward the front door again. A cab was chugging down Sylvan Lane. Cops were shivering, their breath frozen in the air.

"It looks like a helluva good life, Chief."

"In this community," he said slowly, "it's hard to tell sometimes."

"You didn't happen to take any pictures of the snow around the house when you arrived?"

"We had to tramp up the walk from the road to the door so that was messed up." He removed an envelope from the inside of his uniform jacket. "But first thing I noticed was that there was no marks anywhere around the house. So we took some Polaroids, all around just in case."

"You're a real pro, Chief." I accepted the pictures from him. "Wow!"

"Not a mark anywhere, except the ones that we made. The wind might have blown the snow over footprints or car tracks, but I don't think so."

"Medical examiner estimate time of death?"

"He said it was hard to be exact because it was so cold in the workshop. Anywhere between three and ten hours, maybe even longer."

"Not very helpful, is he?"

"But we know Mrs. Turner was alive because she called April Kincaid at seven-thirty."

"So somewhere between seven-thirty and midnight, just when the snow was falling?"

"Right."

A handsome man, in his late fifties or early sixties, hatless and wearing a thin trench coat, climbed out of the cab and, looking bemused, strode up to the cops on the portico.

"OK. Let's see the workshop."

"The stairs are right around the corner from Miss Turner's room here at the south end of the house. Like I say it's kind of weird. They cut off the end of a bedroom here to create the stairway. Mrs. Kincaid raised all kinds of complaints about it."

"But it wasn't her house, was it?"

"Mrs. Kincaid kind of likes her causes. One of them is preserving the local community. She made things miserable for that black TV star who chopped down all the trees; and she protested loudly when the Turners built the addition onto their house. I guess they kind of forgot to get a permit."

"One of those."

"Yeah. They say she put spikes in the trees at the TV guy's house. A worker was hurt, but we could never prove she did it."

"And she was a friend of the Turners'?"

"She could fight you one day, even throw pickets around your house and the next day overcome you with sweetness. That's the way she is. I think I'm on her good list now, but it's hard to be sure."

"I'm going to want to talk to her."

I didn't want a smart defense attorney to catch me by surprise and drag her in as a nutty neighbor who might have killed the Turners.

"You bet."

At the bottom of the stairs that had offended Ms. Kincaid was a stairwell. The steps turned to the left and went down another storey to a door.

"That the way to the garage?"

"Right."

I turned and looked at the massive oak door, which obviously was the one out of which Dermot McLaughlin had cut the panel. The lock was formidable, no keyhole and turnkey affair, but a big mechanism into which you would slip the flat metal disk with corrugated edges. The disk itself lay on the table inside the door in a plastic bag.

"Shouldn't be hard to make a copy of that, should it?"

"You gotta have the right alloy first. It's sensitive to the kind of metal as well as the shape. The company in Switzerland is the only one that makes the stock. Not worth the time or energy for anyone else to try to imitate it even if they could."

I resolved that I would not let the key problem worry me.

"You're right, Chief," I said as I stepped through the doorway and down four steps into the workshop. "It is weird."

The stench of blood and death, acrid, corrosive, sick, assaulted my nostrils. My stomach protested but then gave up on me in disgust.

Cops were dusting the workshop for prints and searching through the closets and bathroom, which were built into the wall between the house and the workshop. A woman patrol officer was taking pictures with a Polaroid and a 35-mm camera. The telltale yellow tape blocked off the north half of the workshop, where floor-to-window drapes, thick and dark gray, had been pulled back.

The workshop itself was a glass and steel addition built on the south half of the back of the house, a storey-and-a-half high. It surely would have disfigured the house, so perhaps Mrs. Kincaid's displeasure was appropriate. However, the only ones who could see it would be boaters out on the lake—and during the winter, perhaps Mrs. Kincaid through the leafless trees to the south. Half of it looked like an air force command and control center—a line of computer terminals, large monitors, and a solid bank of high metal cases, either computers or storage compartments. Behind the computing equipment a group of worktables were arranged to form a square, inside of which was a big leather chair. The tables were heaped high with graphics output, some of them in color. In front of the chair a laptop portable, coverup, and a half-empty coffee cup suggested that someone had left the work station only a few moments ago.

At the end of the table there were two empty soup bowls and a pair of uneaten sandwiches, crusts trimmed away, remnants, no doubt, of the snack Mrs. McLaughlin had prepared for them. I lifted up the corner of a sandwich. Roast beef all right. It reminded me that I hadn't eaten any breakfast—and no dinner the night before either.

Let's see. They were hard at work at five-thirty when she brought the sandwiches and very much alive at the time of the seven-thirty phone call. When did they begin their last nap? Probably not too long after the phone call.

"High-tech invention," I murmured, pointing at the bank of terminals.

"He started out monkeying around in his garage, like Henry Ford, he used to say," the Chief replied. "But he kept in touch with the most recent computer developments. He said they were just another way to monkey around."

"You knew him?" I turned to the Chief.

"Not well. Talk to him occasionally at church functions. St. Matt's."

I glanced at some of the color graphs. They made no sense to me. "A brilliant man, I guess?"

The Chief shrugged his broad shoulders. "That's what they all said. It's a shame that his life had to end this way, before his time so to speak."

"It's a shame any life has to end. Before, at, or after its time . . . OK, let's look at the site."

I peered into the bedroom area, still protected from the glare of the sun by drapes along the north wall and the wall facing the lake. I had seen dead bodies before and was used to the sight and smell of death. This time, even though the bodies had been removed, the sight of dried blood, brown and shiny all over the room, caused my stomach to churn dangerously.

"Charnel house," I whispered.

"Even worse before we took the bodies out. We don't see this sort of thing much up here," he sounded apologetic. "We had several very sick patrol officers, men and women."

The bedroom was functional, not luxurious, the kind of place to which researchers would retreat for naps when they could no longer stare at the computer screen: twin beds, two nightstands, a couple of chairs, a dresser, a vanity table, and a mirror. All the furniture was the same color as the computer equipment in the work area. When the drapes were pulled back, the bedroom would blend nicely with the rest of the workshop. Did an interior decorator design the place for them? Why not?

"Careful," said the Chief. "Don't step on the blood."

"No way . . . How were they dressed when they were discovered?"

"Fully clothed, like they had thrown themselves on the beds for a quick nap, on top of the blankets."

I edged away from the death scene. How could anyone do something like that to parents?

"Why is it so cold in here?"

"John Turner believed in energy conservation. No need to have a house any warmer than sixty in the winter and no cooler than eighty in the summer. You can always wear sweaters or take off your shirt, he said. Although the house and this place are pretty well insulated—that glass is two thick panes sealed together—in weather like we have now you can't hold the temperature at sixty degrees. That's why April Kincaid called them last night."

"I assume that she would approve of energy conservation." I walked over toward the glass wall facing the lake.

"Hard to tell what she approves of and doesn't approve of." Chief Stewart shook his head. "She's . . . she's a little odd. You'll see what I mean when you meet her. But she did worry about them: two elderly people with poor health who paid no attention to time or temperature in a glass house with a blizzard and a cold wave closing in on them."

I looked out the window. It was impossible to tell where

the back lawn ended and the lake began. The snow cover behind the workshop was unblemished.

"Beach out there?"

"The lake is down now, so there's a pretty good-sized beach. That hump in the snow is the seawall."

Could someone have come up the ice-covered beach, surmounted the seawall, and come across the backyard? And then retreated not leaving footprints?

Not likely.

But what if the wind had covered up the footprints with drifting snow?

All right, the killer would still have to figure out a way to get into the house.

"The beach is public, right?"

"Right. However, you'd have to walk a half mile north or south to find public access to it. Of course, in this kind of weather, you might sneak through backyards. But you'd have to park your car somewhere. That's one of the things the Lakewood Police keep a close watch on. People don't like strange cars parked on their streets."

"I'll keep that in mind . . . Do I have it right? No doors to this workshop other than the one we came in?"

"Nope. Only the windows. Look up there. See those metal struts. You push that switch on the beam and the top half of all three walls opens out."

"You try it yet?"

"On a day like this?"

"If we don't experiment with it a defense attorney will want to know why."

"Look out, everyone," the Chief bellowed. "We're going to open this thing up."

"It's cold out," someone protested.

He pushed the top button and almost noiselessly the top of

the building opened up and out—six massive windows on the lake side and two at either end.

Bitter cold rushed into the workshop.

"Hey!" everyone in the room yelled in unison.

"It works all right," I said. "Close it."

Chief Stewart pushed the bottom button. Just as noiselessly the windows closed.

"Ingenious. I suppose it would take a pretty thick rock or brick to smash through one of these?"

"More like a cannonball."

"The machinery?"

"Over there behind the computers, kind of the energy center of the place. Radiant heating."

"Suppose that one of the Turners wanted to walk down to the beach on a summer day. How would they go about it?"

"I don't think either of them paid much attention to the beach. But they'd have to go out the door we came in, down to the garage and out the garage, or up the stairs to the second floor, down to the kitchen and out the kitchen door."

"Couldn't do it directly from here?"

"Not at all."

Perhaps someone could have climbed in from the outside, scaling the glass wall to the windows, maybe using a ladder, and then climbing down on the inside. Assuming that the noise of someone climbing and the blast of arctic air didn't wake the victims, this hypothetical perpetrator could then have killed them, climbed up the wall and escaped the same way he came in. Maybe he could have even used a long pole to push the button somehow that would have closed the window. Then he could have retreated down the beach to his car, which might not have been mired in a snowbank.

A highly improbable scenario. But one a good defense attorney might well propose as an alternative to the one argued by the State of Illinois.

The hole in the scenario was how the windows could be opened from the outside.

"Chief, I know this sounds weird but we've got to examine every possibility. Ask the state police lab to check out whether the windows could be opened from the outside by some kind of sophisticated radio signal."

"Right." He pulled out a notebook and jotted a couple of words in it.

"You might also have them check this whole place to make sure that there are no secret doors that we haven't found. Turner was apparently an electronic genius with a fondness for secrecy. Maybe he built an escape in here that he alone knew about, in case of fire."

"Got it."

"Is that the Kincaid house to the south, the big Dutch Colonial through the trees?"

"Right. She couldn't see this place in the summer. During the winter, though, when the lights were on here, she could see it through the trees. One of her complaints was that the light kept her awake at night, since her bedroom is on the north side of their house."

"She couldn't pull the shades?"

"You'd have to know April Kincaid." He rolled his eyes.

"I'm going to want to meet her. What's her husband do?"

"Bank vice president. Downtown."

The back of the garage was immediately beneath us, and the apartment above it at eye level. The house had apparently been built on a hill—a prehistoric dune probably—and the garage at the foot of the hill, so it was beneath the first floor of the house and the workshop, and the apartment was level with the first floor of the house. The shades of the apartment were drawn. It looked spacious enough.

The big oak tree behind the garage would block the view between the workshop and the second floor of the garage.

However, in the winter, when the Turners were working on their computers, the McLaughlins could look on a slant from the back windows of their apartment into that part of the workshop. Did the Turners mind the possibility of such supervision? Was there some kind of arrangement about keeping the shades drawn in the back of the garage apartment?

"You might check on the McLaughlins, Chief. Did the Turners mind that their servants could peer through the tree and see what they were doing during the winter?"

"They couldn't really see what they were doing."

"Probably they couldn't watch what was on the computer screens, but they'd know they were in there, even catch a glimpse of them. Last night, when Clare woke them up, they could have pulled up the shade and seen the lights anyway."

"I'll see to it, Terry."

"OK. Now I want to see the safe."

"It's here behind the computer. More than just a wall safe."

It was indeed more than just a wall safe. It was rather a massive, freestanding walk-in cabinet, several inches thick and at least seven feet high. A cop was dusting the inside for prints.

"Maybe we'll find some of Clare Turner's prints."

"She didn't say she touched it, Terry; just that she looked inside."

The shelves of the safe were jammed with computer output and models of weird-looking machines and electronic components. A large, ornate box, the inside padded in dark blue cloth had been pulled off a shelf and tipped over on the floor. There were a couple of other empty places on the shelves.

"That's the jewel box, I guess," said the Chief. "It would hold a lot more stuff than we have recovered already."

"I think we also should have someone who can make

sense out of this stuff tell us what John Turner was working on. Maybe some of these high-tech models were more valuable than jewels. It's hard to tell whether any of them have been taken."

"Or photographed."

"Yeah," I agreed. "Or photographed."

I was looking for alternative scenarios that we might have to shoot down to sustain our case against Clare Turner. We did not have at that point a very good case. All circumstantial unless we found her fingerprints on the scalpel or perhaps on some of the larger jewels. We probably couldn't go to trial, but we could force them (her yet nonexistent defense team) to plea bargain. Guilty but mentally ill. Twenty years. In the hospital unit at Dwight. Maybe a hint of clemency later on. Not much punishment and not much of a deterrent for aggravated murder, two deaths, a robbery, and a robber in a private home. But she wouldn't inherit any of the money; and she might not find the dykes in Dwight all that pleasant companions. If worse came to worse we might even go with not guilty by reason of insanity. Off to a psychiatric institution maybe only for a couple of months, though likely for several years if we could swing it. The media wouldn't like such a deal. Neither would we, but it might be the best we could do. She'd lose her inheritance anyway.

Media, always the media. They claim they keep us honest and maybe they do. But they also make us focus on image more than reality.

You do what you can in my job with what you have. Although she might be as guilty as sin, there was no way we'd get a lethal injection sentence on this one.

Which proved how wrong I was.

"You might also find out, Chief, whether Clare Turner ever wore any of her mother's jewels and what kind she has of her own."

"Check." He made another note. "What do you think about the whole business now?"

"I think she did it all right. Who else stands to gain from their death? But without more evidence we're not going to have much of a case."

"You can always pick up more from good routine police work."

"That's for sure; you guys are doing a helluva job. If you need any help from us don't hesitate to yell."

"What about the key problem?"

"What about it?"

"How did she get into the workshop? And then out again?"

"With a key, how else?"

"We don't have an extra key."

"Depend on it, there is one. The state crime lab people can track down the Swiss company and find out about extras. I don't believe there is a key which can't be duplicated, whatever John Turner thought."

"Will do."

In the absence of an extra key or a good argument that there could be an extra key, even our circumstantial case would be pretty weak. Unless there was some way around it.

Locked room mysteries belong in detective fiction, not in real life, to say nothing of double locked rooms which, I supposed, was what this one was. Double locked room if you counted the unmarked snow. It would distract a jury, if the state's attorney and the judge permitted it.

"Your Honor, counsel for the defense is trying to set up a smoke screen with this argument about locked rooms. This is real life, a real murder of two real people, not a detective story to be read on a night when there's no good films on television."

"I quite agree, Counselor. Objection sustained. We'll have no more about locked rooms."

Not very likely, not unless the judge was either dumb or irresponsible. Much more likely, I would hear, "Overruled. The issue of access to the workshop is germane to the case. Unless it can be resolved, I would have to instruct the jury that the state has failed to prove opportunity for the defendant to commit the crime. I might even be forced to dismiss the case."

Not good. Unless we could find the extra key or come up with some other explanation, we'd have no chance of getting a murder one verdict. We'd have to plea bargain.

"Chief." The woman patrol officer who had monitored our conversation in the library came through the door and interrupted my fantasy. "There's a man upstairs who says he's Fred Turner, the brother of John Turner. Do you want to talk to him?"

"We sure do."

As I followed the two cops out of the workshop, I glanced back at the safe.

Sure enough you'd see its open door as soon as you came into the room.

7

"I'M DEVASTATED," FRED TURNER PROTESTED, "I REALLY can't believe it."

Fred Turner was perhaps ten years younger than his brother, much better looking than the man in the pictures I'd seen around the house. About five feet ten with a square, handsome, suntanned face and bright blue eyes. He was wearing a carefully tailored dark blue blazer and khaki slacks, a lot of rings and bracelets, and a large turquoise bolo tie. Despite his fastidious good looks and his expensive clothes, he looked faintly seedy.

An operator, I said to myself, and maybe not totally honest.

"I'm afraid it's true, sir. They're both dead, died in their sleep last night."

We were sitting in the library again, sipping the coffee which Moire McLaughlin was bringing with commendable regularity. This time I agreed to eat a croissant, two of them.

"How did they die?"

"They were murdered, sir."

Chief Stewart was doing the talking.

"Their throats slit by person or persons unknown," I added.

61

"God." He turned pale. "How ghastly."

"I'm sorry, sir, that you had to come home to this."

"Home? Oh, I see what you mean, Actually, while I was raised here, I've lived in Tucson for twenty years. I guess I consider that home. We don't have weather like this." He smiled weakly. "I kept trying to persuade John to retire in our area. But he was indifferent to weather."

"What brings you to Chicago, Mr. Turner?" I asked.

"Hmmm? Oh, I had a business meeting at O'Hare yesterday, at the Westin I believe it was. The meeting took a little longer than I thought it would so I missed the afternoon plane. I decided not to try to fly to Denver and change planes. So I called my wife and told her I'd wait till today when the weather would be clear—poor woman worries about my flying in snowstorms—and give old Jack a ring. I checked in at the Westin, had a bit to eat—I'd missed lunch—and called. The girl answered . . . "

"Mrs. McLaughlin?"

"No, no." He laughed easily. "I forgot the daughter's name in the turbulence of the moment, Clare of course. She said that her parents were at work in their lab but I should come out in the morning after the snow stopped. She didn't recommend trying to work my way through the blizzard."

"Good advice. What time was that?"

"Oh, about seven o'clock or so."

"You decided to come over this morning?"

"That's right." He smiled, happy that I was accepting his story. "When it cleared up this morning, I took a taxi over here and encountered," his voice broke, "this disaster."

"You have our sympathies," I said, trying to sound sincere. I didn't like him any more than I liked his niece, whose name he couldn't quite remember.

"We were not very close." He shook his head as if he still couldn't believe what had happened. "No one could be close to him except Mary. Childhood sweetheart, that sort of thing. Went to St. Gregory High School together when we lived in Andersonville on the North Side of Chicago—Edgewater I guess they call it now, though not if they grew up there."

"I see."

"Mind you, he was a fine man. Absolute genius. Sort of an Edison for our time. Should have had a lot more media attention. Celebrity. Would have none of it. But there was too much going on in his head to pay attention to ordinary human friendships."

"And he wouldn't retire?" I pushed a little.

"Wouldn't know how . . . When I'd stop in here to see him, he wouldn't know what to talk about. He wasn't unfriendly, not a mean bone in his body, always ready to help, but his mind was constantly on the designs spinning themselves out in his head."

"What is your occupation, sir?" The Chief had his notebook out.

"Mine?" He fiddled with a ruby ring. "Oh, I have a number of interests. Real estate, that sort of thing."

"Did your late brother invest in your projects?" I asked.

"Heavens no!" He threw up his hands. "I had better sense than to ask. He turned everything over to a broker at Northern Trust. I could have made him a lot more money. But money was not one of his interests. This house, everything about it, was Mary's doing. Rather good taste, don't you think?"

"Indeed yes."

Good taste and no imagination or flair.

"Do you have any idea who might have done this . . . this terrible thing?"

"We are pursuing our investigation," the Chief said solemnly.

"I hope you're able to find the bastards." He clenched his fist. "Why would anyone want to kill John or Mary?"

"Inheritance?" I asked bluntly.

"I have no idea what he planned to do with the money." Fred Turner blandly ignored the implication of my question. "He's always been very generous to the Church, you know. I suspect that the Archdiocese will get most of it; he and Mary were quite dedicated to the parochial schools. There was a real dustup when the girl insisted on going to Lakewood High School. I'm sure she'll be left with enough money so that she won't have to worry about anything for the rest of her life. I suppose he'll leave me a bit. I never asked about it and he never said."

Too long an answer, too long by half.

"Could you estimate the size of his estate, Mr. Turner?" I asked cautiously.

He threw up his hands again. "He wasn't super rich, though he might have been if he wasn't so cautious in his investments. Let's say fifteen to twenty million, something in that order. Inheritance taxes of course, though I suppose he had good estate planning. Trust funds for the girl."

Both the Chief and I were silent. A lot of money. If all Clare obtained was trust funds, her motive for murder would vanish.

"But I wouldn't think that inheritance," he played with the ruby again, nervously I thought, "would be much of a motive for murder. John's days were numbered. I gathered from the girl, Clare, that he was working very hard because he wanted to finish his latest project. Mary's health wasn't much better. Possibly worse."

Again too long a response.

"Not unless someone needed money instantly," I replied.

"That would be true, of course."

"What do you plan to do now, Mr. Turner?"

"I'll call Margie, my wife, my second wife actually, from here if I may use one of the phones. Then I'll find a decent motel nearby so that I can be present for the wake and the funeral. I presume the Mass will be on Tuesday?"

"The family will have to decide that after the bodies are released." The Chief put on his official voice.

"When will they be released?"

"When our investigation no longer needs them."

"Who is the family in this case?"

"The daughter, naturally."

"I don't know her very well," he said thoughtfully. "She was only three or four years old when we moved to Tucson. Pretty little thing even then. Quiet. She's adopted, you know."

"So we understand."

"If you don't mind . . . ?"

"By all means, sir." Chief Stewart rose and conducted him toward the door of the library. "I'll show you a phone. You will let us know where you're staying, so we can inform you about funeral arrangements?"

"Certainly."

He had made no effort to find out where Clare was or how he might contact her.

While I was waiting for the Chief to return, I prowled the library, coffee cup in one hand, a second croissant in the other. I found a shelf loaded with pictures, a young man in army air forces uniform, the same young man and a pretty young woman on their wedding day, an older man trying to smile in front of a new factory, the same man also trying to smile as he received an award. A cute toddler grinning up at the camera. A silver wedding anniversary picture with the little girl now about four, still grinning.

The elder Turners didn't look quite like a Catholic *American Gothic*. John Turner wasn't holding a pitchfork.

The girl's smile had faded by the time she appeared in riding clothes with a horse, about eight by then. Then another picture with a horse when she was a young teen, still no smile. A prom picture, probably a junior prom, the young woman in a rather daring strapless dress, which displayed elegant breasts to their best advantage, the boy good looking and smiling. High school graduation. A stylized shot, probably from her debut at the Presentation Ball. A very serious college graduation picture. No smiles in any of them.

Next to the pictures, silent sentinels, stood a line of athletic trophies—track, volleyball, tennis. An athlete too. Did she smile when she received those trophies, I wondered.

Despite the cheerful sun and the pleasant warmth that had begun to seep into the library—someone must have pushed the thermostat up—I felt heavy and sad. There was a lot of suffering in those pictures. Two lives passing by all too rapidly; and another one, perhaps tragic almost as soon as it had begun, also doomed before it had a chance.

We are but a breath, the psalmist wrote.

My job, however, was not to reflect on the meaning—or the meaninglessness—of life, but to see that criminals were punished.

I wondered why I had never run into her in the yuppie bars I've been known to frequent. Probably because she was much too serious to be on that circuit.

"What did you think of him?" Chief Stewart broke into my melancholy reflections.

"I think he was delighted at his brother's death."

"Me too."

"Couldn't care less about who did it or about the daughter. Just wants the money."

"Which doesn't prove anything."

"Agreed. Still we must check his story."

"Even if he was staying at the Westin, he could have come over here last night, couldn't he?"

"Rented a car, drove over, talked to his brother, had a fight, killed them both, and got back to the hotel before the storm got too bad."

"After seven-thirty."

"Yeah. Not too likely. Probably not possible. And the McLaughlins said there were no visitors. But we'll want all the details of his movements, if only to fend off a defense scenario."

"Did you notice that Clare answered the phone when he called and not Mrs. McLaughlin?"

"I don't imagine she was on call all day and night."

"We'd better make sure."

I don't think we ever did check that out, not that it would have made any difference in the final outcome.

"He was both delighted and worried, Chief."

"Pretended that he wasn't a potential suspect when he knew that of course he was."

"Sleaze if you ask me, no more honest than he has to be, but not smooth enough to really carry it off."

"I'll check him out."

"I'll take care of that one. I've got a little clout in Tucson. Save you some work."

"Fine by me. Want to walk over and talk to April Kincaid now?"

"Good idea. Then I'll leave you alone so you can get back to your work. But first I want to look in the garage."

We walked down the stairs from the kitchen. They intersected with the stairs from the library in a stairwell in front of the door that led to the garage. The door was unlocked.

Like the rest of the house, the garage was spotlessly clean. Even the tools on the workbench along the wall were arrayed in precise order. The Lincoln town car, 1985 model I thought, glowed as if it had just come off the assembly line. Dermot McLaughlin kept the car in top condition. I opened the door. The leather smelled of polish. I should have someone take care of my car like that.

Clare Turner's Porsche looked distinctly out of place in such company. It was old, rusty, battered, and dirty—clearly secondhand. I glanced at the odometer—165,000 miles. Certainly she could afford something better. Or maybe she thought if she held on to it another couple of years it would become a valuable classic.

No, that didn't sound like Clare.

"This is where your people found the book bag, Chief?"

"In the front seat, on top of a box of Kleenex tissue. It was pretty clumsy to leave it there if she knew the police were coming."

"Clumsy and stupid."

"She doesn't seem to be stupid, Terry."

"All killers are stupid, Chief, except the professional hit men. If they weren't stupid they wouldn't kill. They think they're smart, brilliant even, and folks like us are dumb. So they make silly mistakes and get caught. I suspect our friend Clare had nothing but contempt for us. So she made a silly mistake."

"We'll have to account for the rest of the jewels."

"First of all, counsel for the defense will have to establish that there were other jewels in the safe. OK, let's meet this legendary April Kincaid."

We went back up to the house.

"Chief, I want to show you something funny." An older man in civilian clothes met us in the kitchen. "Take a look at these pictures we found in the safe."

I peered over the Chief's shoulder. On the envelope in neat block letters were the words "paranormal phenomena."

That's all we needed.

The pictures lived up to the label. There were about a dozen of them, taken at various times in various places in the house, usually when there were guests. In each of them a wraithlike substance hovered among the people in the room—amorphous, diaphanous, insubstantial, your classic ectoplasmic phenomenon, right out of a horror film.

Only this wasn't a horror film; it was real life.

I felt a shiver run through my body.

"What the hell . . . !"

"The house is supposed to be haunted," the Chief said calmly. "You hear stories about occasional odd things happening here."

"These are fakes," I insisted. "They have to be."

"How do you fake a Polaroid? Notice something strange about them?"

"The whole thing is strange!"

"Yeah, but look at the way the thing relates to Clare."

He sorted four pictures out of the stack. In each of them, the wraith seemed to be enveloping Clare, almost as though it were trying to protect her.

"Who is the haunt supposed to be?"

"The wife of the family who lived here before the Turners moved in, oh, maybe twenty years ago. She lost a baby at birth, went into a depression, and killed herself. Young woman, first child."

I shivered again.

"Look, Chief, the state's attorney for the county of Cook does not deal with the paranormal. Abnormal all the time, but paranormal never. If we can subpoena this . . . thing, fine. I'll take it, her, whatever seriously. Until then it's out of my jurisdiction."

"You want me to keep these and pass them on to you as evidence?"

I hesitated. Somewhere in the Italian side of my soul there

is deep superstition, the kind that does not necessarily believe in good spirits, but takes the existence of evil spirits for granted. I did not want the pictures, but I did not want to let go of them either.

If we planned to use them in the trial, we'd have to tell the defense and that would destroy us on the spot. Yet if we didn't use them, would we be suppressing evidence? No, I didn't think so.

Besides I was both fascinated and frightened by them.

"Yeah, why not? We might as well hang on to them. I'd get laughed out of my profession if I tried to show them to a jury."

For all my bravado, I was still shivering inwardly. The uncanny or maybe it was the Uncanny scared the living daylights out of me.

"Can do," the Chief said amiably, apparently not disturbed at all by the possible presence of the paranormal.

I still have the pictures. I've had a lot of nightmares about them since then. I've never thrown them away, though a couple of times I've had the match in my hand to burn them. Occasionally I take them out of the envelope and wonder what they mean. Could they tell me something about the case? I'm that desperate to find a solution now to the locked room that I'd believe anything—even that a wraith killed John and Mary Turner.

"All right. Let's deal with the living instead of the dead. On to April Kincaid."

"She's pretty strange too," the Chief warned me.

8

————————

WHAT IF I HAD MET HER IN A SINGLES BAR? Like the Sports Bar on Division Street?

I don't think, Father, that she'd hang out at a place like that. She wasn't the singles bar type. But I see your point.

Look, Father, I'm one of your single men that's tired of being single. I don't go to such places looking for a one-night stand. I go there looking for a wife.

Yeah, I could show up at one of your dances at the cathedral. Or the tea dance at Old St. Pat's. Or the World's Largest Block Party they have over there. I usually make the scene at the latter, since my folks gave up on their own parish.

I'm afraid of finding the wrong woman. I've already done that a couple of times. Maybe I'm afraid of finding the right one too, as far as that goes.

Like you say, I'm ducking your question. I don't want to face the answer I have to give.

But here it is: If I had met Clare Turner somewhere else, let's say at a dance here at the cathedral, yeah, sure, I'd have been interested in her. Like I said, I fantasize about arch-duchesses, especially ones that have an aura of mystery around them, a hint that they are a enigma to be solved, a suggestion that you might explore them forever and still not know everything about them.

Know what I mean?

She would have intrigued the hell out of me—aloof, elegant, self-possessed, mysterious. All right, I would have pursued her.

And how would she have reacted?

I think she would have discouraged me at first, but not enough to drive me away.

Did I know that even on that winter day in Lakewood? Somewhere in the back of my brain I did, sure. But it wasn't a singles bar or a cathedral Christmas or Valentine's dance. It was a murder scene. So I denied the attraction to myself.

That didn't make it go away?

How right you are.

9

WE WALKED DOWN THE ROAD TO 1180 SYLVAN LANE—
only a pair of houses on the block. I glanced back
through the trees that separated the two home sites. Their
black branches were like a screen, which filtered out most of
the view. In the summer it would be quite impossible to see
one house from the other. At this time of year, however, Mrs.
Kincaid would be able to see the lights in the Turner workshop; but even with binoculars, assuming that she had them,
it would be pretty hard to ascertain what was happening.

Not much of a chance for an eyewitness.

We trudged up the walk, already neatly shoveled, to the
entrance of the house. The Chief pushed the bell. Inside so
many chimes sounded that you'd think you were in the Pi-
azza San Marco in Venice.

The door opened immediately—someone had been waiting for us.

"Oh my goodness, come in out of the cold." April Kincaid
spoke with dismay in her voice. "Joe Stewart, you ought to
know better than to walk in the cold on a day like this! Don't
the taxpayers provide you with a patrol car?"

Mrs. Kincaid was a surprise. I had expected an older
woman. In fact she was in her early forties and quite attrac-

tive, indeed sexy, in her gold pajama suit—an outfit that might have appeared in the pages of *Vogue*. She wore too much makeup; the blond in her hair, however skillfully it might have been applied, was overdone; and her wrists jangled with one too many bracelets. Nonetheless, she was slim and trim and well proportioned; she filled out the top of the pajama suit quite nicely. My imagination fantasized about what she would be like without the suit. She would certainly keep a bed warm on an icy winter night.

That reaction to a woman a decade and a half older than I am shows how my involuntary monastic life was twisting my view of the world and the people in it.

Then I noticed that her smile, at first warm and almost sweet, was fixed and that her voice, at first intimate and gentle, was smothering—and her faintly British accent was phony. No, even on an icy winter night, I'd decline with gratitude but still enjoy the thought.

We were seated in the "drawing room" of her outsized Dutch Colonial house, a room done in gold, which seemed to match her clothes, and made to wait while she brought "tea and biscuits."

"Biscuits?" The Chief looked at me.

"Cookies. She's using the British word. She isn't from England, is she?"

"Springfield, Illinois."

"Figures."

The cookies, however, were delicious. I ate all but one of them.

She was sorry that her husband had to go downtown to the bank, but she did not mind in the least being interviewed in his absence. "It's such a terrible thing to have happen in this quiet neighborhood. I told the poor dear, wonderful Turners—who loved the neighborhood as much as I do— that glass monstrosity of theirs would bring undesirables to the neighborhood, but I never dreamed that it would cost them their lives."

"I see," I said though I didn't see at all.

"I always think that it is so important to protect a peaceful neighborhood; it is really as much part of the environment as the trees and the lake and the air and the dear little animals, don't you think?"

"Yes, ma'am."

She was more than just sexy. As our conversation continued I realized that she radiated a subtle, intense, and slightly perverted sexual energy, mostly by slight but unmistakable body movements, hints of a woman in the early phases of lovemaking, perhaps abandoned lovemaking. April Kincaid was a threat, albeit an appealing threat. It would be a rare man in whom she would not excite dissolute sexual fantasies.

"John Turner will be such a terrible loss, not only to this neighborhood but to the whole of humankind, don't you agree, Chief?"

"Yes, ma'am."

"The death of anyone," she rushed on, "is *such* a tragedy, no man is an island you know, but here was a truly *great* man, a prophet without honor in his own country. Such a *humble* man, if you know what I mean."

"Humble?" I said for want of something else.

"Some people thought he was stubborn and, the good Lord forgive me for it, I was one of them. But I came to see through the years that the stubbornness was merely holy *simplicity*. And he was *so* dedicated to the environment. All his efforts in the last days of his life were directed toward energy conservation, a mechanism to improve fuel efficiency in cars. It would eliminate the threat of global warming. I can't think of a more important work, can you, Mr. Scanlan?"

"Energy conservation?"

"Oh, yes indeed. As I said to Rodney—my husband—there are different ways of protecting the environment. I had to learn to accept that his way was more important than mine, although," she frowned and a dark light glinted momentarily in her vague brown eyes, "I do think that he could have built a workshop which fit in better with our neighborhood. We had a little spat over that"—she smiled as though it was a minor and fond memory—"but it didn't interfere with our friendship. And poor dear Mary, God be good to her as I'm sure He will, she helped me in every one of my causes."

"Causes?"

"There are so many causes today, aren't there, Mr. Scanlan? I'm sure an assistant state's attorney would know about them more than a poor little suburban homebody like me—energy conservation, animal rights, the homeless, AIDS victims, disarmament, world peace, the environment, whales, noise pollution. I do my best for each of them," she sighed as though the list had exhausted her, "but it takes so much time and effort. Poor dear Mary helped me all she could. I understood perfectly when the demands of John's projects prevented her from helping me as much as I would have liked."

Was there a touch of asperity in her voice?

"She called you last night to beg off from today's demonstration at the railroad station?" Chief Stewart finally managed to get to the point of the visit.

"Oh yes, and I admit I was a bit upset. Many of my women were canceling with all kinds of excuses because of the weather. I knew Mary wouldn't do that. But I'm afraid I was a little impatient. Protecting the old station is *so* important because it's *so* much part of our community, isn't that true, Chief?"

"Yes, ma'am."

April Kincaid was quite mad. Dangerously mad perhaps—as well as sexually seductive. Had she not put spikes in the trees which were being cut down? Well, allegedly put spikes in trees?

Homicidally mad?

I wouldn't want her on the witness stand if I could avoid it. Yet her evidence would be essential to establish that someone had killed the Turners after Clare came home and after the blizzard had begun.

"She called you at what time, Mrs. Kincaid?"

If I were happily married, I wondered, would I find her subliminal sexual invitations so powerful? Would my head be pounding and my blood rushing rapidly and my fists clenched if there was a wife waiting for me at home?

Probably.

"Just at seven-thirty. I was upstairs in my little scriptorium working on my list of women for the protest and the clock was right next to the phone. Five other women," her face darkened, "called me after that."

"And you called her back later?"

"Oh, yes, dear Mr. Scanlan, more times than I can remember. When I was finished with my calls . . ."

"What time was that?"

"Almost nine o'clock . . . I looked out the window and saw that the snow was just *terrible*. I turned on the weather channel and they said it would plunge to below zero and the windchill would be forty below. Well, here right next to the lake, the windchill is simply *frightful*. I felt a little guilty," ingratiating smile, "because perhaps I had been a trifle rude to dear Mary. And I do so worry about them out there in that glass thing of theirs. They pay no attention to the weather. Poor John thought the room never had to be more than sixty degrees, which is a bit too zealous, isn't it, Mr. Scanlan?"

"How many times did you call?" The Chief took over the interview. He was welcome, I thought, to this crazy lady.

"Oh, perhaps five or six times. There was no answer, which is very unlike the Turners. I went over to the window of my kitchen and looked out. The snow was very thick by then, but I could see the light in their workshop, so I reckoned they were there."

Reckoned indeed.

"You didn't see anyone out there in the woods at that time or any other time?"

"Oh, no."

"When did you stop making the calls?"

"I'd say about eleven o'clock. Then Rodney and I went to bed," a faint smile and a light blush hinted at some activity in bed, "and I tried to sleep. I was worried about them, but Rodney said, like he always does, that they are old enough to take care of themselves. He was wrong, wasn't he?"

"Did you look out the window at any time after that?"

"Only when I woke up about three. I had finally fallen asleep and something startled me. Like a terrible scream. I suppose it was only the wind. That's what Rodney said. But I went to the window and opened the drapes . . ."

"You were able to see the workshop through the snow-storm?"

"I can always see that terrible place." Her mask slipped away and she became for a second or two a very angry woman. "Even when I can't see it, I know it's there. It is *so* ugly. Well, I got my binoculars—I use them to admire the sailboats on the lake during the summer—and I put on my negligee," she flushed slightly at the hint, deliberate I was sure, that she slept in the nude, "and I couldn't see anyone moving about in that *place*. It's very difficult to see clearly, but still I was very worried. I called the number again and again there was no answer. So I called Clare and told her I was worried about her parents."

"How did she react?"

"How does that one ever react?" She almost spit out the words. "She was polite and courteous and utterly indifferent to me and her parents. Rodney, who has read a lot about psychiatry—he says it's very important in the banking business—thinks she has the eyes of a psychopath. Our Elaine was best friends with her all through high school. I was so glad that Elaine went off to Dennison. I thought Clare was such a bad influence. One must be so careful with one's children, must not one, Chief?"

"Yes, ma'am."

"I believe in giving them total freedom, but I also believe in warning them about bad influences in their friends."

"In what way was Clare a bad influence? Drugs?" I intervened again.

"I shouldn't be at all surprised," she snapped the answer. "She was so . . . so *sullen*. She didn't seem to be able to laugh or smile or enjoy life."

"What did Elaine say to that?"

"She said that Clare was not sullen, only shy, but I *know*," her voice rose sharply, "sullen when I see it."

"What was the nature of her relationship with her parents?"

"What relationship? She barely spoke to them, save to argue. She's adopted, you know; blood always tells, doesn't it?"

Apparently adopted children were not on her list of causes.

"They were not close at all. I said many times to Elaine that she was a terribly ungrateful young woman. Why, she wouldn't work together with them on poor John's projects. Absolutely refused."

"What did Elaine say to that?"

"She said that Clare's father was impatient whenever she made a mistake and she'd run away crying. Elaine said he was a perfectionist. But don't geniuses have to insist on perfection from their coworkers?"

"Where is Elaine now?"

"Oh, she's a ski instructor in Vail. She's always *so* loved the outdoors."

"So what did you do after you made the call?" The Chief continued persistently to follow the questions in his notebook.

"Well, I sat and waited for a return call, not that I would expect one from *her*. Finally I saw the snowplow with the lights of a squad car right behind it and I thought it was Father Mike's car after that. I woke Rodney and said something terrible had happened. He agreed so we turned on WBBM and in another hour or so heard the *dreadful* news."

She dabbed at her nose with a tissue.

"I'm trying to be brave, but I really am so distraught . . . More biscuits, Mr. Scanlan?"

"No thanks."

"You didn't see anyone while you watched and waited?"

"*Absolutely* no one. By then the snow had stopped so I could see quite clearly. All the land around the house is so *barren* at this time of the year, if you know what I mean . . . Anyway the killing must have been much earlier, must it not?"

"Why do you say that?"

"Because they didn't answer my phone calls before I went to bed."

"Very likely," said the Chief, shutting his book.

"One more thing, Mrs. Kincaid," I said as we rose. "Do you have any idea who might have killed the Turners?"

Her eyes widened. "It must have been a tramp, must it

not? He came by on this cold night and saw the lights on in that awful place and asked if he could come in out of the storm. They were so kind to the poor, so innocent." She reached for the tissue again. "He saw her jewels and killed her for them. I warned them that it was a mistake to put up that place. But they wouldn't listen to me."

Despite the tissue, she sounded not sad but triumphant.

"She kept the jewels in the workshop?"

"Yes, and I told her not to do that, but she said it was a much stronger safe than the one in her dressing room. But they never locked the safe."

"Never locked it?"

"I would walk by often and see it wide open. What was the point of that fancy lock on the door to that place, if she left the safe open?"

What indeed.

The Chief and I thanked her for her time and escaped.

"Wow!" I said as we walked out into the bitter cold and blinding sunlight. "She's something else."

"You noticed." The Chief laughed.

"Do you think she's a good lay, as well as moving around like a hooker? Does she deliver on what she promises?"

"Would almost have to be, wouldn't you think?"

"I guess so," I agreed. "I suppose she'd have to be pretty good in bed for a man to put up with all the babble."

"He seems to love her. She's not my cup of tea."

"Good fantasies," I said. "Nothing more."

"You suspect her, Terry?"

"Do you?"

"She's a little crazy and perhaps a bit of a nympho, but I don't think she has the stomach for throat slitting."

"Probably not. But I dread the thought of putting her on the witness stand. A jury of twelve reasonable men and women might have a hard time believing she knew what time of day it was."

"That's a problem all right." The Chief sighed. "You want me to check her out just the same?"

"You'd better believe it."

10

I WENT TO MASS THAT AFTERNOON AT OLD ST. PATRICK'S, AS I do most of the unattached Catholic yuppies who live in Lincoln Park. It makes my mother happy, and who knows what kind of attachment I might find there? I was distracted by the case, but I did remember to pray for the repose of the souls of John and Mary Turner.

And I did promise that I would personally bring to justice the one who had killed them. There was no doubt in my mind as to who had killed them. Looking back on it from the perspective of the present, of course, there should have been a doubt.

There were no unattached persons present who seemed to have any interest in an attachment to me. There usually aren't.

The next morning I went out on a little exploration of my own. I drove up the Kennedy to the Edens and turned off at Peterson. Although it was Sunday morning, inbound traffic was already building up. My first stop was at the Sauganash home of Richard Martin, the president and CEO of Turner Electronics. The snow removal crews had done a reasonable job on the main streets and were working on the side streets, but Kildare Avenue was still slippery.

"Nice of you to see me, Mr. Martin," I said, "especially on a Sunday morning."

"We'll miss him terribly," he replied. "I'll do anything I can to help in your search."

Dick Martin was a trim, sandy-haired man of medium height, somewhere in his late forties, with a quizzical grin and twinkling eyes, the kind of mick who a generation ago would have been a precinct captain, perhaps a ward committeeman.

We were seated in his "study," a room dominated by a big computer screen and an even bigger TV set. His wife, whose eyes were altogether too shrewd for my taste, had brought us coffee and rolls. I dug into the rolls.

"Was he still active in the company?" I asked for a beginning.

"Spasmodically." He winced. "He owned 51 percent of the stock and the Leyden trust owns most of the rest. The Leydens are interested only in the return on investment, which is very nice at the moment, so they leave us alone. Jack could legally call any shots he wanted and the board would go along with him."

"These shots were frequent?"

"Infrequent and erratic. Jack never had any taste for administration. He was only too happy to turn that over to others. He hired me fresh out of DePaul twenty-five years ago to run the company day by day. He intervened only when he had a product he wanted us to make."

"You opposed that?"

"Hell, he was an absolute genius. He revolutionized certain aspects of automotive and electronic engineering. Sometimes I argued about his schemes, sometimes not. A lot of them didn't work, some of them did. We lost some money because of his gizmos. But we made a hell of a lot more money because of other gizmos."

"I see. What was it like to argue with him?"

"You had to know how to do it. After a quarter century I knew how to do it. You didn't directly say he was wrong. Rather you suggested more testing." He shrugged. "Our biggest item—it's in almost every GM car and truck in the world—was one that flunked the tests. We made it anyway because he insisted."

"How many of his gizmos worked out?"

Dick Martin spread his hands. "One in forty, one in thirty? That's not a bad rate, you know. Bell Labs doesn't do as well. When one of Jack's gizmos worked, it really worked."

"Did he play the averages that way?"

"Absolutely not. In his mind everything he tried was going to be a revolutionary success. However, when something had clearly failed, he promptly forgot about it."

"What will the company do without him?"

"We'll have to use more orthodox methods for developing innovations." He filled my cup and offered me another roll. "We have a pretty bright R and D staff to take up the slack. We'll have to work harder, and life will be a little less exciting with the old man gone."

"You liked him then?" I took the roll, apricot filling, my favorite.

"Hell yes. He was a little odd, no he was a lot odd, but he was a nice guy and he was very good to me—and to everyone in the company as far as that goes. He never had much in the way of human relations skills, but after a while you took that into account and didn't mind."

"A curmudgeon?"

"Not exactly. Curmudgeons know they're being rude; they do it deliberately. Poor Jack never deliberately offended anyone."

"I see . . . Hard to get close to?"

"Impossible. The only one close to him was Mary. They

were two of a kind, absolutely inseparable. I guess she provided all the affection he needed and vice versa."

"The daughter?"

"Clare? Good kid. Our eldest, Jane, went to Barat with her. Quiet and reserved, but bright and kind and sweet."

"Really?"

"Yeah . . . I don't know how she fit into the family. They'd been married more than twenty years when they adopted her. Mary wanted a child. By then I don't think Jack did. They had all their relationship patterns established. I think they both found her an intrusion. She turned out to be a pretty independent person. I don't think Jack ever really adjusted to her. Poor guy. A lot of fathers I know would be delighted with a kid like Clare. He could never understand why she wouldn't work with him in the lab like Mary did."

"Did you tell him?"

"Sure I did. I said, Jack, she's only a kid. You can't expect the kind of attention to the work you'd get from a committed adult."

"And he'd say?"

"He'd mutter something about concentration and discipline. He gave up after a while."

"Tell me a little bit about his life."

Martin filled my cup again and offered me the last roll on the plate. It was raspberry, not apricot, but I couldn't let it go to waste, could I?

"He was born in 1922 in the Lakeview neighborhood of Chicago—that's north of Uptown, you know—on the wrong side of the tracks, so to speak, though not all that wrong. West of the L, west of Clark Street, good solid German neighborhood, still is in great part. His mother was German. His father, who'd fought in the first war, worked for the Chicago Surface Lines—the old streetcar system. He was a conductor for a while but ended up in the offices as some kind of senior clerk. Kept his job through the Depression, which in those days was quite a feat.

"Jack went to St. Gregory's Grammar School and High School. As you know he's been very generous to the Catholic schools. It broke his heart when Clare insisted on going to Lakewood High with her friends instead of Woodlands or Regina."

"Stubborn?"

"When she wanted to be, at least as stubborn as the old man. Had to be to survive, I guess. She was a pretty happy little tyke till the last couple of years of grammar school."

"Really?"

"A lot of fun to have around the house, actually. Anyway, Jack graduated in 1940. He and Mary were in love even then, but neither of them had any money and Jack's father was sick. Jack worked on the cars for a few months and his father died. Jack saw the war coming and figured he'd volunteer before he was drafted. He joined the army air corps as it was then called because he'd been making model airplanes since before he could read. They made him a mechanic and a few months later he kissed his mother and Mary good-bye and left for Hawaii. He survived the Pearl Harbor attack and later went on to Guam to work on the B-29s.

"He came out a sergeant with a lot of mechanical experience. He wanted to go to college, as did most of the young G.I.s coming home in '45. But his mother, a very strong-willed woman, said the Depression was coming back and he'd better get a job if he intended to marry. So he went to work in a garage on Clark Street and tinkered with gadgets on the side. He sold the patent on one of his filters to Old Tim Leyden, the grandfather of the guy that runs the empire now. Leyden—you might remember that he died right after his eldest grandchild, John, was killed in Vietnam—robbed him if you ask me, but Jack was happy because he was able to buy his own garage, hire people to work it, and fiddle with more gadgets."

"Which he kept selling to Leyden?"

"Right; and Leyden Tools made tons of money on them. In '54 Leyden thought he saw a better way of making money, so he proposed setting Jack up in the electronics business with each of them owning half the company. He even gave Jack an extra point. Leyden's son, the one who married Teresa Leyden, who kept the empire going all these years, had been killed in a jet dogfight over the Yalu River during the Korean War. Maybe the old man wanted a son. They started out in a warehouse on Elston Avenue near where Riverview used to be. I suppose you're too young to remember the Riverview amusement park?"

"The legend lives with my parents. I was raised on Great America."

"There'll never be another place like Riverview." He shook his head sadly. "Anyway, when I came on board ten years later, he had four different shops scattered all over the North Side. I suggested he concentrate them all in a new factory in the industrial district just west of here. He said it would cost too much. I pointed out that the money he would save from duplication of effort would pay for the plant in ten years."

"He buy that?"

"He looked at me like I was some kind of magician, and maybe not too honest a one at that."

"And he said?"

"His very words were: 'What the hell, that's why I hired you. Go ahead and do it.' "

"So he became a very rich man?"

"He did indeed, though I think he didn't pay much attention to that. Mary did and the old lady before she died ten years back. All Jack ever cared about were the gimmicks and gizmos. He was still the G.I. tinkering around in the back of the garage when he wasn't working. In a way he was always the kid playing with model airplanes."

"And he never went to college?"

"Not for a single day. I think engineering school would have ruined him. Like most geniuses he was unorthodox. I don't know many engineers of his generation who caught on to computers early and stayed with or ahead of the developments. You'll find the best of the CAD equipment in his laboratory. A better way of tinkering, you see."

"What was he working on recently?"

Dick Martin shifted uneasily in his chair, the first hint of nervousness I had seen during the interview.

"A new kind of catalytic converter. His greatest invention yet, he claimed. He was extremely secretive about it too. Feared the oil companies. You see, he was always a nut on energy conservation, long before it became fashionable. He wasn't, as you might imagine, your typical post-1960 environmentalist. I don't imagine he gave a hoot about whales or owls or snail darters—if he ever thought of them. But he hated to see energy wasted. His frugal German mother saw no reason for heating a house above sixty in the winter and neither did he. 'Let my employees wear sweaters,' he'd say to me."

"Did you win that argument?"

Martin grinned wryly. "Only by threatening to resign."

"So this new gizmo would save energy?"

He nodded solemnly. "Jack said it would make gasoline three times as efficient."

"Three times!"

"Right. He insisted that if it were installed in a car that gave you twenty-five miles a gallon, you would get seventy-five miles."

"Seventy-five miles a gallon!"

"That's what he said."

"Your R and D people agree?"

"They told me he had finally gone round the bend. Completely cracked. But, while they're very good, they're also very orthodox."

"The oil companies would love it."

"Don't think they didn't know about it. They have spies everywhere—best industrial espionage anywhere in the world outside of Japan. And, given Jack's record, they were worried too. One of them tried to buy us out. Young Tim Leyden was only too willing as you might imagine. Jack wouldn't even talk about it."

"You would not like to be bought out?"

"They'd close us down," he said flatly.

"Who gets control of the company now?"

"A trust fund for Clare and for his charities. I'm the chairman. Management controls the fund."

"So you won't sell out?"

He shrugged. "If the offering price was big enough, you could make a case that we'd have to fulfill our trust. The prices they're talking about would provide us with an endowment far above what we have now. Clare could sue us to force us to sell. Or Tim Leyden. She wouldn't, at least I don't think so. He might, particularly if his grandmother pushed him."

"So it looks kind of bad."

"Not at all." He sighed. "You see, with Jack gone, the oil companies stop worrying about his little magic gimmick, not that they had that much to worry about in the first place. But those guys don't take chances."

"His death, then, is a kind of a blessing for the company."

"I suppose so," Dick Martin said grimly. "But we'll miss him. A lot of people with choked voices have been on the phone to me in the last twenty-four hours."

"Who do you think might have wanted to kill him?"

"Are you hinting that Big Oil might have wanted to do it?"

"They're not nice people."

"They're certainly not. Maybe they wouldn't stop at murder if they had to. But they much prefer using wealth and power and high-paid lawyers. It's cleaner and neater. Besides I'm sure that their R and D people say the same thing that mine do. Jack was over the hill. He wasn't a threat to anyone anymore."

His death, however, also meant that a lot of people would be more secure in their jobs than they were forty-eight hours ago.

Would a defense attorney figure out this possibility? A high-quality one like Mick Whealan, now occupied as president of the Cook County Board, would surely think of it. Most would not. Such a line of defense—blaming the oil companies for framing Clare Turner—would play well in the media and establish reasonable doubt in most juries.

We'd damn well better plea bargain before someone on her defense team thought to ask what John Turner was working on when he died.

"Seventy-five miles a gallon?" I said to Dick Martin as I left his house.

"Yeah. Seventy-five miles a gallon. Funny thing, I kind of half believe it would work. Make the world a hell of a lot better place, wouldn't it?"

11

DRIVING CAUTIOUSLY ON THE KENNEDY AND THE CONGRESS (as we Irish Democrats call the Eisenhower) toward First Avenue in Maywood after I left Dick Martin, I pondered the life story of Jack Turner. What was it like to be a teenager in the Great Depression? What was it like to be in love for five years on a lonely island in the Pacific, thousands of miles away from the woman you wanted to marry? What was it like to come home and end up working as a garage mechanic? What was it like in a few years to become wealthy beyond your wildest dreams? What was it like to have an independent little stranger in your house, a child disrupting your work and your relationship with your wife? What was it like to see your life's blood pumping out of your neck?

A grim end to an astonishing American success story, a story none of whose components I had ever experienced.

By the time I had arrived at the Loyola Medical Center on First Avenue in Maywood, I was depressed, so depressed in fact that I did not notice the patch of ice on the visitors' parking lot, spun around in a hundred-and-eighty-degree skid and missed a Buick Park Avenue by a couple of inches.

I better watch myself, I thought as I walked into the hospital, or I could end up as a patient here.

A wiser admonition would have been that I was too deeply involved in my job and needed a long vacation. Things would be very different now if I had followed that latter advice.

I was free-lancing that Sunday. A state's attorney is not an investigator. That's what police are for. I had no business talking to Martin, although I was sure that whatever police force might interview him wouldn't find out about the new invention. Nor did I have any business snooping around the medical school.

But the case had already become an obsession.

I had to hunt for more than an hour in the hospital and the medical school to find someone who was willing and able to talk to me. He was Dr. James P. Couglin, head of the Internal Medicine Department.

"I don't quite understand the interest of the State's Attorney's Office in this young woman," he said dubiously as he waved me to a metal chair in a small windowless room, smelling strongly of antiseptic.

He was a big man, maybe six foot three, bald with a fringe of gray hair, an enormous frown, and a deep bass voice. He wore a green medical coat and jeans. I thought that I might want him as my doctor but that I would fear him as a student.

"There's been a murder committed, Doctor. Her father and mother were brutally murdered, their throats split."

He made a face, sickened at the picture. "And Dr. Turner is a suspect?"

"Doctor? She hasn't graduated yet."

"It's a courtesy for our upper division medical students. Well," he drummed his fingers on the steel table between us, "is she or isn't she a suspect?"

"I'd be less than honest if I said that she's not a suspect,

Doctor. She was in the house. She stands to gain from their death. Her behavior has been a bit strange. But we're a long way from pressing charges against her."

"So why do you want to talk to me?"

"It'll be an informal and off-the-record conversation, Doctor. I won't quote you. I certainly won't subpoena you. I merely want to get a feel for the girl's personality."

His frown became bigger.

"Off the record or on the record, I don't care, Mr. Scanlan. And I'd be happy to testify in a trial about Dr. Turner's personality and character."

I was taken aback.

"And you would say?"

"I would say that she's an absolutely first-rate student and a poised professional person and that a murder charge against her, of all people, is total nonsense."

I nodded my head. "I'm glad to hear you say that."

Actually I wasn't. I waited for him to continue.

Well, maybe I was. From this point on I can't describe much less explain my ambivalences.

"She's quiet and self-possessed but internally very strong. I can remember an incident in my field in which a senior resident ridiculed her diagnosis, one which was absolutely correct. I'm afraid the young man is a bit of a chauvinist, more than a bit as a matter of fact. She stood her ground. She neither backed off her own position nor answered him in kind. Rather she was both respectful and determined. Many other women students would have fled in tears. No chance of Clare Turner doing that. In the end she made a fool out of him rather than vice versa and everyone knew it."

"Impressive . . ."

"She's also exceptionally sensitive to patients. Most quiet young women of the sort she seems to be are also shy and tongue-tied with patients. I have been surprised how well she empathizes with them, without saying very much at all. It's really quite impressive."

"I was struck by what seemed to be the absence of grief or any emotion yesterday."

He nodded slowly. "That doesn't mean she experiences no emotion, Mr. Scanlan."

"I know that, Doctor."

"It would be compatible with what we see of Clare here. There are many layers of self-protection around her character, though less I think than when she started here. I believe she is in analysis, which, since she plans on being a psychiatrist, is an excellent idea."

"I see."

"Such self-protection is not necessarily dysfunctional, Mr. Scanlan."

"We all have defenses, Doctor. I have tons of them myself."

He laughed. "Quite right. It would be much healthier for Dr. Turner to display grief now. She will have to cope with it eventually. But I would not say that her self-restraint is so unusual as to be abnormal."

"I understand."

"Any other questions with which I might help you?" He had begun to trust me, which was perhaps, all things considered, a mistake.

"Her relations with her fellow students."

He hesitated. "She was not what could be called a loner surely. Nor would one say she was an extrovert. Some students insist on eating lunch alone so they can study during the lunch hour. She was always with others; I can never remember seeing her eating alone. She might have said very little to them, but she was present."

"Did you ever see her laugh, Doctor? Or smile?"

"So that's what worries you? You wonder why a lovely

young woman who must be capable of a radiant smile does not reveal that radiance?"

"I wouldn't expect her to be radiant at the time of her parents' murder, but the absence of facial expressions . . ."

"Yes, I know what you mean." He drummed on the table again. "It did not go unnoticed here. At first we thought she was too serious. I wouldn't say that we were wrong. However, I also learned that she has quite a complex repertory of facial expressions. They were only slight movements but they conveyed a lot."

"I understand."

I didn't really.

"There was a student party once." He frowned, as if he were hesitant about revealing what happened at student parties. "I had been invited out of courtesy, one of those come-early-and-leave-early invitations. Dr. Turner entertained us all with an imitation of my classroom manner. She is quite a good mimic, actually."

"Really?"

"I was astonished. So, I might add, was everyone else. Later she apologized to me for fear she had hurt my feelings. I responded by congratulating her on a superb show. There was devilment in her eyes, Mr. Scanlan. It was gone by the next class. But it had been there just the same and not, unless I'm completely mistaken, for the first time."

"I see."

I didn't really. Not at all.

"You must follow your own professional norms, Mr. Scanlan. All I can say is that you would be gravely mistaken if you judged Clare Turner by her seemingly impassive behavior."

"I understand, Doctor." I stood up. "Thank you for your time and patience."

"Not at all." He shook hands firmly.

I turned to leave.

"One more thing, Mr. Scanlan."

"Yes, Doctor?"

"Will the Bears win the Super Bowl this year?"

"There's not a chance of them getting beyond their division."

"Diminish that chance by one million and you'll have the odds that Clare Turner killed her parents or anyone else."

"I'll keep that in mind, Doctor."

I guess I didn't keep it in mind—though I didn't forget it either.

I had heard two ringing endorsements for Clare Turner that frigid Sunday—she was sweet and she was empathetic. I was not convinced. Maybe I should have been convinced.

I went home and called one of my young assistants. "Peg, find out the details about the Turner will by tomorrow evening."

"Yes, sir," she said. "Right away, sir."

12

THE FIRST THING THE NEXT MORNING, IN MY SMALL AND cramped office—one desk and two chairs to myself because I'm a senior person—at Twenty-sixth and California (the County Courthouse and Administrative Building is five miles away from the center of the city because a county commissioner owned the swamp on which it was built) I thought about resigning. I had been thinking about that every Monday morning for a year.

I'm depressed every time I walk into the building, by the steady stream of drug dealers, released on personal recognizance bonds, coming out of the building, by the appealing little children of the people we try to send to jail, by the bored cops and bailiffs, by the rushing crowds of state's attorneys and public defenders, all with folders under their arms, and by the conversations in the elevators about the next job.

I'm sick of the courtyard of the old stone county jail outside my single window, of the thought of fifty judges and thirty thousand felony cases a year (half of them drug or drug-related charges), of drug dealers back on Halsted Street an hour after we release them, and of the fact that while the majority of judges, prosecutors, public defenders, bailiffs, and cops are white, ninety-five percent of the alleged offenders are black.

"We can't solve social problems," Dan Hills says, "we can win individual victories. Other social systems have to deal with the causes."

We win some. In the corner of my office—blond furniture, blue carpet, green cushions on the two chairs—is an automobile seat with a seatbelt. The seatbelt won't open once you've closed it. A junior high school teacher offered kids—of both sexes—rides home in his car. Then, having trapped them in the front seat, he would sodomize them with a long screwdriver. I took him out of circulation for a while.

Some victory.

Anyway, I decided that I wouldn't quit this Monday. First I would put Clare Turner behind bars at Dwight State Prison for Women, where she could look forward to a life of sexual slavery to black lesbians.

I made my call through to Tucson.

"Pete, do you know a guy named Fred Turner?"

"You bet I do."

Pete was a Hispanic with a Swiss name whose family had been in the United States a lot longer than either the Scanlans or the Fillamarinos.

"Tell me about it."

"An operator. Shady. Not exactly a criminal, but on the edges of it. Drinks too much, may be an alcoholic. Made a lot of money and lost a lot of it. A couple of times. A bit over the hill now, but likes to pretend he's still a player."

"Uh-huh."

"I hear that he's in some trouble. Needs maybe a quarter million or even more to meet some loan payments. If he doesn't he'll lose a lot more than that."

"Like his life?"

"No. The mob isn't involved, but a big hunk of his liveli-hood. What you got on him?"

"Possibility of murder one."

Pete whistled.

"His brother and sister-in-law were killed early Saturday morning. Fred will be one of the heirs. Turns out he was at O'Hare on Friday night."

Pete whistled again.

"Sound like him?"

"Not really. I can't see him planning a murder, especially a bloody one."

"In a fit of anger?"

"Maybe. But he's a pretty weak fellow. Still, who knows about killers?"

"Right. He does need the money, however?"

"Pretty desperately."

"Thanks a lot. I'll keep you posted."

"You coming out here soon? I can still beat you on Tucson National."

"That's not the way I remember it."

I put down the phone and it rang again.

"Joe Stewart here, Terry."

"Good morning, Joe. What do you have for me?"

"A lot of stuff. We're releasing the bodies late this after-noon. Wake tomorrow, Miss Turner tells me, funeral Wednesday."

"OK."

"Will you be in attendance?"

"No . . . what else do you have?"

"The autopsy shows no sign of any other cause of death, no narcotics or anything like that. They both were pretty sick."

"Got it."

"Interpol gives the McLaughlins a clean bill of health."

"From the Irish Garda?"

"Right. We checked their bank account. They have a couple hundred thousand tucked away. No reason to kill for jewels, especially if the Turners didn't leave them anything in the will."

"Figures."

"Fred Turner checks out. He did have a business meeting and he was registered at the Westin. He was seen there that night, but nothing airtight."

"OK."

"Clare Turner does not wear jewelry, so she never wore her mother's."

"Fine."

A living saint, was she?

"Most of the jewelry is still missing, according to the insurance schedule."

"That's interesting. You're still searching for it?"

"You bet . . . No fingerprints on the scalpel or the jewels."

"Damn."

"None besides the decedents in the workshop—except for Mrs. McLaughlin's on the dishes and Ms. Turner's on the lock."

"On the lock?" My head snapped up.

"Just one key. Remember she opened it after Sean McLaughlin cut the hole in the door."

"Right."

I wouldn't dare use that in a prosecution. A jury would know we were short on evidence if I tried it. Dead giveaway.

"No recollection in the community of Ms. Turner using drugs. She seems clean on other misbehavior. A quiet girl they all say. No one ever knew what she was thinking. Some found her a little scary because she was so quiet, but hell that's no crime."

"Not at all . . . Anything on her real parents?"

"Nothing so far. Oh, yes, April Kincaid. No alibi except from her husband, though mind you we didn't ask directly. Someone called me to say she had heard her in the supermarket the other day moaning about the addition to the Turner house—and that after five years."

"Not much to go on."

"That's about all for the moment, Terry, except the media are giving me hell. They want an arrest."

"They always do."

"They've pretty much made up their minds that it's Clare Turner."

"Give us twenty-four more hours."

"Right."

Outside the city was in the grip of a massive thaw. The two blizzards were melting into a vast and messy swamp. All we'd need was another freeze and Chicago would be a large hockey rink.

I put the phone down and it rang again.

"Terry? Dan."

"What took you so long?"

"Your line was busy. What do you have for me?"

"It'll take another day to put it all together."

"The media want an arrest."

"Don't they always?"

"Did this daughter do it?"

"Yeah."

"Do we have a case against her?"

"Pretty thin at the moment."

"The boss is on my back. So is the mayor of Lakewood."

"Look, weren't you the one who told me that you look pretty silly if you make an arrest and then have to drop the charges?"

"Yeah. I also told you that sometimes you have to prosecute a weak case."

"What you actually said was that rarely if ever do we bring such a case to trial."

He laughed. "You and your damn memory . . . Who's representing her?"

"Rollins, Parks, et al."

"Old Chandler Parks?"

"Not that old."

"An asshole."

"My thought to the word."

"They won't have one of their crew go into court will they?"

"We should be so lucky."

"That old phony Elmer McBride?"

"That would be prima facie malpractice. Let's hope they do."

Dan hesitated. "You sure she did it?"

"She stands to inherit maybe fifteen million dollars."

"Wow! And she's adopted?"

"Great case."

No trace of concern for the suspect's possible innocence?

Not much, but, you see, that's not our job, that's the job of defense counsel—and ultimately of the jury. In most criminal cases, even murder cases, there really isn't much doubt about who committed the crime. It's usually the one who stands to profit the most from it or the one who is closest to the victim or maybe both. A child who inherits a lot of money is not only prima facie the first suspect, but the most likely criminal.

We don't go after people about whose innocence there can be no doubt. And we try our best in Cook County not to let the cops phony up evidence that's not valid, even if we're convinced we don't have enough to put a guilty person behind bars.

There are a lot more mystery books than there are mysteries. Usually the problem is not solving the crime, but getting enough proof to win a case.

Do innocent people go to jail? Sometimes, usually because of phony evidence, occasionally because of honest mistakes. But the conversation between me and Dan Hills would routinely have been the proper one. Now I'm convinced that we were not careful enough.

That gets ahead of my story.

I read the various reports that Chief Stewart had faxed me. Damn! Why were there no fingerprints? And where had she hidden the rest of the jewels?

Just before noon, the Chief was on the phone again.

"She just came in and volunteered to take a lie detector test."

"What!"

"Calm as you please. Said she knew that she was under suspicion and that it would make life simpler for everyone if she took the lie detector test."

"What nerve!"

A worthy opponent anyway.

"Said she wanted to get it over with."

"She came alone or with a lawyer?"

"Alone. I told her she'd have to come back with a lawyer. She said she would."

"Who's acting for her?"

"A man named McBride."

"Elmer McBride?"

"I think so."

"She deserves better."

"Strange thing for you to say."

"Yeah, I guess it is . . . They're doing it at District 15 State Police?"

"First thing in the morning. What if she passes?"

"That information can't be used in court. Besides, icy people like her can fool the machine. The most we'll concede is that the test didn't suggest guilt. Inconclusive."

"She thinks she can beat the machine?"

"You bet. Why else do it?"

The phone rang again. "Ter? Peggy."

"No excuses."

"Hey, man," she protested, "I'm six hours early."

"Let's have it."

"Short or long?"

"For the moment short."

"OK. When all the taxes are paid out, she'll have three million up front and a trust fund that should generate a half million a year in current dollars. She's also a life member of the board of the foundation which controls the company. The income from that goes to Catholic schools in the Archdiocese."

"Wow!"

"You said it."

"Her uncle?"

"He'll have a half million to play with. Not too bad either."

"The McLaughlins?"

"Five thousand each."

"Not much."

"No motive there, Ter."

"And if she loses the money because of a murder or manslaughter conviction?"

"The whole kit and caboodle goes to the Archdiocese."

"Would you say God is on the side of a conviction?"

"Can't tell what She'll do, can you?"

"I guess not."

"Do I get to work on this case? I hate the bitch already."

"We'll think about it."

Of course she would get to work on it. But we older folk have to keep things under control—especially when the younger ones are only four years younger.

Just Clare Turner's age as a matter of fact.

13

"DO YOU HAVE A CASE, TERRY?"
Dan Hills was sitting in my office, legs around the back of the chair, chin resting on the top, a coffee cup in his hand—he always comes to your office instead of summoning you to his.

Dan is in his late thirties, a tall, thin man, with thick black hair, a quick smile, and enough charm for five people like me—your central casting prosecuting attorney. He's been the brains of the office for eight years. If he goes into private practice—and he should because he has four kids to send to college—I'm supposed to be the designated replacement. No way I'll take the job. I'm tired of the dirt and grime of being a prosecutor. Worse, I'll never be good enough to carry Dan's gym shoes.

He has three stock openings for the kind of conversation we were about to have.

"You got a case" meant you had his OK to proceed and he'd take the rap if something went wrong.

"You haven't got a case" meant forget it, you shouldn't even have bothered him with this.

The opening gambit with me was somewhere in between.

It meant that I had to convince him and that if he then gave his OK it was my responsibility and I took the rap if we lost.

"We got a case," I replied, "but not much of a case. Just the same I think we gotta indict. The media are screaming for an arrest."

"The kid passed a lie detector test."

"It was inconclusive."

"Yeah, that's what *we* say. But you know as well as I do that we normally let them walk if they do as well as she did."

"She's one of the most self-possessed human beings I've ever met. I think she fooled the machine."

"Yeah, tell me what you got."

So I went through the evidence. It sounded pretty weak. "Look," I summed it up, "she was the only one in the house. She had all the motives. There's a history of family conflict. She's a little odd. Who else might have done it? If we let her walk, we'll never find a killer."

"Any other suspects?"

I went through the list.

Dan shifted back and forth in his chair. Then he sipped his black coffee.

"She's the most likely of the lot," he agreed, "but a defense attorney could have a field day with all of them."

"If he's smart enough to research them."

"That's right," he agreed dubiously. "Who's appearing for her?"

"Would you believe Elmer McBride?"

He closed his eyes and shook his head. "She deserves better."

"We play them as they're dealt."

"Agreed . . . but look, Terry, me fine bucko, if we get a judge with any intelligence he'll dismiss the case at the very beginning."

"I won't let it get that far."

"Plead her?"

"Why not?"

"For what?"

"Guilty but mentally ill. Twenty years. It's better than the rest of her natural life."

"A smart lawyer wouldn't buy it, not with our case."

"Not guilty by reason of insanity. Indefinite time in a hospital?"

"The media won't like that either."

"We point out that she loses her inheritance."

"Yeah," he agreed dubiously.

"When the shrinks let her out, a couple of years maybe if we can lean on them, the media hardly notice. It's one day on the back pages."

He shook his head. "I don't like it."

"I don't like it either. But we can't just let her walk. She doesn't have a good lawyer. This way she loses the inheritance most likely, but she's a free woman in a couple of years and maybe can practice medicine in some other state. And she's got the jewels."

"Why haven't the cops recovered them?"

"Beats me."

"Wait a minute." He sat up straight. "If she was smart enough to hide them, why leave evidence in her car?"

"She didn't expect the snowstorm. She was going to trade them to a fence for some quick money."

"Maybe," he sighed.

"Murderers are dumb even when they're smart."

"I won't argue that."

My brother the priest says that in life there are certain critical turning points, times when you make a decision that will shape the rest of your life—without knowing that the decision is all that important. He says it doesn't matter how bad the weather is or how tired you are or how pissed off you might feel, these are the decisions that really count and there's no excuse for blowing them.

I've often thought, as I recall that conversation with Dan, that I was at that moment making one such decision.

"Look," I summed up my argument for Dan, "even if they won't plead her and even if we get thrown out on a motion to dismiss, we'll at least have the media off our back. We can't let her walk now. They'll scream special treatment for the rich. OK, if the case is thrown out, they can blame the judge; and plea bargains don't get headlines."

"By the time it goes down, people will forget the case?" Dan frowned. "Is that it?"

"You want to announce that we're not going to indict?"

"Not particularly."

"Let a jury of her peers decide whether there's enough evidence that she killed her parents, if it comes to that. Why should we make that decision for them?"

"You know how many trials we'd have if we followed that policy?" He grinned wickedly.

"This is different, Dan. This is the brutal killing of a great if little-known man by an adopted daughter which is front-page news and the lead story on evening TV."

"Underrated inventor." He did his John Madden imitation. "You really want to do it?"

"I think we have to."

He bit on the rim of his plastic coffee cup. "OK," he said, "go with it. But I don't especially like it. I got a feeling in the back of my neck; we're opening up Pandora's box on this one."

"Peggy as a junior?"

He stood up. "Yeah, that's a good idea. Nice contrast for the jury."

When he'd left my office, I had a few brief second

thoughts. The back of Dan's neck was notoriously accurate as a prophet.

Yet looking back on it, I don't think we could have gotten away with not indicting her. The media would have been down on Dan and the Boss. They'd already convicted her.

I brushed away my doubts and dialed an internal number.

"Peg? Terry. I want a locksmith who can take apart this nonsense about a lock for which you can't make an extra key. Find out the name of the company that makes them and see what they have to say."

"Gesselschaftweiss A.G. in Lucern."

"Right."

"Does that mean we're going after the bitch?"

"It sure does."

"And I'm on the case."

"For the moment."

And that was that.

That afternoon I called Elmer McBride with Peg listening on the other phone in my office.

"Elmer, this is Terry Scanlan at the state's attorney's office. We're going to indict your client Clare Turner."

"Who?"

Two o'clock and he was drunk already?

"The woman who slit her parents' throats up in Lakewood."

"Is alleged to have slit their throats."

"Look, Elmer, we don't want to have to bring this one to trial. We have all the evidence we need. Murder one. Aggravated. Two deaths. Robbery. Robbery in a private home. We could go for the death penalty. But there are mitigating circumstances, her parents were real weirdos. We'd be prepared to do a bargain."

That's the way we play it. With someone brighter than

Elmer is these days I'd have been a little more subtle. What can I tell you?

"Ah . . . who did you say you were?"

"Terry Scanlan."

"You haven't worked there for twenty years."

"That's my father, Jim Scanlan."

"Jim old enough to have a son working for Rich Daley?"

"Rich isn't state's attorney anymore. He's mayor."

"That's right." He chuckled. "So you're old Jimmy Scanlan's son."

"That's right, now about Clare Turner . . ."

"You want a plea?"

"All things considered at the present time, we think that would be best."

"What are you offering?"

I hesitated. Make it tough and force them to negotiate? Not too good an idea because I didn't think old Elmer was capable of negotiating. But, damn it, I didn't want her to walk quite so easily.

"Guilty but mentally ill. Twenty years. Maybe some kind of informal agreement about clemency if she shapes up. Say seven or eight years?"

Which meant four or five.

"Very interesting. I'll talk to my client. Be back to you. Jimmy still alive?"

"Very much so."

"He married that gorgeous Italian gal, didn't he?"

"He did indeed."

"Well give them both my best."

"Sure will."

I hung up and then Peg did the same. "Poor bitch deserves better than that," she said.

Peg Burke had long blond hair, a turned-up Irish nose, and a mind like a 386 computer. If I had brought her home to

Mother, that latter worthy would have been delighted, despite the fact that Peg was not Italian. However, Peg was not interested in marriage or even romance at the moment, and anyway, she scared the hell out of me.

"We play with what we're dealt. And I don't want any sisterly solidarity on this case, young woman."

"Fat chance."

I heard nothing from Elmer McBride until the day that we arraigned Clare Turner in the court of Judge B. Michael "Micky" O'Malley, quite possibly the worst fool ever to preside over a courtroom in the county of Cook.

The computer spits out random assignments of judges to cases these days—the presiding judge picks them only when the computer is down. The system is supposed to be unbeatable, but no system is ever unbeatable.

The Administrative Building, where we had our offices—normally two or three prosecutors to an office—was built in the seventies. The County Courthouse next door is an art deco legal temple dating to 1927, complete with black marble pillars, tall bronze lamp stands (which might have held candles), cross-beamed ceilings with floral designs in the panels, and white marble walls. It's your typical TV courthouse but more down at the heels—and covered always with a thick layer of Chicago dust.

The courtrooms, some of them now marred by thick glass security walls, look like chapels, albeit Protestant chapels—benches like pews, marble walls, and dark wood altars behind which the judge sits while, in some cases, a jury sits in choir stalls.

In one such courtroom, Clare Turner looked pale and gaunt—a few hours in the lockup, chained to drug dealers and whores, will do that to you, especially if you're a bright young woman from the suburbs.

"Elmer," I grabbed his cashmere overcoat as he walked

into the courtroom, "I haven't heard from you about my offer for a plea."

"Hmm?" Elmer's expression was empty as Lake Michigan on a winter day, and about as warm. He was a big, florid
man with bushy white hair, expensive clothes, the faint smell
of booze mixed with Ralph Lauren cologne, and the phony
geniality of the stage Irishman.

"I said we'd accept a voluntary manslaughter plea, three
to six years."

"Did you really? Let's see, young man, what was your
name again?"

"Terry Scanlan."

"Ah yes, Jim Scanlan's son."

"That's right."

Now seemed the perfect time for a plea, tie the whole
thing up and get it out of the papers, save everyone a lot of
work.

"And what is it you're asking about?"

I would have been less impatient if I thought he was putting me on.

"If your client is willing to plead manslaughter, we'll let
her out of jail in twenty, twenty-two months."

"Hmn . . . we've discussed this before?"

"On the phone."

"Well, my client is not guilty and will not accept any plea
bargain."

"Have it your way." I turned on my heel and walked away
from him.

I should have offered him the fallback plea—not guilty by
reason of insanity. We would have called for a hearing. She
would have gone off to a hospital for a couple of years.

For some reason my back was up. I didn't want her to
walk on an easy plea.

I doubted that he'd ever discussed the plea with Clare

Turner. A good defense attorney would have realized that we didn't have a strong case and looked for a plea. At the moment, especially in the courtroom of the erratic and irascible B. Michael O'Malley, I might have bought it if I were a good defense attorney.

Maybe not. A really good one would know that he could kill us in a trial. He would have taken the chance of a trial if his client was ready to run the risk.

There was, after all, millions of dollars at stake.

B. (for Boyle) Michael was a mean, fussy little tyrant with a permanent squint and a nasty sneer. He is the kind of small, bald man who sits at the very end of an Irish bar and makes snide comments about everyone who comes in and would get his front teeth punched out every day, if he wasn't such a weak little runt.

So Clare Turner, wearing a gray suit, a white blouse, and her rimless glasses, pleaded, in a cold and confident voice despite the trauma of being enveloped by our criminal justice system, that she was not guilty to a charge of murder in the first degree.

We asked for a million dollar bond.

"These are very serious crimes, Your Honor." Peg spoke for us, glaring at the defendant. "They are not the result of an ordinary domestic quarrel. The court ought to send a strong message to young Americans about respect for parents."

It was bullshit. Clare Turner was not about to run away.

"My client is an outstanding young woman, Your Honor. There is not even a traffic ticket on her record. She should be permitted to continue her medical education. I propose a fifty-thousand-dollar bail."

"You're out of your mind, Mr. McBride," the judge snorted, "if you think you're going to get away with that in my courtroom." He reached for his gavel. "There'll be no bail in this case." He pounded his gavel. "Bailiff, see that the defendant is removed in restraints to the women's section of Cook County Jail." He pounded the gavel. "Next matter?"

So an unprotesting Clare Turner was handcuffed and led off back to jail. The media people rushed from the courtroom.

"I'll be damned," I murmured to Peggy.

"Probably," she replied, "at least for a long time in purgatory for your chauvinism . . . Who is crazier, Judge or Counsel for the Defense?"

"Maybe we're the crazy ones for being in a courtroom with either of them. She'll be out by Monday on appeal."

"A weekend with the bull dykes in county jail, poor bitch."

First time Peg had used the word "poor," a dangerous adjective on the lips of an Irish woman.

A TV person stabbed a mike at me. "The judge seems to be taking this crime more seriously than the state's attorney, Mr. Scanlan."

"We're delighted that Judge O'Malley is concerned about keeping criminals off the street. We wish that other judges would be equally concerned."

I didn't add that in other cases Micky O'Malley showed no hesitancy in putting rapists and drug dealers back out on the street.

Later, eating lunch with Dan Hills at Bruna's, an old speakeasy converted into an Italian restaurant over on Oakley Avenue, beneath the towers of St. Paul's Church (German national), I wondered aloud about the impact on our slender case of B. Michael's unique approach to the law.

"If I were you," he said grimly, "I'd pray that he turns around and throws it out. Otherwise, even if you persuade a jury that there is evidence beyond a reasonable doubt of Clare Turner's guilt, you'll have to try it over again because First District Appellate will find reversible error. Poor

Micky can't help himself, he always commits reversible error. He should have been put out to pasture long ago . . . and can you imagine if an appeal goes into the federal courts? What would Eileen Kane do if the case showed up in her courtroom?"

"Ship us to Alaska if we were lucky . . . You're probably right, Dan," I agreed grimly. "It'll be a charade for the next couple of weeks. But we got him on the luck of the computer draw, didn't we?"

"Did we?" Dan looked at me suspiciously.

"What do you mean?"

He shrugged. "Not sure exactly. But nothing ever happens just by accident in the Cook County court system."

14

WHAT CAN I TELL YOU, FATHER BLACKIE?
I was badly confused. I should have taken myself off the case. The idea didn't occur to me. But it should have occurred to me. I'm a professional, an experienced prosecutor. I should have known what I was doing.

I was fighting off or rather trying to fight off a strong emotional attachment toward a defendant who seemed obviously to be the murderer of her parents. If it were not for the emotional turbulence in my head, and other parts of me too, I guess, I might have been more objective. I might have told Dan Hills that, media or not, we didn't have a case and that we'd be better off if we took the media heat by saying that instead of taking more heat if a jury creamed us.

I suppose I thought I could beat Elmer no matter how weak our case. Maybe I could have too.

Did I ever really admit to myself that I was falling in love with Clare Turner?

No. I dismissed my reactions as lust resulting from prolonged frustration.

Yeah. I know that at the beginning of a relationship it's

hard to distinguish the two. But I was Terry Scanlan, the hottest prosecutor at Twenty-sixth and California. I was not about to let lust interfere with my professional performance.

So I would break down completely later on.

15

THE TRIAL BLURS IN MY MEMORY. I RECALL SNIPPETS OF
dialogue—and moments of astonishment and surprise as
Judge O'Malley destroyed Clare Turner's defense and as I
often stared out of the dirty windows of the courtroom in the
direction of Lake Michigan (invisible in the distance) and
wondered what sense any of it made.

"Your Honor," Counsel for the Defense in his most pon-
derous tones, sounding like a cardinal in the pre-Vatican
Catholic Church, "even the most cursory examination of the
evidence which the State of Illinois proposes to offer
against Clare Turner reveals that to call it paper thin would
be to pay it a compliment. The most they can bring against
my client is circumstantial evidence and that of poor quality.
This absurd trial should be brought to a conclusion before it
begins. Your Honor, with great respect for your wisdom, I
move for dismissal."

Peg and I held our breath. We were both ambivalent. We
did not want to lose before we began. But we did not want to
try this case, not at all if it came to that (though we had never
admitted that explicitly to each other), but surely not before
this judge.

"Don't be ridiculous, Mr. McBride." He pounded his gavel. "Motion denied." Another pound. "The trial will continue."

"The prosecution will show, Your Honor, gentlepersons of the jury, that this foster daughter, for motives of pure selfishness and greed, deliberately and in cold blood slit the throats of her parents and left them to bleed to death in their beds. John and Mary Turner watched their life blood spill out of their throats and regretted in the last moments of their lives that they had ever taken this young woman into their home. We are charging murder in the first degree, and aggravated murder at that—two deaths and a robbery in a private home. We believe that such a crime justifies our asking for the death penalty."

Gasp in the courtroom. No reaction from Clare Turner.

"Ladies and gentlemen of the jury, all the prosecution has to sustain its case is the weakest kind of circumstantial evidence, hardly enough to bring a charge into this courtroom and surely not enough to subject this sterling young woman to the ordeal she must endure. I'm sure that when we have picked apart the State's case, you'll bring in an immediate verdict of not guilty and permit her to return to the career of service to which she has so generously dedicated herself."

"Now, Chief Stewart, my learned and gifted young colleague in his direct examination drew from you the statement that a panel had been removed from the door to the workshop at the back of the Turner house.

"Can you tell us who removed that panel?"

"Mr. McLaughlin, sir."

"Ah. And why was this necessary?"

"To gain entry to the workshop so as to ascertain why the Turners did not answer their phone."

"Could not a key have been used?"

"No, sir. The key was inside the workshop."

"But surely there was another key somewhere in the house?"

"No, sir. It was a special lock, made by Gesselschaftweiss in Switzerland."

"Well, I know about Swiss watches, Chief, but Swiss *locks*?"

"Yes, sir. The lock was opened by a metal disk. You had to write to Switzerland to obtain an extra copy."

"Were you able to verify that there was not a second key to this particular lock?"

"Yes, sir."

"Now, Chief Stewart, if the door to the workshop was locked and the key was inside it, how could the defendant have obtained access to the workshop and murder her parents?"

This was the ball game. Dubious about my chances of winning it, I objected.

"Your Honor, this is a murder trial, not an Agatha Christie locked room mystery novel."

"Sustained."

"Your Honor," adjusting his tie clasp, and tugging on his French cuffs, Elmer McBride turned to the jury and then slowly back to the judge, "this matter is crucial. I hope to show that my client did not have the opportunity to kill her parents. If she did not have the opportunity, then all the circumstantial evidence that the prosecution has so diligently gathered becomes meaningless."

He was laying the groundwork for an appeal. B. Michael ought to have known that. He ought to have permitted the questions about the locked room to continue. But he didn't seem to care about being reversed or about the impression his ruling might make on the jury.

"I've made my ruling, Mr. McBride. As the state's attorney has said this is not a trashy mystery story."

I knew now how Tom Foran felt during the legendary Chicago Seven trial. He watched a good case be destroyed by the pettiness and stupidity of Judge Julius "The Just" Hoffman. The only difference was that my case was much weaker. I probably would not need my expert witness, a lock maker who claimed that he could made a duplicate for a Gesselschaftweiss lock.

"We won that one," Peg whispered in my ear.

"How do you think the jury is reacting?"

"They don't like either of those old men."

"I agree."

"And Clare Turner?"

"Cold bitch . . . but, I have to admit, kind of elegant too. Dragon Lady."

"One more question, Mr. McLaughlin. When you were summoned by Miss Turner to open the door to the workshop, did you try to open the door with the door handle?"

"No, sir." His big forehead furrowed as though he didn't know we were going to ask the question.

"Why not?"

"Didn't Miss Turner say that the door was locked?"

"Did she?"

"Didn't I just say that?"

Damn, what they did in Irish courts about this habit of answering a question with another question.

"Please answer by not asking a question, Mr. McLaughlin."

"Yes, sir."

"Yes, sir, what?"

"Miss Clare said the door was locked."

"So what did you do?"

"I tried to break it down, and like I said then I got a drill and a saw and cut a panel out of the door."

"I see. But you cannot testify with certainty that it was locked."

"No, sir."

"Thank you, Mr. McLaughlin."

McBride attacked at once.

"You've just said, Mr. McLaughlin, that you can't testify that the door was locked?"

"That's right."

"But you can't say that it was unlocked either?"

"No, sir."

"In your experience was it always locked when it was closed?"

"Almost always, yes, sir."

"Almost?"

"Once or twice I found it open, but not very often."

"It was usually locked when it was closed."

"Yes, sir."

I held my breath. But Elmer didn't pursue the subject.

"Dr. Morris, I ask you this: is it your conclusion that the cause of death was a sharp weapon in the hands of someone who was very skilled in its use?"

"Yes, Miss Burke, it was a clean incision, very quickly made by someone who knew what he was doing."

"He or she?"

"Yes, ma'am."

"Now, Dr. Morris, is this scalpel, State's Exhibit 7, the kind of weapon that might have been used?"

"Yes it is."

"What sort of instrument is it, Dr. Morris?"

"It's a surgical scalpel."

"The sort that would be readily available to a doctor?"

"Yes, ma'am."

"Or a medical student?"

"Objection."

"Overruled. You may answer, Dr. Morris."

"Yes, ma'am, it is."

"Dr. Morris," McBride fingered the buttons on his vest, "did I hear you say that it was a medical scalpel which killed the two victims?"

"No, sir. I did not say that."

"I must be mistaken. What did you say?"

"I said the wounds could have been made by a medical scalpel."

"Ah . . . the wounds were compatible with the use of such a weapon."

"That is correct."

"Well, now, sir," he puffed out his chest, "are there any other kinds of weapons which might have been used?"

"I suppose so. Sharp weapons."

"An ordinary kitchen knife?"

"If it was sharp enough and used skillfully enough, yes."

"Thank you very much, Doctor."

"Can you tell me, Officer Crawford, where you found this scalpel, the one with material on it that the state crime laboratory identified as blood of the same type as that of John Turner?"

"In a book bag, Ms. Burke."

"The kind of bag that college or graduate students use?"

"Yes, ma'am."

"In fact, it is the bag here on that table labeled State's Exhibit 11."

"Yes it is."

"Where did you find this bag, Officer Crawford?"

"In a Porsche motorcar in the Turner garage."

"A *Porsche*?"

"Yes, ma'am."

"That's a very expensive car, isn't it, Officer?"

"Objection!"

"Overruled."

"Yes, ma'am, I believe it is."

"Was there anything else in the bag, Officer?"

"Yes, ma'am."

"What else did you find?"

"Jewelry."

"State's Exhibit 12?"

"Yes, ma'am."

"I see. Anything else?"

"Yes, ma'am. A pair of plastic gloves."

"State's Exhibit 13?"

"That is correct."

"The kind of gloves that doctors or medical students use?"

"Objection, Your Honor. My respected colleague is asking for an opinion."

"Overruled. And stop sputtering, Mr. McBride. If you continue your attempts to disrupt the smooth flow of the prosecution's case, I'll be forced to hold you in contempt of court. You may answer, Officer."

"Yes, ma'am, I believe it is."

"No further questions. Your witness, Mr. McBride."

"Now, Officer Crawford, I'm sure a quick-witted and intelligent young woman like you would have observed all the important details in that garage."

"I tried to, sir."

"Did you happen to notice the odometer in that expensive Porsche motorcar?"

The woman cop hesitated. "Yes, sir, I did."

"And how many miles that expensive car ate up in its lifetime?"

"I'm not sure of the exact number. It was certainly over a hundred and fifty thousand miles."

"Objection, Your Honor, the question is irrelevant. I admire Ms. Crawford's attention to detail, but it has no bearing on the case."

"A little late in coming, Mr. Scanlan, but I will sustain it."

"No further questions."

But Elmer had made his point.

I would remind the jury later that in his testimony McLaughlin had said that he never tried to open the door himself when Clare Turner summoned him.

That was my locked room explanation—the door had been opened with an electric toothbrush and had remained open until Clare and McLaughlin had entered it. There had been no need to cut the hole in the door.

We had searched the house for an electric toothbrush but were unable to find one. An investigator hinted that maybe we should plant one. I wasn't even tempted. Not much anyway.

"So, Sergeant Reed, you conclude that this set of prints you found on the safe in the Turner workshop are, beyond any possible doubt, the prints of Clare Turner?"

"Yes, sir."

"And you searched for prints on this book bag."

"Yes, sir."

"You found prints?"

"Yes, sir, many prints old and new."

"Of one person or many?"

"Only one, sir."

"And whose prints might those have been, Sergeant?"

"Clare Turner's, sir."

"I see. No further questions. Counselor?"

"Yes, thank you very much, Mr. Scanlan. Now, Sergeant, I have only one or two more questions for you. First of all, were there any fingerprints on the scalpel or the jewels that are State's exhibit, let me see, I have a hard time keeping the numbers straight . . ."

"Get on with it, Mr. McBride."

"Yes, Your Honor, you must forgive an old man who needs to use his glasses . . . Ah, yes, Sergeant, exhibits 8 and 9."

"The jewels didn't yield much in the way of prints, such items rarely do."

"And the scalpel, this exhibit here, which the State seems to think is the murder weapon?"

"No, sir."

"No prints?"

"No, sir."

"None at all?"

"No, sir."

"Very interesting . . . Now just one more question: did you find Clare Turner's prints anywhere else in the Turner workshop?"

"No, sir."

B. Michael looked at me as if he expected another objection. I ignored him.

"Very interesting. Now would the single set of her prints on the safe be consistent with her opening wider the door of an already open safe to see if anything had been taken?"

"Objection. Speculative question."

"Sustained. The point, Mr. McBride, is that the fingerprints were there."

"Yes, Your Honor." He sighed loudly. "No more questions."

Another point for McBride. Despite persistent interference from the judge, much of it an almost deliberate effort at reversible error, he was demolishing our case. No great credit was owed to him for doing that. A law school freshman could have done the same thing.

"Now, Mr. Leroy, would you tell me what kind of lock this is that we have marked State's Exhibit 14?"

"It's an elaborate form of your basic Caba lock."

"Where are these locks made?"

"In Switzerland usually."

"I see. And what are their advantages?"

I had hesitated about putting our locksmith on the stand after Judge Boyle had cut off McBride's efforts to raise the question of the locked room. However, the issue had been planted in the heads of the jurors, and it seemed like a good idea to respond with our technical expert.

"They have five tumblers, sir, and they cannot be opened with any ordinary lock-picking mechanism. Moreover the companies that make them provide only one key, unless you send them a sworn statement asking for another key."

"I see. So they're highly effective locks. Would you recommend them to someone who wanted to protect a special room in their house?"

"No, sir."

"Indeed. Why not?"

"You can open them with an electric toothbrush, Mr. Scanlan."

"Really?"

"Yes indeed."

"We have a battery-operated electric toothbrush in the

courtroom. Would you mind demonstrating how you would open this lock, Mr. Leroy?"

"Certainly. First I will lock it . . ."

"Hold it up please, Mr. Leroy, so the jury can see."

"Yes, sir . . . The five tumblers slip into place as you can see and the lock seems pretty firm. Then I jam the toothbrush into the keyhole like this . . . and the tumblers fall open. You might just as well not have a lock."

"So the single key strategem is useless if you have an electric toothbrush?"

"And know how to use it, yes, sir."

"Thank you, Mr. Leroy."

I wished he hadn't used the first phrase of his response. Too late now.

"Mr. Leroy," Elmer seemed to wake from a nap, "would you demonstrate for the jury how you secure that lock with your electric toothbrush?"

"Secure it?"

"Yes, sir, lock it."

"You can't lock it with the toothbrush, only open it."

"It only works one way then?"

"Yes, sir."

Judge Boyle was fuming. But I was not about to object and call attention to the weakness of our argument.

Elmer McBride must have been a hell of a lawyer in his sober prime.

"Do you happen to know where this toothbrush came from, Mr. Leroy?"

"No, sir."

"You don't know that it came from the Turner house?"

"No, sir."

"No further questions."

• • •

"Which one of the Kincaids do you want, Peg?"

"How come the choice?"

"I can't make up my own mind."

"Do you think she's sexy?" Peg eyed me closely.

"The daughter?"

" 'Course not, idiot. The mother."

"I don't know," I lied. "Why do you ask?"

"Curiosity about men's tastes I guess."

"Well," I decided to tell her the truth, "I think most men would find her very seductive in a kinky sort of way."

"Yeah." She nodded, as if understanding. "I think some women would too . . . I'll take her."

I had more sense than to ask why.

"Are you quite sure, Ms. Kincaid," Peg asked, "that it was seven-thirty when Ms. Turner phoned you?"

"Oh yes, quite sure, I had just made out my schedule for the evening you see."

April Kincaid was wearing a gray knit dress with a turtle-neck collar, the kind the fashion writers would call "demure" because in fact it was just the opposite. She had not abandoned her seductive little movements. The jury didn't like her much.

"You make a schedule each night?"

"Oh, yes, I make three schedules for each day, morning, afternoon, and evening and then revise them in the course of the day."

"I see. That's very efficient. What had you scheduled for that evening?"

"I intended to call those who would join my protest in the morning, then to catch up on some of my records, and then, ah, converse with my husband."

A little sexual innuendo for the courtroom.

Peg charged right over it.

"And can you remember exactly what Ms. Turner said?"

"Pretty much. I'd heard the excuse from her often before, poor thing. They were working on one of Mr. Turner's inventions," she shrugged, pushing out the top of her dress, "and she couldn't leave the house."

"Would you have any doubts that it was Ms. Turner's voice on the phone?"

April seemed surprised: "Oh, no, not at all. We had spoken hundreds of times on the phone since we've been neighbors. I would have known her voice even if she hadn't identified herself, which she did on this occasion."

Peg, playing the crisp, no-nonsense professional woman, guided her skillfully through the testimony, minimizing April's sexual impact.

"What was Ms. Clare Turner's reaction when you woke her with the call at 3 A.M.?"

"She sounded annoyed. Of course I *had* awakened her, hadn't I?"

"Did she refuse to check up on her parents?"

"Well, not exactly. But she seemed reluctant to get out of bed."

"So what did you say to her?"

"I told her about the cold wave and the storm and said that I was worried about them."

"And her reaction?"

"She sighed impatiently and then agreed to go down to the workshop."

"I see. What happened then?"

"Nothing really. I waited till she called back. I thought she would at least have the decency to tell me what she found. When there was no call, I went back to bed, and, ah, after a while I fell asleep."

"And you learned of the murder?"

"From the morning radio news."

"No further questions."

"Trash," Peg murmured when she returned to our table.

"Now let me get this straight, Mrs. Kincaid." Elmer was being the courtly gentleman for the lovely lady. "The jury and the judge and the attorneys visited Lakewood yesterday to inspect the Turner house. Yours was the one right next door, was it not?"

"That's right." She smiled sweetly at Elmer.

"Some distance away, however, as I remember it. Big lots in your lovely community."

"Yes."

"You could see the lights of the Turner workshop from your bedroom window? It seemed to me the trees pretty much obscured any view in that direction."

"Objection, Your Honor. Where is Counsel going with this line of questioning?"

Elmer walked over to our map of the Turner home and the area around it. "I'm just trying to clarify in my own mind, Your Honor, the layout at the scene of the crime."

"Very well, but don't delay us with too much attention to the layout. I'll overrule the objection."

"When there are leaves on the trees, one cannot see the light from their laboratory. But it was the middle of winter."

"Ah yes. So it was. But then in the middle of the night, you'd have the blinds drawn in your bedroom, would you not?"

"Certainly." She bristled.

"So the light wouldn't bother you very much?"

"The light was a constant affront." Her lips tightened. "It violated the privacy of our neighborhood as did that terrible glass monstrosity. I couldn't stand to think of it. Even with our drapes drawn it was a total violation."

"Really?"

"They had no sense of aesthetic beauty," she erupted. "I warned them that the workshop would attract tramps. What happened to them served them right!"

"How would you explain that statement?"

"Objection!"

"Sustained. Mr. McBride, that is a totally improper question."

As we left the courtroom at the end of that day, Peg snarled, "McBride is an asshole."

"I won't deny it, but why?"

"All right, he made April look like a crazy. He should have pressed on and made her look like a killer."

"I don't think the judge would have let him."

"Probably not, but he's a clever old geezer. He could have conveyed a lot more to the jury if he wanted to."

"If he thought of it, Peg, which he probably didn't."

"What do you want to bet she would undress in that room with the drapes open?"

"You think so?"

"You don't?"

"Hadn't thought of it."

"McBride should have asked her."

"The judge would have had apoplexy."

"But the jury would have heard the question. They'd know the answer too, at least the seven women would. That would make her seem very suspicious."

"You shouldn't be planning their strategy, Peg. You should be thinking about ours."

"I know." She sighed. "Not that it matters. The jury, except maybe for the foreman, is already on her side."

"I don't think so."

"Believe me they are. They might not have doctoral degrees, but they're smart. They know we don't have shit for a case."

• • •

"Now, Miss Kincaid, as a close friend and classmate of Clare Turner's through high school, how would you describe her relationship with her parents?"

Elaine Kincaid was pretending to be a reluctant witness. Actually she loved the attention.

"They were, you know, fighting all the time."

"I see. About what?"

"Everything. They wouldn't give her any freedom."

"And she was angry at them?"

"All the time."

"Did she ever threaten them?"

"Not exactly."

"What do you mean?"

"Well, she said once that they were elderly and she had to be nice to them while they were still alive."

"Indeed. They opposed her attending medical school, did they not?"

"Yes, they did. They thought she ought to take over the family giving."

"Giving what?"

"Money to charity."

"Did the conflicts lessen as she grew older?"

"I think they got worse."

"Objection. Pure conjecture."

"Overruled."

"Did Clare Turner have a temper?"

"A terrible temper. She kept it in most of the time, but when she exploded, she really blew her stack."

"Could you give me an example?"

"Well . . . I remember once when she missed a shot that cost us a basketball game, she wouldn't talk to anyone for three days."

"I see. Can you think of any other times, perhaps when she was angry at her parents?"

"Objection. Counselor is leading the witness."

"Overruled. Her relationship with her parents, Mr. McBride, as you perhaps have not noticed, is what this case is all about."

"Uh, well, I remember when she wanted to go away to college and they, like, wanted her to stay home, she was so mad that she goes she was thinking of running away. She even goes like she wished they had never adopted her."

"Did she, in your recollection, ever threaten to kill her parents?"

"Objection. Your Honor, the state's attorney's line of questioning is an outrageous violation of the right of a defendant to a fair trial."

"Overruled. It's your behavior, Mr. McBride, that is outrageous."

"Once, when she was in high school and they wouldn't let her go to the dance she, you know, told me that she was so mad that she could kill them."

"Kill them?"

"Yes, Mr. Scanlan."

"In so many words."

"Yes."

"No further questions."

"Now, Miss Kincaid, did you really think that she would go home and murder her parents when she said that?"

"I . . . I wasn't sure."

"Don't a lot of young people say things like that when they're angry and don't mean them literally?"

"I guess so."

"Did you tell your parents?"

"No." Her lip turned into a stubborn pout.

"If you thought she meant she would kill her parents and

you still didn't tell your parents, wouldn't you have been partially responsible for their deaths?"

"I suppose so."

I should have objected, but the whole trial was a foolish and silly game.

"So you really didn't think she meant it seriously?"

"Well, you know, kids say things they don't really mean after they say it."

"I see . . . Now isn't it true that you and Clare Turner were both candidates to be queen of the senior prom?"

"Yes."

"And who was the queen?"

"She was."

"Isn't it true that your friendship ended the day she won that election?"

"Objection, Your Honor. Irrelevant."

"Better late than never, Miss Burke. Sustained. This trial is not about senior proms, Mr. McBride. Do I have to remind you again that it's about murder?"

"Your Honor, I hope to show that this witness has reasons to hate the defendant."

"I have made my ruling, Mr. McBride. Proceed with your questions."

Once more, however, Elmer had made his point.

"Would you state your occupation, Mr. Lyons?"

"I'm a security consultant, Mr. McBride."

"I see. Any specialty?"

"Locks."

"Good. Now I wish to ask you some questions about the lock on the door to the Turner workshop, State's Exhibit 14."

"Objection, Your Honor. I thought we had ruled out this romantic nonsense about locked room mysteries."

"We certainly did, Mr. Scanlan. I'll excuse the witness from further testimony."

"They don't like it," Peg murmured, nodding in the direction of the jurors.

"I don't blame them."

"What's he trying to do?" Peggy demanded. "Set a record for the number of reversible errors in a single case?"

We were in Dan Hills's office. None of us felt good about the trial.

"The media are hostile to the defendant," I noted, "but they're beginning to have doubts about Boyle Michael. Did you see the law column in today's *Trib*?"

"The Patty Hearst phenomenon." Dan shook his head. "Rich young women are guilty till proven innocent. O'Malley is a dummy but he knows that. He's playing to the crowd."

"Do we try it again," Peg asked, "when it's bounced back after appeal?"

Dan shook his head. "I'm not sure we'll get that opportunity."

"I'm not sure either," I agreed. "Our case, as problematic as it might be, doesn't matter anymore. The jurors aren't listening to me. They're listening to O'Malley and McBride."

"And whom do they like?"

"McBride," I replied. "B. Michael is winning the defense's case for him."

"You're a medical student, Ms. Turner."

"That's right, Ms. Burke."

The courtroom was tense, expecting a good show, a battle of the titans between two bright, attractive, and self-possessed young women.

"So you've had experience with surgery?"

"Experience?"

"You've participated in operations?"

"During my surgical clerkship, I scrubbed for a couple surgeries."

"Clerkship? Scrubbed?"

"I'm sorry for the jargon, Ms. Burke. During the last two years of medical school we spend six-week periods in various hospital services, familiarizing ourselves with what happens in them. Scrubbing means that we go through all the preparations, such as washing our hands with disinfecting soap and donning surgical clothes."

"The green clothes we see on TV?"

Peg did not look at the defendant, not once. Clare Turner, on the other hand, did not take her eyes off the junior prosecutor.

"That's right."

"Dramatic events, are they not?"

"Sometimes."

"You actually participated?"

"No, Ms. Burke, I watched. From a distance."

"You never helped the surgeon to do an incision."

"Oh, no."

"How did you feel during an operation?"

Clare Turner hesitated. "Scared."

"Why?"

"I worried about the patient dying."

"Did one ever die while you were in the operating room?"

"No."

"I see . . . Did you ever think of being a surgeon?"

"Oh, no."

"Why not?"

Peggy was preparing to blindside the defendant. And doing an excellent job at it.

"I . . . didn't think I could tolerate the strain."

"Of cutting into another person's body?"

"That's right."

"I see . . . So you never used a scalpel on a live body?"

"No . . . I couldn't possibly . . ."

"Even in an emergency?"

"Maybe."

Judge Boyle was frowning. Was the state's attorney trying to make a case for the defendant?

"So you never cut into a human body with a scalpel."

"No."

"Then you didn't take an anatomy course?"

Trap sprung.

"Yes, of course, I did. In first year."

"I see. So you do have considerable experience in wielding a scalpel."

"On a corpse."

"Still, it was once a human person."

"Yes, I know."

"So you were not telling us the truth about never using a scalpel."

"I was telling the truth. Your questions were in the context of an operating room."

A deft dodge out of a trap, one which, for all Peg's skills, was a clumsy trap.

But we didn't have much.

"Were you good at it, Ms. Turner?"

"I never liked it. I used to go back to my apartment and vomit . . ."

"I didn't ask whether you liked it. I asked whether you were good at it."

Elmer should have objected then and there. He didn't.

"I suppose so. I don't know."

"Isn't it true you received an A in your course?"

"Yes."

"Didn't your instructor commend you for your skills with a scalpel?"

"Yes."

"Were you not approached by surgeons who had heard of your skill? Did they not suggest that you might have a very successful career as a surgeon?"

"Yes. But . . ."

"But what?"

"I didn't want to be a surgeon."

"Why not?"

"I'd be afraid of hurting someone."

At that point Elmer asked for a recess.

"Draw," Peg murmured.

"She didn't panic when you closed the trap."

"Nope. Didn't figure she would. The jury likes both of us, thinks we're the only sensible people in the whole show. They're not sure about you yet. But they like her more than they like me."

"Tasteless."

"I'm not so sure."

"Now, Miss Turner, how would you characterize your relationship with your parents?"

"I loved them, Mr. McBride, and they loved me."

"I see. Would you characterize this love as demonstrative?"

"No, sir. They were quiet and shy people. I guess I'm like them."

"There was no conflict then?"

"No major conflict; we didn't shout at each other. I never ran away. They respected my freedom. I respected their right to try to talk me out of something I wanted to do. I went to the high school that I chose and to the college they chose."

Her voice was clear and firm without being loud, but her

delivery was mechanical, almost as though she were reciting from memory. As usual her emotions were invisible. I studied the faces of the jurors. Pretty clearly they liked her.

"Did they ever refuse a request from you for money?"

"I never asked for money from them."

"Did you ever quarrel about money?"

"Yes, sir. About my medical school tuition."

"Oh?" Elmer feigned surprise.

"I wanted to pay for it out of my regular allowances. They wanted to pay it themselves. My father was really upset with me for rejecting their generosity."

"I see. Now who won the argument?"

"They did. I apologized for being insensitive."

"Did you kiss and make up?"

"There never was much kissing in our family, Mr. McBride."

"Do you know of any reason why anyone would want to murder your parents?"

"No, I don't. I don't believe that either of them had an enemy in the world."

"So you can't think of anyone who might have killed them?"

"No, sir."

"Did you kill them, Clare, as the State claims?"

"I did not. I loved them. I miss them."

But there was no sign of grief or love in her manner. The media would have a field day on the "ice princess" as they were calling her. Nonetheless the jury looked impressed.

"Now I'd like to ask you about access to your father's workshop. Who could have had access to it that night?"

"No one, Mr. McBride."

"No one?"

"No, sir. They locked themselves in and the key was inside."

"Then how were they killed?"

"I don't know."

"Can you tell me something about that key and lock?"

"Objection, Your Honor. You have repeatedly ruled that the issue of key and lock is irrelevant."

"Objection sustained, Miss Burke. If you raise that issue once more in this courtroom, Mr. McBride, I will instruct the bailiff to remove you to the county jail for contempt of court."

"Your Honor, I simply want to note for the record that once again you have denied me the opportunity to persuade the jury that my client did not have the opportunity to commit this crime."

"It may well be that the Court of Appeals will be interested in mystery puzzles, Mr. McBride. I'll warn you for the last time that I do not want this distraction in my courtroom."

"Very well, Your Honor." Elmer turned away with a smile.

And well he might smile. Of the whole jury only the foreman—an accountant named Crane Ladd, short with a large black mustache and a superior smile—nodded his head in approval. Unless I was spectacular in cross-examination, there would be no need for defense to appeal.

"Now, Dr. Turner . . . it is Dr., isn't it?"

"I won't graduate till next year."

"I see, but medical students are called 'Doctor' in the hospitals, are they not?"

"It's an honorary title."

"Should I address you as 'Dr. Turner' or 'Miss Turner'?"

"I am not a medical doctor yet, Mr. Scanlan."

"Very well then. Now, tell me, how long have you been using drugs?"

"I don't use drugs."

"Oh, I thought you told Chief Stewart that you did." I fumbled through a stack of papers, pretending to search for a quote.

"I told him that I smoked marijuana once or twice in high school and sniffed cocaine a couple of times when I was in college."

"So you admit using drugs?"

"A couple of times."

"You realize that those were violations of the law."

"Yes."

"Did you tell your mother and father about these crimes?"

"No."

"What would they have thought if they had known about them?"

"Objection. These questions are irrelevant to the case."

"Overruled. Defendant will answer the question."

"They would have been very upset."

"Do you think that someone who has been guilty of crimes against federal and state narcotic laws should be trusted in the medical profession, Dr. Turner?"

I turned to face the jury.

"If they've stopped using the drugs, yes."

I whirled on her.

"And you've stopped. Are you sure of that?"

"Yes."

"Why did you stop?"

"I didn't like the effect of the drugs."

"Not because you were violating the law."

"That was part of it."

"What else?"

"I didn't like losing control."

"Ah? Do you lose control often, Miss Turner?"

"I don't think so."

"You don't *think* so?"

"It depends on what you mean by often."

"Once a week?"

"Oh, no."

"Once a month?"

"No."

"A couple of times a year?"

"Maybe."

"Did you lose control before you killed your parents?"

"I didn't kill them, Mr. Scanlan."

"Then what was the last time you lost control?"

"I got mad at a traffic policeman who was delaying traffic. I swore at him."

"To his face?"

"Oh no."

Out of the corner of my eye I saw that the jury was not buying my trickery. Peg shook her head. Damn it, woman, I don't have to be told. Moreover, I was not shaking Clare Turner one bit. She figured that she was a match for me.

"You spoke of your *allowance* from your parents. Could you tell me how much that was?"

"Objection."

"Overruled."

"Twenty-five hundred dollars a month."

"Did you say a year?" Astonishment in my voice.

"A month."

I went through the motions of calculating. "That's thirty thousand dollars a year!"

"Yes, sir."

"Would it surprise you, Miss Turner, to know that most of the people in this courtroom, in this city, don't earn that much money?"

"I know that I've been very fortunate."

"I would say so . . . Now, Miss Turner, have you ever worked, I mean at a real job?"

"I worked as a switchboard operator at my father's plant after I was a freshman in college."

"Would you call working for your father a *real* job?"

"I guess not."

"Anything else?"

"A volunteer in Lakewood Hospital to make sure that I wanted to go to medical school."

"So you never had a real job, a job at which you had to work to earn a living or put yourself through school?"

"No."

"And yet your income was thirty thousand dollars a year, tax free I assume?"

"Yes."

I shook my head in disbelief. "As you say, you've been very fortunate."

Peg was nodding. I thought so. Envy was always a powerful motive.

"Now what were your plans after you graduate from medical school?"

"Go into a residency program."

"In what field?"

"Psychiatry."

"Why?"

A booby trap for you, Clare Turner.

"I was impressed by my own therapist."

And you walked into it!

"Ah, you're saying you have been under the care of a *psychiatrist*?"

"Yes."

There was still no change of facial expression. Or rather such minute changes that you could barely notice them.

"Were you hospitalized?"

Did that tiny lip movement mean that she knew she had been tricked?

"No."

"How often did you see your therapist?"

"Objection."

"Overruled. Answer, please."

Clare Turner hesitated for the first time.

"Young woman, I directed you to answer the state's attorney's question."

"Four times a week."

"For how many years?"

"Four years."

"The fees are about a hundred dollars an hour now, are they not?"

"Yes, sir."

"Nice work if you can get it."

I laughed and so did the jury and the courtroom. You never go wrong running against psychiatry.

"Let me see, Miss Turner." I again pretended to be doing arithmetic. "That's four hundred dollars a week, times fifty-two weeks, twenty thousand dollars a year, eighty thousand dollars for your trips to the psychiatrist. Your parents paid for this I suppose."

"Yes, sir." She was not flustered in the slightest. I was banging my head against a solid cement wall. I was also fighting the fire storm of ambivalences raging in the back of my head.

"You must have been pretty sick to require that kind of treatment."

"Is that a question?"

"Yes it is."

"Objection."

"Sustained. Reword the question, Counselor."

Sure, but I'd made the point.

"I suppose you spoke a lot about your conflicts with your parents to this man?"

"Woman."

"All right," I rolled my eyes, "woman."

"Yes."

"She side with you against your parents?"

"Psychiatrists don't take sides."

"What *do* they do?"

"They help you to understand why your relationships are what they are and perhaps how to change them."

"For eighty thousand dollars! I thought you told Mr. McBride that you loved your parents and that they loved you."

"Yes."

"But despite that love you had to spend eighty thousand dollars of their money to understand it better?"

"Love can always improve, Mr. Scanlan. I wanted to be able to love them better—and my own husband and children should I ever have them."

It was a perfectly sensible reaction to my idiot questions.

"You were adopted, were you not, Miss Turner?"

"Objection."

"Overruled."

"Yes I was."

"By a man and a woman who showered you with good things and indulged your every whim?"

"By a man and woman who were very good to me."

The judge interrupted to call it a day.

"Well?" I asked Peggy.

"You didn't make things worse for us. I think we have two jurors on our side, six against, and the others undecided."

"Outcome?"

"Hung jury. We'll have to do it all again."

• • •

"If you didn't put the bag with the scalpel and the gloves and the jewels into your car, Miss Turner, who did?"

"I don't know."

"You were planning a vacation to Costa Rica the following week, were you not?"

A bit of information we had acquired from her travel agent.

"I was."

"Had you told your parents?"

"No."

"Why not?"

"There was a benefit ball for the Archdiocese they wanted me to attend."

"You had paid part of the money for the fare."

"That's right."

There was another slight movement of her lips, seeing my trap perhaps but unable to escape it.

"Your bank account was low. So you couldn't pick up the cost of the trip from petty cash?"

"No."

"Did you kill your parents who had overwhelmed you with generosity so you could enjoy an expensive vacation?"

"I would have paid the rest with my credit card."

A few members of the jury smiled. Peg frowned. I had overreached.

"Who benefits from your parents' deaths, Miss Turner?"

"I do. My uncle Fred does. The Archdiocese does."

"That's all."

"Yes."

"Do you believe that your uncle Fred might have killed his brother?"

"No."

"Cardinal Cronin?"

Titter in the courtroom.

"No."

"Then who?"

"I don't know."

"There are a lot of things you don't know, are there not, Miss Turner—who besides you benefits from these gruesome murders, who put your mother's jewels in your book bag, whose medical scalpel slit their throats, whose gloves protected that scalpel from fingerprints?"

"Objection. Your Honor, Counsel is browbeating my client."

"Overruled." The judge yawned. "Defendant will please answer the question."

"Will you please repeat the question, Mr. Scanlan?"

At that moment I was suddenly consumed by overwhelming sexual desire, mixed with deliciously sweet tenderness. I was falling in love with the defendant. Her eyes flickered as though she had read my mind and my imagination. For a fraction of a second my eyes and hers locked. Her emotions responded to mine.

I could deceive everyone else, but I could not deceive her, and I could no longer deceive myself.

"I asked you to explain," I groped for words, "how it is that you don't know who killed your parents and who put the evidence in your car."

"I don't know, Mr. Scanlan, because I have no explanations of why anyone would kill my parents or why anyone would want to suggest that I did it."

I was badly shaken by the emotions that had erupted within me. My fantasy probed enthusiastically at the delights of taking off her clothes and making gentle love with her.

I glanced at my notes on the prosecution's table. Peg looked up anxiously at me. I saw the word "grief" on one of my yellow legal-sized pads.

"When did you stop grieving for your parents, Miss Turner?"

"I'm still grieving for them. I will always grieve for them."

"And feel guilty?"

"Of course."

I pounced. "Of killing them?"

"Of what we all feel when our parents are gone, of not loving them enough, of not telling them often enough that you love them."

I was in bad shape; I couldn't let her off the stand on that note. What could I say?

"Do you expect the jury, Miss Turner, to believe that even though you were the only person who might profit from your parents' deaths, and even though the instruments and the profits of death were found in your bag and your car, and even though no one had a motive for making you appear to be the killer, do you expect the jury to believe that you did not kill your parents?"

She paused and looked at the jury.

"I don't think it proper, Mr. Scanlan, for me to have any expectations about the jury's beliefs. I hope they find me not guilty, because I did not kill my parents."

"No further questions."

"What the hell happened to you?" Peg demanded as we left the courtroom.

"Brainstorm, blackout. Was it noticeable?"

"I saw it, she saw it. I don't think anyone else."

"How bad was I?"

"Not up to your usual, I'm afraid. You didn't change anyone's mind and you pulled things together nicely at the end. We'll have to see what your friend Judge O'Malley says to the jury."

"I can hardly wait."

16

Sure, Father Blackie, that's when I knew I should get out. In fact, I knew I should have asked Dan Hills at the very beginning to turn the Turner indictment over to someone else.

But by then it was too late. You can't quit at the end of a case. Maybe after, I should have asked to go on the Chinese Wall, but not then.

There were two different people inside me, one of them was a very lonely man who hungered for this lovely young woman. The other was a veteran prosecutor who was convinced that she had killed her parents. The two people weren't speaking to each other.

It was only later, when I began to know her better, that the prosecutor in me began to believe what Dr. Couglin out at Loyola Med had said. There was no way she could be guilty. But to this day, to this minute, I can't prove that.

17

I RUSHED DESPERATELY FOR THE ELEVATOR. SOMEONE HELD the door for me. As I stumbled in—and dropped a file of notes—I saw that the someone was Clare Turner. I hesitated, preparing to back off.

"It's a public elevator, Mr. Scanlan," she said calmly as she picked up my file and handed it to me.

"Thank you."

"You're welcome."

Tension, professional, sexual, human, pushed down on my chest. She was watching me with casual interest—and I was making a fool out of myself.

"You're very good at your job," she said calmly. "Very good indeed."

"Thank you." I felt my face flame.

"Should there ever be a next time, I'd much rather have you on my side than on the other side—you and that bright and lovely blond woman."

"I'll keep that in mind."

We both knew that our gonads had set up a chemistry between us that someday, one way or another, we would have to deal with. Also we had begun to admire one another.

She can't be a killer, I thought for a moment.

Then the prosecutor took over: that's for the jury to decide.

Somewhere inside of me a hope began work, a hope that the jury would decide for her. I fought it with all my might.

But that seditious hope would not go away.

The door opened on our floor; I stood back to let her out first. The two of us almost collided with Peg Burke.

"Good morning, Miss Burke," Clare Turner said lightly.

"Good morning," Peg stammered. Then when Clare had walked down the corridor toward the courtroom, she turned to me. "What the hell was that all about?"

I tried to explain.

"A bitch," she reflected, "but damn it, Ter, a classy bitch."

"I'm afraid the jury will think so too."

"There can be no possibility of reasonable doubt in your minds, ladies and gentlemen of the jury. Only Clare Turner had the motive, only Clare Turner had the opportunity, only Clare Turner possessed in that house the stolen jewels and the murder weapon. If she did not kill her parents, then who did? Who got into that house in the middle of a blizzard and snuffed out their lives with a skillful swipe of a medical scalpel? She said in her testimony that she had been very fortunate. I think we might agree with that assessment. Few young women her age have been so fortunate. Perhaps her parents were a little old-fashioned in their ways, but in this day and age is that so wrong? And if they were old-fashioned, is that a cause of murder?

"Clare Turner, with her thirty-thousand-dollar-a-year *allowance* and her eighty-thousand-dollar psychiatric bills, could not wait to get control of the incredible sums of money her parents, adoptive parents to be precise, had left her. She could not wait to gain control of her father's company. She could not grant her parents the few years of life that might have remained to them. By her own admission she has had a drug problem, she has need of psychiatric help, she feared a loss of control.

"I put it to you that on that cold and windy night with snow falling all around, she lost control and in her impatience to inherit her parents' wealth, she cut her parents' throats and watched triumphantly as their living blood bubbled out of their arteries. She is certainly guilty of murder in the first degree, and I'm sure you will render that verdict—to protect other indulgent parents who have spoiled a child by loving them too much. Think of such parents when you decide in your conscience what verdict to render, a verdict which you and you alone can reach."

"Not bad," Dan, who had come up to the prosecutor's table for the first time, whispered, "not bad at all."

"They don't hate you. They even like you," Peg added, "but they like her more."

And I love her. Thank God no one knows that, except probably Clare Turner herself.

"I call to your attention, my patient friends," Elmer McBride was drunk, but not so noticeably drunk as to affect the jury, "the simple fact that motive is not enough to convict a man or a woman. Nor is circumstantial evidence. Anyone wishing to cover their tracks could have obtained a medical scalpel and a pair of gloves. Almost anyone could have found the defendant's book bag. Is it not utterly obvious that such a cache of weapons and loot is a plant? Would a woman as calm and as intelligent as Clare Turner be so clumsy in leaving proof of her guilt? Find out who tried to frame Clare Turner and you will find the real murderer.

"Until then, you must ask yourselves how she was able to pass through a locked door and kill the parents she loved so dearly. The state's attorneys, admirable and skillful young prosecutors that they are, have failed completely to account for that phenomenon. Find out who had a way of getting into that locked room and you'll know who the killer of John and Mary Turner really is.

"Unless the State can explain how she got through the locked door—and it patently cannot do so or it would have long since—there is not only reasonable doubt about my client's innocence, there is no case at all against her. You have, I submit with all due respect for your patience and integrity and intelligence, no choice but to lift from this grieving young woman the burden of the undocumented charges, which the State in its misguided zeal for justice has brought against her. Tell them by your verdict that the police forces of this state should go out and search for the real killer."

"Elmer has been better than I thought he would be in court," I told Dan Hills. "It's too bad he didn't think of alternative scenarios."

"Doesn't have enough gray cells left to do that—drowned them all in alcohol."

"He didn't win over Crane Ladd," Peg said glumly, "but Elmer has ten of them on his side."

"Hung jury," Dan said. "Not your fault, Ter, Peg. You did your best with what you had. You were right, Ter. We had to indict."

"Have to try again?"

"Don't know. We'd better sleep on it a week and reassess."

That night my mother called me to tell me that "that lovely girl is not a killer, Ter, you should know that."

When your mother is not on your side, you're in real trouble.

"It is my solemn task this morning," Judge O'Malley sounded like an angry schoolteacher with a class of below-average students, "to make some observations about certain points of law which might be useful to you in your deliberations.

"First, I must warn you against taking seriously the histrionics of the attorneys involved in this case, particularly lead Counsel for the Defense. Such histrionics may well deserve our admiration and make us aware that we are in the presence of a man who by his own admission is one of the great defense lawyers of our time. Nonetheless, the facts and the law of the case are simple and you should not let elaborate verbal display blind you to the patent truth."

Having committed one more reversible error, the most incredible of all of them so far, he turned to the cards on which the State had printed the appropriate jury instructions for a first-degree murder charge and droned through them as though it were a useless exercise in a matter where the outcome of jury deliberations should have been obvious.

"Wow!" said Peg as the jury withdrew. "That was a caricature of instructions to a jury."

"They could win reversal on the basis of that alone," I groaned.

"He should not be permitted to sit on the bench."

"He had strong political sponsorship . . . How long do you give them?"

"Less than a day."

Peg was wrong. The jury took six days. The only one who did not seem frazzled through the long wait was Clare Turner. I couldn't keep my eyes off her. Apparently no one else noticed. Peg certainly didn't and she didn't miss much.

Finally they came in, looking worn and angry.

"Well, now," the judge snapped at them, "have you *finally* reached a verdict?"

"We have, Your Honor." Crane Ladd sounded triumphant.

"My God," Peg murmured, "we won."

"On the matter of State versus Clare Turner in the charge of the murder of John Turner, how do you find?"

"Guilty, Your Honor, of murder in the first degree."

A loud gasp swept the courtroom. Clare Turner's jaw tightened slightly.

"And in the matter of the State versus Clare Turner in the charge of the murder of Mary Turner, how do you find?"

"Guilty, Your Honor, of murder in the first degree."

"It took you long enough to reach your verdict. Nonetheless I must congratulate you on its wisdom. I hereby revoke the defendant's bond and direct that the bailiff remand her to Cook County Jail. I will hear motions for punishment in this courtroom a week from today at ten-thirty."

Peg and I ignored the reporters as we left the courtroom.

"We have no choice but to ask for the death penalty, as we said we would," the state's attorney said firmly. "The media are quite properly demanding that we treat her like any other person convicted of such a crime. Equal justice under the law."

"The jurors say," Peg observed, "that it was ten to two for acquittal and that Crane Ladd badgered them into the guilty verdict."

"That might be appropriate grounds for defense appeal. It ought not to concern us."

He was right. We had to do what we would do in any similar case—ask for the death sentence, knowing we'd get something less.

"The social workers," Dan Hills said, "are recommending twenty-five years to life. That means she'd be out in twenty years."

"Fine," said the state's attorney. "I presume Judge O'Malley will follow their recommendations. But we will look terrible if we propose that instead of reluctantly accepting it."

"Terry?" Dan looked at me.

"The Boss is right. We have to ask for the death penalty, though I presume we'll be hoping that he doesn't grant what we want."

"You agree, Dan?" the Boss asked, not confident enough of his own instincts to insist on the decision he had made.

Dan stared out the dirty window of his office. "I guess so. I'll admit I don't like this case. Something about it smells, though I'm not sure what it is. O'Malley's sentence won't stand, I'm sure of that, so I don't suppose it makes any difference what we ask for next week. When he's reversed, the First District Appellate panel will take the heat, and we won't. But let me ask you this"—his eyes shifted away from the window and swept the three of us like laser beams—"what if all appeals fail? Are we prepared to send that young woman to the room where they give lethal injections?"

Dead silence. The Boss gulped. "In that case, I think we would join the defense in a plea for executive clemency."

"By that time," I added, "the weight of public opinion will shift in her favor."

"Good." The Boss rose. "We're all agreed."

"Do you realize what we did in there?" Peg demanded as we walked down the hall.

"Sure. We said we'd ask for something we didn't want and that if we got it we'd step in at the last moment and try to prevent it."

"We're not supposed to do that, Ter."

"I know. I know."

"Have you ever done it before?"

"No."

"Why did we do it this time?"

"Maybe because we all have doubts."

"Reasonable doubts?"

"Vague doubts."

"That shouldn't do it, should it, Ter?"

"Nope."

"So it's her. She's spooked us all, hasn't she?"

"I guess so, Peg." I sighed. "This is an odd case."

"I don't like it."

"Neither does Dan."

"Would you seek an indictment, if you had it to do over again?"

"Absolutely," I said firmly.

But I wasn't so sure.

Vague doubts.

And intense love.

"Your Honor," Counsel for the Defense, a young woman Peg's age who had been silent through the trial, said, "we believe that since this is Ms. Turner's first conviction and because she has the talent to expiate whatever crime she may have committed, that the court would do a service to society by being lenient. We accept the probation commission's recommendation of twenty-five years to life."

"Is that all?"

"Yes, Your Honor."

"Mr. Scanlan?"

"The State believes, Your Honor, that a crime like this, so senseless and so brutal, requires the death penalty. Two lives have been snuffed out, productive and generous lives, anything less than the death penalty will send a signal to young people in this state that they can capriciously murder their parents and expect to escape with only nominal punishment."

"Miss Turner, do you have anything to say to this court before sentence is passed?"

"Only that I did not kill my parents."

Everyone in the court leaned forward. This was the climactic moment of the trial, even if most of us thought that the trial verdict would soon be reversed.

I knew from the sneer on the judge's face what he would say. He'd been waiting for this dialogue all through the trial, all through his life on the bench—his first opportunity to bask in the light of having given the death penalty. I felt sick to my stomach.

"It is what I might have expected from you. You are a cold and heartless young woman, Miss Turner. That has been apparent from the beginning. If you showed the slightest trace of remorse, I might have been inclined to be more lenient. As it is, I will do my duty as I see it.

"Clare Marie Turner, I direct that you be remanded from this courtroom to Cook County Jail. I further direct that on or about November 15 of this year you will be put to death by an injection of lethal chemicals into your body as a punishment for your heinous crimes. May God have mercy on your soul."

I think she swallowed once. Then she turned to console her lawyer, who was crying.

"My God, Terry." Peggy's hand grasped mine. "What have we done!"

"God have mercy on our souls."

18

THE SUMMER DRAGGED ON, HOT AND DRY. I WROTE A LETTER of resignation but did not submit it. Peggy and I avoided each other. Clare was released on bond, pending a hearing by the First District Appellate Court. The November 15 date was fictional. In the worst of circumstances it would take many years before a sentence was carried out. Moreover, since the death penalty was reinstated in Illinois, it has only been enforced once. The justices of the State Supreme Court have apparently decided that, whatever the legislature and the people of the state want, they do not want the death penalty.

According to the media, Clare, free on appeal, had returned to medical school to finish her work so that she could graduate by Christmas.

In response to a reporter who asked whether she felt any resentment against the State's Attorney's Office, she said, "Not at all. They were only doing their job. I wish that they had not done it so well."

And Judge O'Malley?

"I didn't understand some of his rulings."

Maybe that was the kind of person she really is, I thought as I poured over the documentation, looking for a hint of another explanation. I had become, on the State's time I fear, another Counsel for the Defense. I heard that Rollins, Parks, et al had been fired and replaced by a topflight lawyer, Diana Clarke.* Better late than never.

The appeals panel was problematic. Judge Steven Burns had never seen a defendant who wasn't guilty or a conviction that wasn't irreversible. One vote against her. Judge Myra Dawson was bright and honest and sensitive to the risks of judicial abuse. Surely she'd vote for a new trial. Judge Conrad Block was not a man of strong opinions or great talent. Quite the contrary, he was a political hack. But he knew enough about the law to be able to recognize reversible error. One probably in her favor. He'd make the decision I didn't make when I heard about the lie detector test.

Did I now believe she was innocent?

I was split in two. My head said that of course she had done it even if we didn't have enough evidence for conviction, not to say a death penalty. My gut, my heart, whatever, said that she had been the victim of incredible bad luck and that the real killer was still at large.

"Have you thought any more about what we do when *Turner* comes bouncing back?" Dan asked me one morning in the men's room, a couple of weeks after the trial.

"When or if?"

"Who knows how Blockhead will vote? But it will never get by the State Supreme Court, never in a million years."

"Maybe."

"You think we ought to try it again, Terry?"

"You assume there'll be another judge?"

"If the defense doesn't ask for one, we will."

"A decent judge will throw it out of court, Dan."

"Do we give them that chance or do we take the heat of electing not to retry?"

*See *Love Song*

"I guess I'd suggest your usual advice—wait and see what happens."

He nodded. "I'd usually go along with that. I guess what I'd want to see is what the First District says about our case."

"Fair enough."

I was in no mood for work or for summer vacation. I didn't eat much and I slept very little. My family lost patience with me. It was suggested a number of times by a number of different women members of the family that I find some nice girl. I replied that they had all vanished from the face of the earth.

One of my law school friends offered me his house at Grand Beach—he'd made a lot of money in corporate law— for a weekend. "For you and a friend."

"How about just me?"

"Fine," he said. "What's happened to the last playboy of the Western world?"

"He hit his head on a rock."

I loafed on the porch for most of Saturday and didn't sleep that night. Early Sunday morning I forced myself out of bed, put on jeans, a sweatshirt, and running shoes, and trudged down to the beach. I was out of condition and incapable of running, but a good walk to New Buffalo on the sand, I thought, might clear my head.

It was one of those strange summer days on the Michigan Dunes when fog rolls in from the lake and settles on the dunes for a quarter mile in from the lake. The fog ebbs and flows over the beach, sometimes so thick that you can barely see ten feet ahead of you and sometimes thinning out so that you can see patches of blue sky above it.

It was, I thought, perfect weather for a mystery, but I'd had enough of mysteries.

I walked a long way, almost to New Buffalo, and began to feel better. I should take a couple of weeks off, I told myself.

Suddenly out of the fog, the hound of the Baskervilles charged right at me. I recoiled to escape the huge beast, only to discover that she had a stick in her mouth and wanted to play.

She ground to a halt when she saw me and dropped the stick, considering me as a possible player.

Tail wagging, she picked up the stick and stalked around me, defying me to try to take it away from her.

She was nothing but an overgrown puppy.

"Here, girl." I snapped my fingers.

Delicately she approached me. I patted her head. Her tail picked up its beat. I reached for the stick. She was not about to give it to me without a tussle. We struggled. She pulled it away and retreated a few feet. She rested her huge jaw on her front paws and raised her rear end, better, I suppose, to wag her tail.

In a house that tail would be hard on lamps.

"OK." I shrugged. "If you don't want to play, neither do I."

I began to walk away.

She rushed ahead and stopped in front of me, offering me the stick again—or rather a chance to wrestle for it. I began to tug. She tugged back, obviously having the time of her life.

Finally she deigned to let go. I hurled the stick in the direction I had come.

With a happy yelp she chased it into the mists. In a few moments she trotted back, utterly complacent with herself.

"Good girl." I patted her again, engaged in the ritual of tugging the stick away from her, and tossed it in the lake. She charged the water like it wasn't there, and swam furiously toward the stick, then turned and paddled back in.

This time, after I had taken the stick, she shook the water from her long hair and gave me a shower.

"Hey, cut that out!"

She jogged in front of me, looking back to make sure I was following her. The fog cleared away, revealing someone in white slacks and a maroon sweatshirt sitting on a log. The dog ambled up to her and dropped the stick.

Only when she looked up did it occur to me that the dog's name was Fiona.

"Good morning, Counselor," Clare Turner said. "My pooch is promiscuous. She'll play with anyone who will throw the stick for her."

"Fiona."

The dog barked, delighted that I knew her name.

"Irish wolfhound. She looks scary, but she's a pussycat."

The irony of our situation silenced both of us. I had tried my best to convict her of murder. I had battled her frigid calm in the courtroom and seemingly lost. But I had in fact won. I had asked for the death penalty and had won that too. We should hate each other.

But now we were alone in the mists of a summer morning on a quiet beach, observed only by a friendly wolfhound. The ambivalences we felt toward each other struggled desperately.

I should bid her a polite good morning and walk back down the beach, my face burning with embarrassment.

Fiona walked over to me and nuzzled my thigh. I was supposed to sit on the log next to her mistress.

I patted her. The dog, that is.

"I'm afraid you've caught me beyond the boundaries of jurisdiction, Counselor. You can add that to the reasons for revoking my bail at the hearing week after next."

"I won't do that."

"I know you won't."

Again we hesitated. I told myself that I should get away from her as fast as my feet could carry me.

"Let's say," I sat down on the log next to her, as though it were the most natural thing in the world to do, "that this whole chance encounter is off the record and never happened."

"Fair enough." She patted the panting dog. "Nice doggy. Did the state's attorney make you run into the lake? Shame on him. I hope you soaked him really good . . . Now sit down like a good girl while I talk to this stranger you found wandering the beach."

"Did McBride tell you that we offered a plea?" I blurted.

"A plea?"

"A guilty plea on a lesser charge. A couple years in jail. We might have gone further than that. We had a lousy case."

"Before the trial?"

"That's right."

"No, he never told me."

"That by itself is enough for your new lawyers to demand another trial. Failure of counsel to provide effective help."

"It wouldn't have mattered. I wouldn't have accepted such a deal." She was watching me closely, trying perhaps to figure me out.

"You realized that McBride did not serve you well? He was good on his feet, but he should have prepared an alternative scenario, pointed the finger at someone else."

"Aren't you breaking a lot of your own rules?"

Was I ever.

"This conversation never happened."

"I understand." She rested her chin on arms folded across her breasts.

"Some appeals court is going to throw out the verdict. I assume that your Diana Clarke told you that."

Fiona spread herself out on the sand in front of us and rested her giant jaw once more on her front paws, demanding attention. I reached out and petted her head. She gurgled appreciatively.

"She did. I don't know that I believe her. I mean I think she believes it and I think it's reasonable to believe it, but there seems to be an inevitability about everything that has happened . . . Tell me, Terry, do you believe I killed my parents?"

A straightforward enough question. Was this all possibly a dream?

"I don't believe we had a convincing case. I expected it would be dismissed before a trial could begin."

She nodded. "But you had to seek an indictment because of media pressure?"

"Something like that."

How could this woman be so reasonable and understanding about a prosecution that had produced a death penalty for her?

"I've learned a lot," she said, "about myself and about the world, so it hasn't been a complete waste."

"What did you learn?" I looked into her deep brown eyes, still uncertain what thoughts and feelings lurked behind them.

"Being chained to the other women in the prison bus is a useful experience for a pampered medical student from Lakewood. You realize how fragile and artificial the walls around your nice little life really are."

She had picked up a stick and was tracing designs in the sand.

"I see."

"And the other women in the jail, their eyes filled with hate for me because I am white and rich—I realized how much reason they have to hate."

"They're not poor because you're rich."

She rubbed out a design and then began again.

"No, but they're poor through no fault of their own and they have reason to be angry."

"Did they try to assault you?" I tried to make the question sound matter-of-fact.

"A karate chop or two stopped that," she said, equally matter-of-fact.

"Remind me not to try anything."

She rubbed out another design. "No danger of that . . . As I said in the elevator, you're a pretty good lawyer. You'd be even better if you watched more carefully for signals from that cute little blonde."

She said it with her usual immobile face. But her eyes were dancing. At least, I thought they were. Was she kidding me? Could Clare Turner actually joke?

"That's what Peg says."

"I'd bet you haven't had any breakfast. Can I make you a cup of coffee? I have some homemade cinnamon rolls up-stairs."

"I don't know whether I ought to do that."

"Look, Terry, this encounter is in the fog and the mists, out of ordinary time and space. I'm not going to try to seduce you. Not today anyway."

"Well . . ."

"Suit yourself."

"I'm dying for a cup of coffee."

"And a cinnamon roll?"

"More than one?"

"As many as you want."

"You know I shouldn't."

"I know. I shouldn't have asked you."

There was no question about what I would do.

We stood up together, turned toward the steps, and climbed out of the mists into a fresh summer sunlight. My heart was beating furiously. So, I assumed, was hers. Fiona bounded up the stairs ahead of us, turning around a couple of times to make sure her two friends were following her.

I felt that it would be perfectly natural to take her hand as we ascended the dune.

I didn't, but it seemed like a good idea.

The house, Dick Martin's as it turned out, was a square, modern place, neat, clean, and efficient with none of the early-twentieth-century quaintness to be found in Grand Beach.

I sat in the kitchen watching the fog roll back on the lake as Clare brewed the coffee and heated the cinnamon rolls in a microwave. Every movement each of us made suggested enormous sexual energy.

"Have a roll." She extended a dish toward me. "I made them last night."

"Only one?"

"As many as you want."

I took three.

"You're a good cook." I wolfed one of the rolls down in a single swallow.

"Only if you like cinnamon rolls every morning. I do."

Her expression was guarded, as if she regretted inviting me for breakfast. We were back in Lakewood in the cold of winter.

She was, I reflected, an extraordinarily beautiful woman.

"Sorry you invited me up?" I tried to make it sound like a casual question.

She checked on the coffee.

"It'll be a minute," she said. "Do you like it strong?"

"It's too strong when the spoon bends."

"Milk or sugar?"

"As black as midnight on a moonless night."

"Do you like pie too?"

"Yes, but I'm not Special Agent Dale Cooper from 'Twin Peaks.' "

"Funny. You kind of look like him." She poured some coffee into my cup. "Not as cute."

"You're not Lara Flynn Boyle either," I said, remembering my fantasy from the day of the murder.

"I guess not."

"Much more attractive."

"Oh?"

"More voluptuous." I said the word I had shied away from in my previous response to her. "Nineteenth-century archduchess."

She blushed. "I think on your lips that'a compliment."

"It sure is."

"Thank you." She continued to blush. "Despite my public image, I enjoy being admired."

I wanted her as desperately as I had ever wanted anything in my life.

"You didn't answer my question."

"I'm not on the stand now, Counselor." She glanced away from me.

"Sorry." I grabbed for another cinnamon roll.

"Fiona, don't beg, it isn't polite!"

The pooch had placed a vast paw, very gently, on my thigh and looked up pleadingly.

"Just a piece?" I asked her mistress.

"All right."

I gave the wolfhoud half a roll.

"That's all!" Clare ordered.

Quite satisfied with herself, good dog Fiona sauntered away and curled up in the corner to devour her treat with delicate aplomb.

"Nice dog."

"Nicer than her owner?"

"No way. Almost though."

We both laughed nervously.

"I'll answer your question." She refilled my cup. "Yes, I am sorry I invited you. Not completely sorry though." She looked back at me and took off her glasses. "I haven't made up my mind yet."

"I'll leave if you want."

"Not till you finish your coffee."

She continued to inspect me intently. I was paralyzed. If she didn't make the first move, there wouldn't be one.

"Why did it have to be you?" she said as she put the cup in front of me. "Of all the men in the world, why you?"

We both looked away from each other.

"A good question."

"From the first moment in the library."

Her hand snaked across the kitchen table and grabbed mine, as if she would never let it go.

"Yes," I agreed, acknowledging for the first time to myself what I had always known to be true.

I squeezed her hand.

"Chemical secretions in the bloodstream, I suppose. Lots of them."

"Do you think that's all it is, Clare?" I asked, using her name for the first time.

"No, Terry." She offered me with her free hand a plate with two more delicious cinnamon rolls.

"Really homemade?"

"Yes, in case a prosecuting attorney should happen by."

Now I recognized the little movement of her lips and the sparkle in her eyes which meant laughter.

I put down the coffee, stood up, and then we were both in each other's arms, not kissing, not caressing, just clinging to each other for strength and consolation and warmth.

Then we both were weeping, not hysterically, not violently, merely soft, gentle grief.

"I haven't cried since high school," she sniffed.

"You have a lot of tears to which you're entitled," I choked.

"Are you crying too, Terry Scanlan?"

"Yes."

"How wonderful!"

We continued to cling to each other. Her breasts, firm and free under the sweatshirt, were a torment and a delight.

"I love you," I said, knowing the truth of those words only in their utterance.

She hugged me even more tightly. "And I love you, oh so much."

Fiona sniffed at us and decided that this peculiar human behavior was not very interesting. She curled up in a patch of sunlight and went to sleep.

"Are you frightened?" I asked Clare as I soothed and caressed her with my hands and my lips.

"Of you? Certainly not."

"No, of the trial. And the sentence."

"Terrified. Everyone thinks I'm calm and self-possessed, just like they think I don't grieve for my parents. I'm scared stiff. I hide it pretty well, but I know I'm going to die."

"No you're not. There'll be appeals and reversals and retrials. The Illinois Supreme Court has de facto overturned the death penalty."

"That poor man died last year."

"Only because he gave up on appeals."

"I could be the second one."

"No you won't."

"I feel trapped." She shivered in my arms. "Like it's all planned and laid out and there's no escaping it."

"You've been unlucky," I argued, "nothing more. I won't let them hurt you."

Big deal knight errant.

"It seems fated. At each step of the way I seem to win but I lose. I'll be back in jail in a week, you know that."

"No you won't."

"Are you sure?" She buried her head even more deeply into my chest.

"No, I'm not. But I promise we'll get you out. And we'll protect you."

It was a huge promise and one that I could not keep.

"I don't care," she said. "These minutes of love with you make it all seem worthwhile. Oh, my darling, I love you so much."

"You really are a romantic."

"Would you not have guessed it?"

"Not for a moment."

"Now you know . . . fortunately I'm in the right company."

We did not make love, somehow that didn't seem appropriate, but in our kissing and caressing, our weeping and our reassuring, there was a promise that some day we would unite our bodies.

What we did that morning was both more than and less than lovemaking. Though I fondled her wonderful breasts, and kissed them and nibbled at them, physically we went no further. In that sense our love was less than lovemaking.

Rather we healed and warmed, comforted and challenged—which actions go far beyond physical love. We began something that we both felt in the heat of the moment would never die.

We broke our embrace to eat the cinnamon rolls and drink the coffee. Then we embraced and wept again.

"You're my first man," she sighed as we embraced on a

couch on the porch of the house and watched the last traces of fog slip out into the lake, where they waited as a solid and threatening bank about a mile offshore.

"Am I?" I bent over and kissed her breasts.

"It's not only that I'm a virgin, though I am that as you can probably tell. You're the first man I've let near me. I've been afraid of men."

Her rigid self-control had vanished. She laughed. She cried, she giggled, she sighed, she even came close to smiling. Clare Turner was a deeply sensuous woman, but a lover needed to be gentle and slow in awakening her sensuality. There was no rush.

"You don't seem afraid of me."

"I'm not." She held my hands against her breasts. "Not in the least. I not only love you. I like you. I enjoy you. You respect me."

"Do you call my licking your breasts respectful?"

"Oh yes."

"I've never been so captivated by a woman," I admitted.

Fiona stirred at our feet, pondered our embrace skeptically, sniffed at Clare's sweatshirt, which had fallen in front of her, and ponderously returned to her nap.

"We're boring the mutt," Clare said.

"You're not boring me."

"Your mother must be a wonderful woman." She pulled my hands back to her body.

"She is, but how do you know?"

"Because you respect women so much. That's why I knew that I could risk myself with you, even the first day when you were so busy being the tough prosecutor."

"I'm not aware of being so respectful."

"But look at the way you are with Peg Burke in court. She's intelligent, she's pretty, she's ambitious, she's pushy and bossy. You don't put her down, you're not threatened by her, you treat her like an able young colleague, which she is. I like that."

"You don't miss much, do you?"

"I didn't miss the way you looked at me either." She snuggled closer to me, cuddling up comfortably.

"How did I look at you?"

"You absorbed me with your eyes, you took my clothes off in your imagination, you played with me."

"All respectfully?"

"Most respectfully, even reverently."

"What a strange young woman you are!"

"Dear God, I don't deny that!"

"You knew I was thinking all those things about you?"

"Of course. And you knew that I knew. Our eyes kept locking as if we were in a bedroom instead of a courtroom— not that I've ever been in a bedroom with a man."

"I think you might be someday in the not too distant future."

"I devoutly hope so."

"I'm trying to figure out whether you've changed."

"Changed?" She lifted an eyebrow.

"Are you the same woman I met last winter in Lakewood?"

"Do I act like her?"

"Yes, but then again no."

She laughed. "Same answer I'd give."

We clung to each other desperately. Why did this interlude ever have to end?

Why not make love with her then and there?

Because she was not ready, nowhere near ready, and because I'm old-fashioned and a romantic besides.

It was necessary that there be many sessions of foreplay before we went to bed together, and probably a ceremony too.

If that makes me seem strange, then I guess I'm strange. Besides I enjoyed the foreplay.

"You almost broke down completely at the end of your cross-examination," she continued. "What happened?"

"Overwhelming sexual desire?"

"Really? For me?"

"No one else."

"How marvelous!"

"I don't think anyone else noticed."

"Oh, no," she agreed. "Not even Peg, who I think has begun to like me."

"I think so too."

"You shouldn't stay all morning, Ter." She sighed. "The Martins will be back before noon."

"I'm not quite finished fondling you."

"You can fondle me whenever you want and as long as you want for the rest of my life."

"A promise?"

"Absolutely. So long as I'm not just a fetish."

Feminist rhetoric.

"Do you think you are?"

She arched her back in pleasure. "No, not at all. I am a woman who is admired and loved, even as she loves."

I wonder now how we managed to express so much love in so short a time under such threatening circumstances. Perhaps the fact that we were legal adversaries in a matter of life and death made the love more poignant and hence more powerful.

Clare was a strange woman, much stranger than I had realized—and hence more fascinating. Imponderable and appealing.

A mystery, perhaps a lifelong mystery.

"You're mine, Terry Scanlan," she said as I helped her put her sweatshirt back on. "All mine. I've captured you."

"Pretty confident."

"I wasn't sure I could seduce you. But when God and Fiona brought you to me, I knew I had to try."

"Was I easy?"

"A pushover."

"So that was what the coffee and the cinnamon rolls were all about."

She kissed me vigorously, her lips lingering on mine.

"Did you think otherwise?"

"No."

"All right."

"I have indeed been enchanted," I admitted. "I don't want to escape."

"Don't try."

I held her slim waist in my hands and returned her kiss.

"Do you want to make love with me now?" she asked simply.

"You don't have to do that to enchant me."

"I know."

"You're not ready for that yet, Clare."

"I know that too."

"Then why the offer?"

"I want you to know how much I belong to you."

"I understand."

"I'm so happy." She sighed contentedly.

"I've never been more happy," I said, again knowing it to be true in the act of saying it.

"Did you think I was a cold fish," she curled up to lean against my chest, "when you first met me?"

"I confess that I did."

"Most people think that." She dug her fingers into my arms. "I'm really not. But I know I act that way. My shrink says I do it to protect myself, probably because of what happened, whatever it was, when I lost my natural parents."

"She does?"

"Uh-huh. She says I'll always be more reserved than a lot of people, but that's not necessarily all bad, so long as I can open up to those I like and those," she choked a bit, "I love."

"I'm glad to hear that."

"I mean they never say you're going to be all right because that might make you lay back, but she implies that when I find the right man, I'll probably do pretty well."

"Do you think I'm the right man?"

"Oh, sure."

Silly question.

"Does she?"

"She thought you were an asshole."

Was that a giggle?

"And she still does?"

"I told her the way you treat Peg and she kind of changed her mind. But, I'm the one who has to decide about you, not her. Right?"

"Right indeed. So I'm currently on approval?"

She punched my arm lightly, very lightly.

"Approved."

If you want to get out, I told myself, get out now or forever hold your peace.

I didn't get out.

We had accomplished a lot in two hours. We had set up a lot of the conditions for a possible common life.

I realized that peeling off the mysteries around Clare Turner would be even more fun that removing her sweatshirt. It would also be a lifelong task.

Neither of us forgot about the murder charges against her. Neither of us forgot that I was responsible for those charges. But the love which had exploded between us was so powerful that those legal realities seemed puny.

Finally I kissed her good-bye and, accompanied part of

the way by Fiona, walked back to Grand Beach, with bright dreams of how I would save my love.

Before the day was over I began to have my doubts. Had I been taken in? Had I been seduced? Had I been tricked by a careful plot?

Yes, of course I had been seduced. She claimed that she had seduced me and she was proud of it.

But if it were a plot, it had come rather late, had it not?

Then I realized that the woman whom I had hugged and kissed and caressed on the dune was the woman about whom Dr. Couglin and Richard Martin had talked the day after the murder, not the one I thought I had confronted on the day of the crime.

Why had I misread her so completely? Was I afraid of her sexual appeal?

And if my judgement was that clouded, should I not get out not only of the case but of the State's Attorney's Office?

I would never be another Dan Hills. I didn't have the right combination of genes and character to become a compassionate prosecutor.

In my dreams that night I agonized over the question. The next afternoon, when Dan dragged us over to a bar called Jean's just north of the court (where cops and prosecutors hang out, and the occasional public defender that has the nerve to come in through the back door that the rest of us use), I still hadn't made up my mind.

"All right, guys." He sipped on his Diet Coke, whose austerity was marred by two slices of lime. "What are we going to do about this motion to put Clare Turner back in jail?"

"Why?" Peg asked. She was drinking Jameson's, straight up, probably because that was what I normally drink in Jean's.

"Because the Boss insists. That sob story about her continuing her medical education has two columnists on our backs. They're demanding she be treated like any other convicted murderer."

"Under the same circumstances, another one would be out on bail," Peg insisted.

"The papers won't buy that."

"Myra will vote for continued bail," I said, "and Burns will vote to give her a lethal injection immediately. So it will be up to Blockhead."

"I think we gotta do it." Dan shook his head sadly. "I hate to think of her going back into that place. We'll try to make it as easy as possible for her if Block changes his mind."

"We're letting someone else make the decision again," Peg protested.

"That's our job, Peg." Dan rested his chin on the top of his glass. "We don't have much choice."

"Look, Dan," she said. "You can fire me, you can ask for my resignation, but I won't do it."

"Conscience?"

"Call it that if you want. That poor woman has been sentenced to death on the whim of a crazy judge. If we don't stop it, then maybe no one else will. I can't live with that. And I certainly can't live with putting her back in county jail because some columnist demands that we do, when she is no threat to anyone."

"You realize that the Illinois Supreme Court has permitted only one death penalty in this state since it was reinstated?"

"Yes. I don't want her to be number two."

"That's most unlikely." His frown deepened. "Our job is not to determine guilt or innocence, but rather to prosecute to the best of our ability those who seem to have committed crimes."

"I understand that, Dan." Peg sighed, now much older than her twenty-five years. "In principle I agree with you.

But this case is different. There's something wrong about it, something strange, peculiar, evil."

"Ter?"

I finally got around to doing what I should have done before the trial. I put myself at long last on the wall.

"Peg and I haven't talked about it, Dan. But she's had the courage to say what I think."

"I see." He sat up straight and stared at the mirror behind the bar. "You think she didn't do it?"

"Yes," said Peg promptly.

"There's a reasonable doubt in my mind," I added. "She's not been very lucky."

He continued to stare at the mirror. "I quite agree that the case has never smelled right, but I haven't been able to put my finger on what I don't like about it."

"It's been too easy, Dan," I said. "Elmer McBride, B. Michael O'Malley, Crane Ladd, and now Conrad Block. We keep winning when we shouldn't win."

"Maybe." He nodded. "Maybe that's it . . . OK. I'll get someone else to plead our motion. No one gets fired. No resignations accepted. If you two can find a hint of evidence that we can use, I personally will go into court and ask for a new trial."

Not one man in a thousand in Dan's position would have been so humane.

His humane attitude didn't help Clare much. Judge Block voted with Judge Burns to revoke bail. Clare went back into the hellhole of county jail. Maybe some of the bull dykes would learn not to try to rape a person with a brown belt in karate.

Was Clare fated as she thought or just unlucky as I thought?

I was beginning to believe that she might indeed be doomed. My boast that I would take care of her was hollow.

As a state's attorney I can't even visit her. I feel that I have betrayed my love.

We do talk on the phone. She doesn't feel betrayed. Oddly enough, when we talk, she sounds happy.

I knew she was innocent, now beyond any doubt. But I couldn't prove it. I couldn't find a hint of evidence that would justify Dan going into court and asking for a retrial.

I wrote another letter of resignation. Dan looked at it and suggested I see Cardinal Cronin. That's why I'm here, Father Blackie. Will you be able to help us?

Please.

ENTER BLACKIE RYAN

19

———

"**Y**OU OF COURSE OBSERVED," I SAID WITH THE LONG SIGH I reserve for such occasions, "the curious incident of the dog who barked in the night?"

Despite his melancholy, Terry Scanlan smiled. "No dog barked in the night, Father Blackie."

"That's what was curious."

"A quote from Sherlock Holmes."

"The classic *Sherlockismus*, as described by Monsignor Ronald Knox in his *Essays in Satire*. The point here is that the fabled Fiona did not bark in the night."

"Why should she?"

"A murder in the house and an Irish wolfhoud, a sensitive and intelligent species—as the ethnic name demands— remained silent?"

"She might have reacted to a stranger, but Clare wasn't a stranger. So are you suggesting that the nonbarking dog is evidence that Clare really is guilty?"

"Perhaps. Other interpretations, however, are possible."

He stared at me, mystified.

The young man's problem was that, as much as he loved her, he had been unable to shake his initial paradigm of Clare as criminal. Unless he did that he would be unable to find another and more pleasing paradigm.

Pleasing to him. Monstrous in itself.

"I'm sure that somehow the locked room is part of the solution."

"Indeed."

"But I can't figure it out."

"That, in itself, is not a serious problem." I poured some more raspberry tea. He had not yet reached the state of acceptance in my office where he was a potential candidate for a sip of my Bushmill's single malt. "But it does raise some very serious questions."

In truth, it was simplicity itself to resolve the locked room problem. However, such a solution did not automatically point out a killer.

When my friend Rich, now our gloriously reigning mayor, was state's attorney, on some occasions he consulted with me on similar problems. Unfortunately, his successor was not aware of that practice. If I had been consulted earlier in this unfortunate matter and had been able to suggest an alternative paradigm, the present situation might not be what it was.

There were two possibilities, it seemed evident, either one of them monstrous; and in either case, Clare Marie Turner was a remarkable woman, more remarkable, I was willing to wager, than her poor besotted lover sipping his tea had yet realized.

"The foreman's name was Ladd Crane?" I asked, reaching for a Vatican letter the back of which had been serving as notepaper for me.

"Crane Ladd," Terry replied, seemingly mystified by my question.

"The worthy appellate court has yet to render its decision?"

"They're in no rush; they never are."

"Indeed."

"We've had the guards keep a careful watch on her. So far all right."

"No rape attempts?"

"One so far. A bull dyke learned not to fool with someone who has a brown belt."

"Prudent."

"She's at grave risk. We have to get her out of there."

"Her attorneys?"

"They have a motion before the supreme court."

"Indeed."

"Do you think she's innocent, Father Blackie?"

"Arguably . . . All the principals are still in Chicago?"

"Yes, though the McLaughlins have a job offer in Florida which they want to accept. We have no reason to ask them to stay around."

"It will not be necessary, I think, to speak with them."

"Then you're going to help?"

I looked up in surprise. "Is the Pope Catholic?"

"I'm beginning to think there might be an evil fate dogging her."

Fate was not the word I would have used.

"I think that unlikely . . . You did indeed try to find out whether her natural parents were still alive?"

"Yes. We couldn't find out who they are or were. Dick Martin has the impression that Jack Turner believed that they were dead."

"Ah."

"Is that important?"

"Arguably."

That Terry Scanlan didn't grasp its importance proved how deeply mired in the previous paradigm he was. We can't live without paradigms because they organize reality for us.

190 / Andrew M. Greeley

But the organizations are durable and tenacious. We often cannot give them up even when we want to.

"Anything I can do to help, please let me know."

"I shall." I ushered him down to the first floor and out of the cathedral rectory into the autumn splendor of North Wabash Avenue with perhaps unseemly haste. There was work to be done.

My first intervention was a phone call to my brother-in-law, Redmond Peter "Red" Kane, Pulitzer Prize–winning columnist.

"Red, you are familiar with the Clare Turner case?"

"Sure, Blackie, I live in Chicago. My wife is still a federal judge."

"Your opinion?"

"The conviction will be reversed. Boyle O'Malley should be locked up."

"Yet the young woman is in county jail, although she certainly will not flee the jurisdiction and is no threat to the common weal."

"The state's attorney is afraid of a columnist at another paper with whose name I will not stain my innocent lips."

"Ah."

"Your implication is that another columnist should expose this injustice?"

"It would be a good work, Redmond."

"Then it shall be done. Tomorrow morning's paper."

"Excellent."

"Are you involved in this matter, Blackie?"

"Usually well-informed sources say that I am."

"Lucky Clare Turner."

"Arguably."

"You'll keep me informed?"

"You can rely on it. Give my best to your good wife, the virtuous Judge Kane, née Eileen."

"I shall."

One move for our side.

I then punched another number into the phone. I was, as should be obvious, activating a group of people who are amused to dub themselves "The North Wabash Avenue Irregulars."

Complete with sweatshirts with a portrait of the cathedral on the front and, alas, what purports to be a portrait of the cathedral rector on the back.

"Reilly Gallery," a gentle voice said on the line.

"I thought I'd dialed 911."

"Father Blackie!"

"I think that's who it is."

"You're looking for a cop?"

"A retired commissioner will do, even one who has become an artist."*

"Remember we're having supper at my apartment next week."

"God forbid I should forget."

Anne Marie Reilly's husband was Michael Patrick Vincent Casey, a retired cop who has become a successful artist specializing in impressionistic depictions of Chicago neighborhood scenes.

A cousin of the Ryan clan—his mother and my late mother, Kate Collins Ryan, were sisters—Mike is known as "Mike Casey the Cop," the title implying that there is another Mike Casey related to the clan.

However, he is the only one.

It has been suggested by some that he is my Watson or Flambeau or Captain Hastings. His wife, however, contends that I am his Tonto.

"Blackie?" He was on the line.

*See *Angels of September*

"Tahi, Kimosavi," I said, citing Tonto's line to the Lone Ranger.

"What mischief are you up to now?"

"I'm seeking information about a certain accountant, one," I glanced at the Vatican document, "by the name of Crane Ladd."

"I'm sure my friends could find that out."

"Admirable."

"The Turner case?"

"Indeed."

"We're in it?"

"We?"

"The Irregulars."

"Arguably."

"I thought there was a bad smell about that one."

"So it would seem."

My third call was to City Hall, indeed to the office of the corporation counsel, the city's chief legal officer.

"Ryan," he said.

"That's my name."

"Bro!"

"Odd. I was about to call you."

"You just did."

"Admirable coincidence."

"What can I do for you?"

"I seek some data about certain legal colleagues."

"All lawyers are liars," he said, deliberately indulging in a philosophical contradiction.

"First, a certain Terry G. Scanlan."

"He's too good to be a lawyer."

"Ah."

"But he's a damn good one. From the West Side and went to Holy Cross. His father worked for Dan Ward when he was state's attorney. One of his brothers married Jim Donlan's daughter. Her mother is a sister of John Dargan, whose son is at Bishop and James . . ."

My brother Patrick, a.k.a. Packy, delights in tracing lineages and connections.

"Tell me more about the young man."

"First rate. He's been out there at Twenty-sixth and California too long. The Boss likes him and wants to bring him over here, maybe in my office."

"Ah."

"He's smart, sensitive, and loyal. A bit of an idealist, which is hard to be out there, dedicated and absolutely incorruptible. If he has any fault as a lawyer, it is that he thinks too much."

"Serious character deficiency."

"His mother is a Fillamarino, Italian. Her father—"

"Is he married?"

"No . . . Women are one of the subjects about which he thinks too much."

"I see . . . Now as to certain judges, namely Boyle Michael O'Malley and Conrad Block."

Packy was silent for several seconds. Arguably the most perceptive member of the clan Ryan, he misses very little. So he knew what I was about. He decided that as corporation counsel, he did not want officially to ask any questions.

"Two scumbags."

"Corruptible?"

"You'd better believe it."

"I thought all corruption had been removed from the Cook County courts."

Packy laughed bitterly. "It's not as bad as it was twenty years ago, or even a couple of years ago, before the Feds began their scams. Still, if you have the right connections, there's almost nothing you can't get fixed, from a parking ticket up to murder one."

"All the judges are fixable?"

"By no means. Many are as honest as the next person, some even more honest. The trick is to have one of the fixables assigned to your case."

"Who brokers these procedures?"

"The boys usually. It's kind of a cottage industry."

"Boys" is a synonym for "mob," "Guys on the West Side" (with a jerk of the head in the direction of Taylor Street), and "Outfit."

"Ah."

"One of the West Side bunch that's under indictment now is the guy who fixed that case where the muscle man beat up a woman cop. You remember, the judge is no longer employed in the criminal justice system."

"A reassuring fact."

"I mean they have a regular scale—a hundred thousand big ones for certain divorce cases, eighty thousand for a murder, ten for armed robbery, five for use of cocaine."

"Even after the present investigations and indictments."

"Sure. They don't talk about it in chambers anymore, lest they be bugged. And they're wary of someone coming in off the street that might be wired by the Feds. They're also pretty careful about the restaurants where they eat because they know that the regular spots will be wired."

"How is the money passed on?"

"It used to be that you left it in the toilet stalls in washrooms or in the desk of the judge's office when he walked out. Now they do it away from the court—on a bridge over the river at night or in a Halsted bar. Someplace where they're sure there won't be a hidden video camera."

"They're good at keeping up with the technology."

"You better believe it . . . Mind you, Bro, I'm not saying that it's any worse here than in any urban court system. The difference here is that until recently it was so open."

"Indeed. Now, let me ask you one more question. Your friends on the West Side are capable of a fix to obtain a conviction?"

"I've never heard of that. They're into the business of saving the guilty, not destroying the innocent. It's an interesting idea all right, but a little too baroque for them. They have more direct ways of dealing with those who have offended them."

"I see. But if someone wanted to go baroque . . ."

"If the price were right, there's certain young bucks who might try it. The Big Tuna and the Lackey wouldn't approve. They would say that such behavior was immoral."

"And mean it?"

"Sure, everyone has a moral system, Bro. It's just that some are different than the one you preach."

"Catholicism is a religion, Bro, not a moral system."

"Tell that to the Big Guy in the Vatican."

"If the occasion arises, I will indeed."

"Good luck in what you're doing."

"I'm grateful. And my best to your patient and saintly wife."

"Remember you're having supper with us the week after next."

"I shan't forget."

"Hey, wait a minute," Packy said before I hung up. "There is one case where an innocent man was convicted."

"Ah?"

"A kid, twenty or so, was indicted for rape. Thin evidence. Bench trial at the recommendation of defense counsel. The judge found him guilty. Then the defense lawyer, the kid's own lawyer, told the kid's mother that for fifty thousand the judge would reverse himself. She came to us. We gave her five thousand. She went to the defense attorney's office and put the five big ones on his desk. He pulled a curtain and behind it was a glass partition. The judge was there and he waved at her."

"Incredible!"

"We indicted both of them. They were found not guilty, mostly because of instructions yet another judge gave to the jury."

"And the young man who was accused of rape?"

"He walked. We found the real rapist."

"How fortunate for him."

"That was pretty much a private little scam, though we suspect that the judge used it many times, always with frightened people that were probably innocent. His license plate was BTNG—bench trial, not guilty!"

"Indeed . . . and were your friends on the West Side involved?"

"Not directly. There was a scumbag of a low-level capo named Joe Seritella who was the go-between."

"I'll remember the name."

"Now don't forget supper. You know how much Tracy likes you."

"I would surely not disappoint that virtuous and admirable woman."

For some odd reason he laughed. "I'll call your assistant next week and remind her."

"Admirable."

Terry Scanlan thought that the mysterious Clare might be a victim of Fate.

Patent nonsense. "Fate" and "fix" both begin with the letter "F." I would have to remind the worthy assistant state's attorney of that fact.

If, however, the model I was testing fit the data, it was not thereby proven true. I still had to learn why someone would choose, to use Packy's word, such a baroque technique.

There was one last call. To the reigning matriarch of our clan, Mary Kathleen Ryan Murphy, M.D.

"Punk? You're not going to cancel out on supper tonight, are you?"

"Certainly not."

Someone on my staff would surely have remembered.

"I wish to seek your professional opinion on a matter of some importance."

"Another one of your cases?"

"Possibly."

"So?"

"You are aware doubtless from the press of a murder case tried recently in the county of Cook, the State of Illinois versus Clare Turner?"

"I have absolutely no comment of any sort on that case or anyone or anything related to it."

So, the suspicion of both the worthy Terry Scanlan and myself was justified.

I am not at all surprised when various members of the clan find themselves without any prior planning and coordination involved with the same people who for whatever reason need help. There is no intrinsic necessity which brings us together in such matters. It rather seems simply to work out that way.

"Indeed," I commented.

"You'd better believe indeed."

"I suppose I should have anticipated that."

"I'll say one thing, however."

My sister Mary Kathleen always ends a conversation with her "one thing."

"And that is?"

"Only assholes would think that poor child was a killer."

"Arguably."

Both Ryan siblings ended the conversation with feelings

of satisfaction. My task now was to determine what sick and twisted reasoning went into the scheme to destroy Clare Turner.

Normally one searches for the beneficiary. But in this particular case it hardly seemed likely that the Catholic Bishop of Chicago, a Corporation Sole, was responsible.

20

THE CARDINAL WAS READING THE BIBLE, A MOST UNUSUAL behavior for a Cardinal prince of the Roman Church.

It was early the morning after my conversation with the distracted Terry Scanlan. That night, as directed, I supped at the matriarch's house and admired (for perhaps the one millionth time) her first two grandchildren—Cormac and Conor Maher, sons of my virtuous niece Caitlan and her husband, one Kevin Maher.

I escaped from the two young, redheaded hellions with my sanity barely intact.

"The mysterious Clare Turner doubtless asked for your help in search of her natural parents," I began with the usual "soft" opening style that I use to accost the Cardinal early in the morning.

He looked up at me with one eye and closed his Bible.

"Arguably," he murmured, imitating my currently most favorite response. He did not, however, ask how I was aware of that, knowing that such a question was bootless.

"You were able to assist her?"

He closed the Bible, finger in place at the page he was reading.

"This question is germane to your investigation?"

"I rather think so."

He took off his glasses and waved me to the chair in which I was already sinking.

"It was not a Catholic Charities adoption in this archdiocese, that's for sure. Nor in any diocese near here. There was something mysterious about it all right. I assume her parents knew where she came from, but they refused to discuss the matter with her."

"You thought her search prudent?"

He considered the question very carefully, as if it were perhaps a search he himself might have understood from personal experience.*

"Who a person is, Blackwood, is more a social and cultural question than a biological one. The curiosity an adopted child has later in life is understandable, though no good can usually come from investigating it. Still, if one must search one's origins, then I guess that's one's right. I didn't try to argue with her. I did what I could and it wasn't much help."

"In her case it would be a matter of something more than biological origins. She has the impression, I am told, that she was perhaps two years old when she taken from her natural parents. Even if one does not subscribe to the radical Freudianism of my virtuous sibling Dr. Murphy, something of the personality and character have been formed by that time."

The Cardinal nodded and gave up on his Bible. He rose from his vast easy chair and poured me a morning cup of the powerful Irish tea to which he is devoted.

"You think this is important to the case?"

"It's a very strange affair. When one encounters such, one searches for other unusual components. Clare's origins are also strange."

"You're convinced that she's innocent?"

*See *The Brother's Wife*

"I think it highly likely."

"She is a rather remarkable young woman, actually. One might expect great things of her in years to come."

"She might be a much better investment than whatever monies would accrue to us if she were deprived of her inheritance?"

"It's a risk I'd take."

"It is said that she is cold and unemotional."

"Bullshit, Blackwood. Again I say, bullshit. Even a person as innocent of pastoral knowledge of human nature as a cardinal can tell that there are towering emotions beneath the surface of that young woman. Your friend Terry Scanlan has been swept up by a maelstrom of womanly passion."

"A fact which, I believe, he begins now to perceive."

"Can he cope with her?"

"Oh, yes, I rather think so."

"What do you propose to do?"

"Poke around a bit at first. Can you remember anything specific from your conversation with her?"

"You're not going to visit her?"

"Not for the present. I want to collect some impressions first."

"She says she remembers sunlight, but no water. Blue skies. A pretty woman and a nice man. Another woman taking her away. Then gray skies."

"The desert?"

"So I thought. I tried the dioceses of Tucson, Phoenix, and Santa Fe. No luck there either."

"Anything else?"

"A vague sense that her natural parents died, or were killed."

"Ah."

"Don't think I haven't considered that possibility . . ."

"You have spoken with her?"

"Visited her in jail."

"Indeed!"

"One of the corporal works of mercy, you may remember, Blackwood. 'I was in prison and you visited me.' "

"I vaguely recall that text."

"I was about to turn the matter over to you when Dan Hills called about Terry Scanlan. I thought it better he tell you about it."

"Doubtless."

"Will you get her out of this mess?"

I permitted my eyes to open wide. "Do you have any doubt about that?"

He merely laughed.

A bewitching young woman, I thought as I ambled back to my own rooms. Not only Terry Scanlan, but also the Cardinal Archbishop of Chicago. Well, if one needed a father figure with which to identify, one could do much worse than Sean Cronin.

Back in my room, I searched for the mass of materials which the indefatigable Terry G. Scanlan had left for me. Typically I could not remember where I had put it the night before, my desk having long since been preempted by the galleys of my new book, *The Achievement of David Tracy*, a volume the sales of which will not provide enough royalty income to buy 1 (one) bleacher seat for a Chicago Cubs game.

I finally found them where I had left them: in the bathtub, which has been unused for most of the last half century because a separate shower stall (with six nozzles) was installed by one of my predecessors of happy memory.

I searched through them and found an envelope with the inscription "Paranormal Phenomena."

Sure enough, just as described, I found pictures of an ectoplasmic shape lurking in various corners of the Turner house, in some cases curling affectionately and protectively around Clare, especially it seemed to me around those parts of her body which might be described as sexual—or perhaps in this era I should say gender distinctive.

Unlike Terry Scanlan, I have no psychic propensities and am not troubled by such phenomena. Nonetheless, I do experience a certain sense of unease when I witness the uncanny.

These pictures were uncanny. It was most improbable that they were fraudulent. Something strange had happened in that house. Some power or force, some residue of past experiences perhaps, was determined to protect Clare Turner.

In service of the wishes of my Lord Cronin, I have had some prior experience with such photographs. I do not necessarily attribute to them anything supernatural as that word is normally understood.

Rather my tentative model is that they result from the interaction of present and past memory vibrations, often focusing on some particularly psychic individual, especially a young individual.

What does that last paragraph mean?

I'm not altogether sure.

In this case, it might well be some lingering memory in Clare's psyche of her natural parents. Perhaps lurking inside herself and manifesting itself externally without her awareness.

William James, my philosophical mentor, would have had no problem with such an explanation.

I put the pictures in my safe (installed by the same predecessor). Although it is never locked because I have long since forgotten (if I ever knew) the combination, it is nonetheless a place where I put valuable materials that I want to be able to find at a later time without too much searching.

Or, perhaps, I thought, a memory in one of the Turners of the truth of Clare's early years.

I packed the materials from the case of the State of Illinois versus Clare Turner in two large shopping bags and asked Melissa, who has charge of the door to the cathedral rectory, if she would have them delivered to the Reilly Gallery. Thus my Flambeau would have all the material (save the envelope with the Polaroids) and I wouldn't have to worry about losing it.

I called the home of Richard Martin and found that he had not yet left for the Turner Electronics plant and that he would not mind talking to me. Moreover his daughter Jane was also at home and would not depart before noon.

I boarded my 1955 turquoise-and-white Chevy Bel Air (a present from my siblings, all of whom share a weakness for classic cars, to which I am immune) and nosed my way down Wabash to Ontario and then over to the JFK Expressway and headed north.

The Martins, father and daughter, were waiting for me anxiously, the teapot already prepared and the croissants with butter and raspberry jam already laid out.

"I'm *so* glad, Father Blackie," Jane said, "that someone is trying to help her. She didn't do it, I *know* she didn't do it."

Jane Martin was a tightly packaged bundle of youthful and attractive Irish womanly energy and hence blessed with an intense sense of moral outrage against all evildoers, especially those who oppressed her friends.

"Ah," I said, knowing from long experience with such as her that one had best give them their chance to speak because in fact one has no other option.

"I *mean* she thinks that nerd Terry Scanlan is a nice boy; and I go, He's an asshole!"

"Jane," her father protested, but not all that seriously.

"Well, he *is* an asshole."

"I believe I have heard that comment before."

"How can you fall in love with someone who's trying to inject lethal chemicals into your body, I mean I ask you, isn't it gross!"

"He may have become a convert to her cause."

"That's what she says, but I don't believe it. Of all the people for her to flip over, although I admit he is kind of cute."

"Arguably."

"*Anyway*, that's typical of Clare. Always doing something strange or weird."

"And wrong?"

"Oh, no way. I mean she's, like, always right when she does something strange. Like going into psychoanalysis or medical school or something really weird. So I suppose she's right about Terry Scanlan too. But she's still in jail, isn't she?"

The biggest dog in all the world ambled into the room, sniffed at me, permitted me to pat her head, and then curled up at my feet.

"Fiona?" I asked.

"She's pining for Clare. She eats hardly anything and just kind of droops around. I'm worried about her, Father."

"It'll be all right, Fiona," I foolishly assured the mourning dog and unobtrusively slipped her a half of a croissant, which she delicately removed from my fingers.

"Can anything be done about it, Father?" Dick Martin asked.

"Certain counterforces have been unleashed."

"Like Red Kane." He held up the day's *Herald*.

"Ah." I took the paper from his hands.

"Our state's attorney, egged on by a certain columnist at another paper whose intellectual range is limited to sentences of eight words, has told us that Clare Turner must remain in county jail in the name of equal justice under the law.

"Every lawyer in town who can read and write (no more than half of the total population of attorneys) knows that Judge Boyle Michael O'Malley's conduct of Ms. Turner's trial was a farce. Judge O'Malley's record for reversals is the highest in the history of Cook County. Whether Ms. Turner is guilty or not of the murder of her parents remanis to be seen. My sources tell me that the State's Attorney's Office was willing to plea bargain for a sentence which would have put Ms. Turner in jail for a year and a half. That says they have no real case against her.

"Why then is she languishing in county jail? Is she a threat to the common good? Is she likely to run away? Or is she paying a price because she happens to be rich and attractive and certain envy-ridden columnists get their kicks by keeping rich young women in county jail?

"If Ms. Turner wasn't rich, she probably would not have been indicted. She would certainly be finishing her medical education. This is equal justice?"

The Ryan family rides again!

"Interesting," I muttered.

"And, look." Jane grabbed the paper from me. "Look at this. Medical school students from Loyola and Northwestern picketing the state's attorney's home. Isn't that neat?"

Northwestern, huh? The inestimable Mary Kate was on the staff of Northwestern as well as Little Company of Mary. So. Sometimes you don't have to make suggestions.

"Counterattack," I murmured.

"She's a wonderful young woman, Father," Dick Martin echoed his daughter's enthusiasm.

"She doesn't think people like her," Jane protested, "isn't that crazy? And that bitch Elaine Kincaid testifying against her made her believe it too. But when she sees pictures of the kids supporting her, she'll change her mind, won't she? Why, even Terry Scanlan has fallen for her, hasn't he?"

"Oh?"

"Well, she says he has."

"Truly?"

The premise had been changed. The alleged love between Clare and Terry was no longer a proof of her weirdness but now of her appeal. I am not inexperienced with such changes of premise when the dialogue partner is Irish and womanly.

As your man Jimmy Joyce put it, a word can mean two thinks; and the "thinks" is not a typo.

"It would only prove that he has good taste," she said defensively, shifting her premise again. "Clare may seem quiet and creepy but she's actually a magic person."

"So I am told."

That such magic had not been displayed to greater advantage at the trial proved that Elmer McBride had indeed blown the defense. Perhaps, however, the behavior of the judge would have precluded such a strategy.

"I mean, she's different, but, Father, anyone would be different who had to put up with her parents. Like Daddy says, they were nice people, but as parents, ugh. She's different all right, but classy. Like totally."

"Indeed."

Thus without my having to ask a single question, I had learned from Jane Martin what I had wanted to learn. The last remote possibility that Clare Turner was responsible for her parents' deaths could now be discounted. The picture of Ms. Turner was now complete. Terry Scanlan has missed it totally in his first encounters, poor worn and lonely young man.

Alas, that did not tell me what resourceful and ingenious monster was responsible.

"Did she ever discuss her natural parents with you?"

"Never once. I mean, I knew she was adopted, but she never said anything about them to me."

"Mr. Martin?"

"Not a word."

"Assuming that the charges against her can ultimately be rejected, what role will she have in her father's firm?"

"Well, she will be chair of the Turner Endowment which will control more than half of the voting stock in the company, so she will be decisive. Young Tim Leyden, who represents his family on our board, will not bother management as long as we make a profit, which we are certainly doing just now. If Clare wants she can become chair of our board. We'll certainly offer it to her."

"And if she declines?"

"Then I suppose I'll become chair as well as CEO. It wouldn't make any difference, so I'd just as soon have her as chair."

"Ah . . . then you see her influence as entirely positive?"

"Oh, yes. Jack Turner was a smart man, never forget that. He wanted her to be active in the company for a long time. She wouldn't agree because she didn't want to be a rich socialite . . ."

"Her very words," Jane interrupted.

"But now, he's kind of trapped her. She'll preside both over the Endowment and the company because she loved him."

"And be a doctor too," Jane added. "I told you she was magic."

"This Mr. Leyden . . ."

"Tim."

"Yes indeed. He is acquainted with Clare?"

"He knows her, not very well, but he's outraged by what's happening to her. He's the one who suggested that she become chairman. I gather she's on some committee of the Cardinal with Tim's mother."

"So the Leydens have no reason to oppose her influence in the company."

"Quite the contrary, they assume, correctly I might add, that the firm needs stability in this transitional time and that Clare represents stability. Mind you, we're only a small part of the Leyden empire."

All very interesting and most likely true. Mike Casey's assistants would confirm it for me. Management of Turner Electronics had no interest in putting Clare Turner in jail and excellent reason for keeping her out of jail.

I thought that probable to begin with, but one needs to approach cautiously a mystery of such vast evil as the one which confronted me.

I bid the Martins good-bye and permitted the fabulous Fiona to escort me to my car. I shared with her the croissant that I had secreted in my pocket. She wagged her tail happily. We were friends for life. If I had not escaped into the Bel Air, she arguably would have licked my face, a favorite amusement of her species.

It might be necessary, I thought, to insist that Terry Scanlan pay his respects to Fiona. Surely the matchmaking pooch was at least entitled to that.

I drove up Edens Expressway and over to Lakewood, a suburb which was so far north that in my childhood in Beverly on the South West Side of Chicago we firmly believed it was on the fringes of the Arctic Ocean.

With some difficulty I found Sylvan Lane. Despite my deep prejudices against any community north of Madison Street, I had to admit that the changing leaves of early autumn created a stunning impact. One was not on the great American prairie but in dune country, a place which at this time of the year could hold its own with any other locale in the world.

Even Beverly, which was constructed on an earlier set of dunes—back when Lake Michigan was Lake Chicago (so named not by the occasional human that might have wandered past the dunes but by contemporary geologists) and extended several miles farther than it does now. And Beverly was much more crowded.

Clare Turner had grown up in this beauty, surrounded by all the comforts and conveniences which modern wealth could buy. She lived a life of more spectacular glory than the richest queens of yesteryear—and also mastered karate.

All she lacked was a family environment of warm and open affection—and perhaps also a milieu of sympathy for the enthusiasms of youth.

For all that, she had become a young woman with a mind and a will of her own. And a sexuality which, when properly aroused, could respond with devastating effectiveness.

Her earliest experiences, I wagered, must have been of intense love.

Thus her survival and her healthy sexuality.

I finally found 1120 Sylvan Lane. It was, as advertised, an enormous house.

I parked in front of the place and walked around. The sun was high in the sky and the lake, some twenty-five yards behind the house, glowed in rich purple.

The glass monstrosity which had been Jack Turner's workshop was indeed as bad as the ineffable Mrs. Kincaid had complained. The curtains were drawn so it was impossible for me to see inside it. At some point in the not too distant future I would want to explore the house.

As I was coming around the house, I was almost overcome by an extraordinary feeling—the strongest feeling of the uncanny which I had ever encountered in my life. There was a force or an energy in that house which wanted me to enter.

The energy—I can think of no other word—was not malign. But I would not use the word benign either. Rather it was worried. It wanted help.

I promised that I would be back. It seemed to recede.

I leaned against my trusty Bel Air, shaking from the odd experience. As I have said I am not particularly psychic nor especially sensitive to the paranormal. I am a philosopher not a mystic. If I see solutions to puzzles rather quickly, it is an empirical rather than a contemplative skill.

Once or twice in my career I have felt such experiences, once in a house in Long Beach, Michigan, where a death had occurred.*

But never had I encountered such a powerful psychic energy. More and more mysterious was this case of Clare Turner.

"Good morning, Father," a sweet voice sounded behind me. "Are you interested in buying this house?"

Ms. Kincaid, dressed in jeans and a low-cut white swimsuit with an open shirt over it—an ensemble which confirmed Terry Scanlan's impression of a strong if slightly kinky sexuality—approached the car.

"Oh, no, I'm just wandering around, communing with the spirits."

"Oh?"

"Ugly glass thing in the back, isn't it?"

"Oh yes. The poor people who built it died last winter."

There wasn't much doubt about why her husband remained married to her. Her subtle body movements confirmed the supposition by Chief Stewart that she would be good in bed. Her seductiveness was so low-keyed as to be

*See *Happy are the Meek*

subliminal, but it was intense. A man in the same house with her would soon go crazy with desire.

"So I've heard. Violently, I understand."

"Such a shame. And their daughter was the one who killed them. Cut their throats."

"Really?"

As we talked April Kincaid became an open if subtle invitation to sexual activity, indeed to sexual assault. Take me, the signals said, take me violently and do what you want if you dare.

A celibate develops certain disciplines and self-restraints which fend off ordinary sexual signals. But this one was far more than ordinary. April Kincaid had stepped out of a pornographic—or perhaps a sadomasochistic—novel.

Thank you, but no thanks.

"Yes, she was tried and convicted and is in prison now."

"Extraordinary!"

Had Jack Turner been a victim, which is to say had she turned him into a victimizer? Unlikely but who knows? Did she have a reputation in the community for extramarital flings? Would her commitment to causes from whales to trees be an outlet for excess sexual energy or perhaps an expiation for it?

Some questions would have to be raised with Terry and Chief Stewart.

"Oh yes, my daughter testified in the trial. She did her best to help the poor young woman, but the child was so obviously guilty that my daughter was no help."

"There must be some ghosts in this house."

"It is odd that you should say that, but I have sensed that too. In fact, even before the death I felt that something was not quite right about the house. Since then, I've felt it more strongly. I live over there, you see, just beyond that stand of trees."

"Interesting. So I suppose you were in this house fairly often?"

"Oh yes, *very* often."

"Well, it's been nice talking to you."

"Could I make you a cup of coffee, Father? Or perhaps a pot of tea?"

"No, thanks. I have to rush back. I understand the house is for sale."

"Yes it is. But no one wants to buy a house where there has been a murder. It's likely to be on the market for a long time. Are you sure you wouldn't like some coffee?"

You better believe I was sure.

21

ANNE REILLY POURED ME A CUP OF HER APPLE CINNAMON tea, which she believes is an acceptable alternative to Bushmill's or Jameson's. Since Anne, now turning sixty, is one of the most attractive women I know, I do not dispute the point with her. She also insists on cleaning my glasses with a little spray container she keeps in her gallery for my visits, a task she performs whether my glasses need to be cleaned or not; as a point of fact, I will confess, they *always* need cleaning. The ritual is finished when she kisses my forehead.

Her appeal is less kinky than that of Ms. Kincaid but far more powerful.

"There," she said approvingly, "now you're all ready to consult with the Lone Ranger."

Anne then went back to the sales area of the gallery and left me and her husband in his small studio, where he was working on a painting of an intersection with a bar, a church, and a funeral home on three corners.

Mike the Cop, a man the same age as his beauteous wife, looks like the late Basil Rathbone playing Sherlock Holmes—tall, thin, handsome, and with shrewd eyes that miss nothing. He normally wears three-piece Italian suits, but at work, as he was today, he appears in jeans (designer of course) and an artist's smock, enough to persuade you you were perhaps in the Montmartre district of Paris instead of on Oak Street in Chicago.

"The woman is a distraction," he admitted with a false sigh of resignation. "A man can't get any work done."

I sighed in response. "Isn't it always the way."

With Anne Reilly in my studio I would get nothing done either, though I don't have a studio. On the other hand the availability of such a woman on the condition that I have a studio might well persuade me of the necessity of purchasing a studio.

"Crane Ladd," he said, returning to his palette, "is not a very bright man."

"Ah?"

"He has purchased three certificates of deposit at three separate institutions, each for a hundred thousand dollars. All with cash."

"And himself an accountant?"

"Not a very bright accountant, I'm afraid. He could have laundered his money in an offshore account. Grand Cayman perhaps."

"He may yet do that."

"And leave a paper trail the IRS will have no trouble following . . . Should one of my associates question him about this sudden wealth?"

Mike does not exactly run a small but highly efficient investigating agency from his wife's gallery. Not exactly.

"No harm would come of that. I suspect, however, that he has been warned not to contact whichever friend of friends originally made him an offer, a warning that he would be wise to honor."

"Probably it was a one-way contact."

"Indeed. But we have confirmed what I had suspected. He was corrupted at some time during the trial. The friends of friends would have perhaps desired a more intelligent man, but they had to work with what opportunity provided."

"So it looks pretty much like the fix was in."

"I think we can take that as given."

"Why didn't young Mr. Scanlan consider this possibility?" Mike applied a dab of paint to the facade of the church and, by so doing, transformed the whole painting.

"Everyone knows that our friends," I gave the requisite nod of my head in the direction of Taylor Street, "can fix trials in the county courts almost at will. However they engage in such behavior to free the guilty. Why would they do it to incarcerate the innocent? As my worthy sib the corporation counsel notes, they normally have less complicated ways of eliminating people."

"Even then," he dabbed the funeral home, "it is not very likely that the State will execute Clare Turner."

"It may be enough for their purposes that she be incarcerated. Or there could be an accident in prison."

An observation which shows how negligent the mistakes I was about to make really were.

"Moreover, a mob hit might raise certain questions."

I nodded in agreement. "Whoever is behind this affair has planned it very carefully."

"You don't think the Outfit people are acting on their own?" Mike looked away from his canvas and considered me with his keen blue eyes. "You think they're subcontracting?"

"Certain lower-level soldiers are acting for a certain medium-level capo who in turn is in contact, perhaps indirect, with the principal in the matter."

"Makes sense." He returned to his brushes. "But who and why?"

"That," I sipped my apple cinnamon tea and reflected

again on the virtues of the admirable Annie Reilly, "remains to be seen."

"Who would want her dead?"

"That again remains to be seen . . . but do you think that one of your young men could ascertain for me whether Richard Martin, the president and CEO of Turner Electronics, would have benefited greatly from a sale of the firm to any of the more prominent oil companies?"

Mike the Cop whistled. "Do you think that's the story?"

"Arguably. He seems quite content with the possibility that she become the chairman of the firm. Perhaps he is content. And then perhaps he is not content. Minimally, we must exclude him from the list of suspects."

"You're fishing?"

"Oh yes."

The wondrous Annie returned, as is her custom, with a plate of chocolate chip cookies.

"The woman can cook too." Mike discreetly admired her rear end as she left the room, not so discreetly however that she was unaware of his interest.

"Wondrous," I murmured as I munched on my first cookie.

"Any other assignments?"

"You might find out from Tucson how the decedent's brother fares, whether indeed his brother's death has improved his fortunes."

Mike nodded agreement. "OK. But neither Fred Turner nor Dick Martin seems the type to engage in this sort of fix."

"Perhaps not, but they both might benefit from it . . . There is one more thing, but I'll give young Mr. Scanlan some work to do. He needs to be distracted. May I use your phone?"

"We'll put it on the bill!" Mike laughed and returned to his canvas.

"Terry? This is Father Ryan . . ."

"I just talked to her, Father. She is scared. She says that some of the other women are looking at her strangely, especially since the demonstration against us began this morning."

"Ah . . . can't you find a reason to remove her from danger?"

"We've persuaded the warden to make sure that there is always a guard or two around her. That should be enough, but she's worried and so am I."

"And your employer? How is he reacting to the pressure?"

"He can't believe that there are protesters in front of his house. He thought he was on the side of the good guys."

"Most unfortunate . . . He will succumb in the near future?"

"I think so. I just hope it is soon enough . . . How are you coming?"

"I have a question for you to propound to Chief Stewart: is it not true that Ms. Kincaid has engaged in certain impulsive but discreet affairs with the men in the community— very discreet and very impulsive, and perhaps not a little kinky?"

"Do you really think that, Father?"

"I would not exclude the possibility. Moreover, I suggest that you go over the testimony of the McLaughlins to determine whether John Turner left his workshop anytime in the course of the day he was killed."

"You don't think . . ."

"We must consider that possibility."

"Of course . . . We should have thought of it."

"Wrong paradigm . . . I'll be at the cathedral rectory this evening engaged in various pastoral activities. If you can't get through to me, leave me a message and I'll be back to you."

"You have a cynical imagination, Blackie," Mike the Cop said when I had hung up the phone.

"Human nature, Mike, as I hardly need tell you, comes in many varieties, not all of them virtuous."

"I have noticed that."

"So you think that Clare is the victim of someone who wants to cover up their own guilt?"

"Arguably . . . though I think it more likely that Clare herself has been the target all along."

"That's diabolic, Blackie."

"Indeed. It is also up to this point successful."

It was not a particularly busy evening at the cathedral. I talked to two happy couples who were planning marriages, attended three wakes, met with the finance committee and the young adults committee, confirmed a young woman's desire not to have an abortion, reassured parents of a teen whose average had dropped to 3.75, and appeared briefly at a high school basketball game.

Terry Scanlan phoned me at ten-thirty.

"You were right, Father Blackie."

"It has happened before on occasion."

"The wives of Lakewood consider April Kincaid to be a virtuous woman. There is not a taint of suspicion among them. However, an occasional discreet whisper between men, say in the country club locker room, paints a different picture."

"Ah?"

"She seems to invite deliberately rather violent assaults that the men involved find most rewarding. If in fact the whispered rumors are true she does not have long-term affairs, only brief interludes."

"Very cleverly planned, I should think, if she's able to keep them so secret."

"So the Chief says . . . He doubts that John Turner was one of her victims or victimizers, whichever the men might be."

"Both I suppose . . . Yet Turner did go for a walk in the course of the early afternoon that day?"

"He did indeed."

"In which direction?"

"In the direction of the Kincaid house, but, Father Blackie, he was your classic nerd, interested only in his work."

"A work about which she knew in some detail?"

He was silent for a moment. "She did know he was working on energy conservation, I remember that."

"Indeed."

"I wouldn't think she was the type that would appeal to a man like him."

"It is written that the bigger they come, the harder they fall."

"But that doesn't mean that she would kill him, does it?"

"Who knows what threats he might have been making?"

"Threats?"

"Consider this scenario: Jack Turner is caught up in one of Ms. Kincaid's little amusements. Unlike the other victims and victimizers, he is not prepared to enjoy the interlude and forget about it. He wants a consistent relationship. She declines, perhaps laughs at him, he threatens her with exposure, she finds her marriage and her position in the community jeopardized . . ."

"That's possible. But how did she get into the locked room?"

"How does anyone get into the locked room? And you

will remember that we know only from her that the Turners were still alive at seven-thirty."

"It's all possible," he said hesitantly. "Difficult to prove . . . Do you really believe it?"

No, I didn't really believe it.

"Someone, perhaps you, should have a conversation with her in which she is asked directly what she and John Turner talked about that day."

"All right, I'll do it . . . I'm not sure . . ."

"And I would urge caution on you. She is a pathetic and driven person, but also quite likely dangerous to both herself and others."

Anyone who would consider me a possible victim has to be truly pathetic.

At eleven o'clock I drifted into the Cardinal's room. He was working on a stack of correspondence.

"No rest for the wicked," I observed.

"That's your problem."

"This committee on which the admirable Ms. Turner served, when does it meet again?"

"Tomorrow afternoon, as a matter of fact."

"It is a shame that you won't be able to see them tomorrow, isn't it? A crisis call from the Apostolic See, perhaps?"

"And I'll have to send along, as a replacement, my dutiful and docile auxiliary bishop?"

"Indeed."

"They will be disappointed." He grinned.

"Doubtless."

"You surely don't suspect any of them?"

"Hardly . . . I'm still seeking impressions, chance remarks, little hints."

"Touching all the bases?"

"Precisely."

He took off his glasses. "Do you have suspects, Holmes?"

"A number of them. However, none that I find persuasive. There's something important here that eludes me."

"I'm astonished."

I ignored this sally as not deserving comment.

"I believe it may have to do with the mystery of her origins."

"That may be insoluble."

I thought of the strange vibrations I encountered before the more obvious and more human vibrations which emanated from April Kincaid.

"Perhaps."

"Blackwood," he said as I was about to leave his study.

"M'lord?"

"I want that young woman cleared and set free."

"Naturally."

"See to it!"

That instruction, half fun and full earnest as my late mother would say, made it official.

Women, I informed the Almighty during my night prayers, are strange creatures. Consider the varied impact on various people of Clare Turner, April Kincaid, and Annie Reilly. Sex is, I reminded the Deity, a most troublesome technique for continuing the species.

And for teaching us how to love.

22

MIKE CASEY WAS ON THE PHONE WAITING FOR ME WHEN I returned from the funeral Mass.

"You were right about Dick Martin, Blackie."

"Ah?"

"The relevant oil company very much wanted to buy Turner Electronics. Still does as a matter of fact. They would give your friend Mr. Martin a substantial bonus in stock options for remaining with the firm in his present capacity."

"Bribes for supporting the sale?"

"Crudely put but true."

"In what amount?"

"Enough to take care of him and his family at a higher standard of living than the present for the rest of their lives."

"Indeed!"

"So they must have been very worried about the converter on which Jack Turner was working."

"Doubtless."

"But . . ."

"Yes?"

"But he seems to have turned them down flat."

"Even after the death of Jack Turner?"

"Yep. Moreover he has persuaded the other members of the board to agree with him."

"In expectation of a higher price?"

"Possibly. But the oil company thinks that the rejection is final. They're quite concerned, as you might imagine."

"It does not seem like financially rational behavior. After all, what would be wrong with such a sale?"

"Martin may be a sentimentalist. He might want to honor Jack Turner's memory."

"Or he might think there is even more money to be made with the converter."

"It could be that too . . . and speaking of more money, Fred Turner has apparently experienced a turnaround in his fortunes."

"So?"

"Our Tucson contacts tell us that he managed to pay off his creditors, probably from loans in expectation of his inheritance, and then get in on the ground floor of the construction of a new retirement community. They say he will do very well on that."

"Until his next mistaken venture."

"The story of his life . . . It also develops that he owns some stock in Turner Electronics."

"Indeed!"

"Non-voting stock. So he can't effect the future of the company. It was held for him in trust till his brother died. Now it's his to do with what he wants."

"Is there more non-voting stock?"

"Some distant cousins apparently hold it too. It's all in the will. I guess the state's attorney's people didn't find it interesting."

"Would its value go up if there was a sale of Turner Electronics?"

"Sure, if there was the prospect of increased dividends—or

if the buyer wanted to pick it up just so that things would be tidy. The point is that a speculator might buy the stock on the chance that its value would go up, although it's not listed on any exchange so it's hard to estimate a value."

"He hasn't sold it yet?"

"No, but my friends in Tucson tell me he's doing a lot of talking about it."

"The oil companies are still interested?"

"Yes, indeed."

"And the decision will be made by?"

"The Turner Endowment."

"Of which Clare Turner is the chair?"

"Whether she is ultimately sent to jail or not."

"Very interesting . . . As always, Mike, your information is invaluable."

"I'll remember that when I send the bill."

He was jesting. Because there is never a bill. He figures he owes me for Annie Reilly, in which respect he is doubtless correct.

Me and God, and the latter much more than the former.

"Some mail, Boss." One of my young associates dropped a vast pile on my desk. "It should keep you out of trouble till lunchtime."

"Indeed."

As I separated the letters which I might eventually open from those which I would immediately consign to the wastebasket, I pondered the new information about Fred Turner, Dick Martin, and Turner Electronics. I did not know what to make of any of it. There would surely be a great deal of money to be made. But it did not follow that either man was capable of murder for it.

Nor could I immediately picture either of them—Martin on the basis of my conversation with him and Fred Turner on the basis of reputation—as capable of the elaborate and evil plot which I had begun to postulate as essential to explain the deaths of the Turners.

The house phone rang.

"Father Ryan."

"A Mr. Scanlan to see you, Bishop. He doesn't have an appointment."

"You know very well, Melissa, that I do not receive anyone who does not have an appointment."

"Yes, Bishop. I have sent him up."

"Excellent."

"Sorry to bother you, Bishop," he said. "And sorry I haven't used the right title."

"I answer to almost any title . . . A cup of tea?"

"If you have something stronger . . . ?"

The young man looked distraught, so I opened my secret liquor cabinet—behind a watercolor of the cathedral by Mike the Cop—and removed a Waterford tumbler and a half-empty bottle of Jameson's (twelve-year special reserve).

"Thanks, Father." He sighed as he sipped from the tumbler. "I'm not normally a drinking man."

"April Kincaid?"

"As you would say, indeed!"

"She turned on her rather peculiar charms?"

"I don't know whether I didn't notice them the last time or whether she put on a special show for me this time . . . It wasn't quite enough to make me forget about Clare—no one will ever be able to do that—but it was a harrowing experience."

"All very subtle and understated, I daresay."

"An invitation to violence. I know that sounds strange but that is what it was."

"Violence against her?"

"Yeah, underplayed of course, but intense—take me if you're strong enough to overpower and violate me."

"A little demented?"

"Oh yes. But that made it even more appealing."

"This happened after she admitted that she was involved with John Turner?"

"Yes . . . How did you know about that?"

I resisted the temptation to say that it was "elementary."

"She knew that he was involved in an energy conservation invention. I would doubt that John Turner would talk about his project to anyone outside of his firm and his family—unless it were some variety of pillow talk."

"She broke down as soon as I accused her. She denied that it was an affair. They played a little kissy face at the annual Christmas party, which was pretty much the Turners' sole contribution to the social life of Lakewood—he was showing her around the workshop to prove how important his work was. Then he started walking over to her house in the middle of the day. She says she begged him to stop and shoved him away when he tried to get too friendly."

"You believe her?"

"She may understate what happened at the party. But she's probably telling the truth about trying to get rid of him later on. He had a weak heart, if you remember; she could hardly risk his dying in her house."

"Did he threaten her with exposure?"

"She claims not." He sipped the Jameson's with great caution.

"Presently she's terrified?"

"Almost incoherent. Obviously she should have shut up instead of spilling the beans to me."

"Indeed."

"I should have thought of the possibility that something like this was going on. So should Chief Stewart. But John

Turner was such a rigid character that an affair seemed most unlikely."

"He probably wanted little more than an admiring and attractive audience who would reward him with some affection. Besides one would be hard put to persuade a jury that she is the type of person who would be capable of slitting the throats of two people, merely to protect her reputation."

"I suppose so."

"It was, after all, the defense's task to seek other scenarios, as you have said."

"I know that . . . She is really a very sad person. Kind of a nympho, I guess."

"Or possibly someone who is trying to resist the aging process at all costs."

I thought for a moment. All I had done so far was to restore to the list of suspects names which had been crossed out earlier. Richard Martin, Fred Turner, April Kincaid—all now appeared to have motives which had not been perceived before. It was not clear that any of them had opportunity. Nor was it clear that any of them was capable of mounting the carefully orchestrated plot that I had begun to suspect.

"If I were you," I said, "I would call Chief Stewart and suggest that Ms. Kincaid might be suicidal and that he should keep an eye on that house."

"Do you think she will really try to kill herself?"

"More likely as an attempt to beg for help. Alas, sometimes such pleas are not well timed."

"I'll call him from my car."

I pointed at the phone. "Call him from here."

"Now?"

"Now . . . A wounded spirit is in grave danger."

I left the room and called Mike Casey on my private line. "Can any of your splendid associates find out whether that miracle converter Jack Turner was designing might have worked?"

Mike whistled. "That's a tough one, Blackie."

"I would wager that someone at Turner Electronics knows."

"I'll see what we can do."

"Give my best to your virtuous wife."

"She might reject the adjective, but I will."

Back in my office, I found Terry Scanlan looking thoughtful and discouraged.

"He seemed to understand what I was talking about."

"Excellent."

"Does she fit in the picture at all, Father?"

"Possibly . . . Tell me, what did your associates discover about the converter on which Jack Turner was working?"

"We turned it and his computer output over to the firm. It was theirs by right because he was working on it with their money. They told me that it didn't work, wouldn't work, couldn't work."

"You had others look at it?"

"Some state police technicians looked at the model. They couldn't make heads or tails out of it. Thought it was a sort of Rube Goldberg contraption."

"And the other materials in his safe?"

"They're still there as far as I know. In his will he left all his work materials—those in the workshop as well as those in a big archive room out at the plant—to the Turner Endowment. He wanted them to build a museum."

"No steps in this direction have been taken yet?"

"Everything is on hold because of Clare."

"So if I wanted to go up there and snoop around?"

"The house would be pretty much like it was the night of the killing. I could get you a set of keys."

"Excellent. I shall of course ask Clare's permission."

"You're going to see her?" His eyes lit up.

"Of course . . . Now what else . . . Oh, yes, I believe you told me, did you not, that the McLaughlins have found other employment?"

"In Florida. Clare kept them on salary until they could find another job. The Turners neglected to provide for them in their will."

"A pity . . . I think it might be useful for you to inquire from the Garda Sciochana, as the Irish for some reason call their cops, what employment the McLaughlins enjoyed before they went into domestic service."

"If you think it is important . . ."

"Arguably it is . . . Has the pressure to release her yet affected the state's attorney?"

"It's not that easy. We can't go into the First District Appellate Court and ask that bail be restored. Her lawyers have to do that. Then we can say that we have no objection, which at this time we certainly will. Even then, however, the court can still refuse."

"She should be moved elsewhere, perhaps to some federal detention facility, for her own protection. Cannot that be done administratively?"

"I've been pushing it. Dan Hills agrees. The Boss is hesitant."

"It is absolutely imperative that it be done as soon as possible."

"I'll see what I can do."

"Excellent." I rose. It was time for him to leave and me to go down to lunch.

Also my head was whirling. There was too much data, too many avenues to be explored, too many suspicions, too many possibilities, too many leads that had been ignored for too long. Moreover, while I had my own explanatory paradigm, nothing I had learned since my first talk with Terry

Scanlan fit that paradigm. I was still following the old assumption that John and Mary Turner were the victims of murder because someone stood to gain from their deaths. My new and very different assumption had yet to be tested.

"Do you have any ideas . . .?"

"A general model with a lot of missing details."

"When will you see Clare?"

"If all goes according to plan, tomorrow."

"I wish I was going with you."

"I'm sure she does too."

I stopped him at the door. "One more question, Terry G. Scanlan. You will recall the envelope with the Polaroid pictures?"

"The one labeled 'Paranormal Phenomena'? How could I forget it?"

"Did you or any of your associates have, ah, any encounters with such phenomena while you were working in the house?"

"With *ghosts*?"

"With psychic vibrations of any sort?"

"Not I surely. If anyone else did, they didn't mention it."

"You might make some discreet inquiries."

"If you say so." He shivered slightly. "That stuff scares me."

"Indeed. But the energy in the picture seems rather more benign than not."

Terry Scanlan departed the cathedral rectory quickly, escaping into the autumn thunderstorm on Wabash Avenue as perhaps a saner place.

Arguably a correct conclusion.

23

"**C**OCKTAILS AT FIVE," CARDINAL SEAN CRONIN INFORMED me. "Light supper at five-thirty. Business during cocktails, chitchat over supper. More brief business over the coffee. *Omnes exeunt* no later than seven-thirty. Got it, Blackwood?"

"Possibly."

"Not what the Ryan family thinks of as a great evening, is it?"

"The Ryans are not numbered among the super rich."

"Arguably." He favored me with his crooked grin. "I know, I know, merely comfortable professionals. Anyway, don't think of these folks as idle rich. They are very bright, very diligent, and very generous. They are not priest fans. They get no kicks from hanging around clergy. They are not head usher–types at all. They are barely impressed with cardinals and not likely to give undue respect to an auxiliary bishop."

"Even one with a Ph.D. and three important publications?"

"They come to the house up on North State to do their work which is important to the Church. They do it, are rewarded with a drink or two and a light supper, and are on their way."

"Indeed."

"I do my best to stay out of their way."

"Yes, I can imagine that."

In the same sense that a 747 stays out of the way when it's landing at O'Hare. Or a Mercedes 600 on the JFK Expressway.

"Let me run through the names."

"That would be useful."

"The chairman of the Catholic School Fund is Gene Renahan, he is a commodity investor . . ."

"Gambler."

". . . who takes long-term positions in oil and has made some five hundred million dollars, conservatively speaking, in that activity. He credits his success to the math he learned in Catholic schools. He founded this group and is one of the two members who chairs the investment committee. He is married, but only recently and has a small child whose gender escapes me. He is the son of a police officer and does not act like a rich man. Nor does he act like a genius. Take my word for it, Blackwood, he is both."

"Takes one to know one."

"The other investment man is Casimir Piowar, the president of the Ogden Park Bank. He is third-generation Polish wealth, studied at Harvard and Oxford, and is one of the most cultivated human beings I have ever met. About forty-five, but snow-white hair. No Polish jokes please. His wife and two children, both teenagers, died in an auto accident a couple of years ago. He hasn't quite recovered."

"Poor man."

"Equally tragic is Mrs. J. John Leyden. She is the daughter-in-law of Old Tim Leyden and the mother of Young Tim. She's around sixty-five I would say, dedicated Catholic, and as smart as they come. She lost a husband—air force colonel in Korea—and a son in Vietnam. Her daughter and son-in-law, he was a marine officer I believe, were killed in an airplane crash shortly thereafter, and then her father-in-law died. Her faith tends to miracles and special revelations and such like, but it keeps her going. She was the one who brought the late John Turner on board, and he in turn yielded his seat to your friend Clare Turner. Jack Turner and Old Tim were business associates."

"So I have been told."

"Finally, Marcantonio Rovere, the restaurant entrepreneur. About fifty. Six kids, all in Catholic schools. Lots of shrewd common sense. Definitely not connected. The Outfit tried to muscle in on him once and he warned them off fairly effectively. I didn't ask how."

"I wouldn't want to know how."

"Now what do you expect to learn from these people?"

"I'm fishing," I confessed. "Looking for hints and impressions about Clare Turner before I finally meet her myself, presumably on the morrow. She continues to be an enigma."

"You think so?"

"Look, on the assumption that she didn't kill her parents, an assumption which *causa argumenti* I am willing to accept, someone went to a fair amount of trouble to make it look like she did kill them. Was it merely to hide the identity of the killer or was there some special animus toward Clare Turner?"

"I'm not the mystery solver, but it seems to me that it would surely be the former. Who could possibly hate Clare?"

"If we knew the answer to that we might be far along toward a solution."

"You don't think any of my committee are killers, do you?" The Cardinal frowned dangerously.

"What would any of them have to gain?" I responded. "But they might disclose some aspect of Clare's personality that would give me a hint of where I ought to look next. Or perhaps something she said about her search for her natural parents."

"She didn't talk much about it."

"All the more reason why the few remarks she might have made would be important."

Before I set forth on the hike a mile up State Street to 1555 North State Parkway, I phoned Mike the Cop.

"Nothing yet on the converter," he said. "It sounds like a wild idea, if you ask me."

"Indeed . . . What do you know about one Marcantonio Rovere, probably born Della Rovere?"

"Owns classy restaurants."

"Connected?"

"Not in the ordinary sense of the word."

"Oh?"

"They tried to push him around once. Blew up his car. So he blew up the car of one of the boys. They decided that it was better to leave him alone. They hang around his restaurants sometimes. They'll tell you he's a man of respect."

"Aha . . . Now would you be able to ascertain for me how much in the way of oil company shares the Ogden Park Bank has in its portfolios?"

"That shouldn't be hard."

I was doing nothing more than extending my list of suspects, though in this case the suspects were so remote that my interest in them was probably absurd.

I did manage to find a pectoral cross and a ring (the latter given to me by Lisa Malone, the actress and singer)* and

*See *Happy are the Clean of Heart*

dressed in a proper jacket which more or less matched my trousers. It did not seem altogether proper to appear in such distinguished company clad in a Chicago Bear jacket.

Melissa stopped me at the door as I was about to venture forth.

"You don't need the umbrella, Bishop. The rain has stopped."

"Capital." I deposited the umbrella, which I could not recall having picked up, next to the switchboard.

"And there's a call for you. Mr. Scanlan."

"Yes, Terry."

"Bishop Blackie, you're scary."

"That's not an original thought."

"April Kincaid tried to kill herself this afternoon."

"Indeed!"

"OD of sleeping tablets. Chief Stewart rang the doorbell at just the right time. They pumped out her stomach at Lakewood Hospital. Her husband's with her. They both seem convinced that she needs help."

"Fascinating."

"The Chief tells me that she wept a lot over the death of the Turners."

"Ah?"

"It's incoherent, but apparently there were some odd things happening at the Turner house that day, about which she did not tell us."

"You will interview her again tomorrow?"

"I sure will . . . You still planning to see Clare?"

"God willing."

"I haven't told her about you."

"Don't."

I usually do not get lost walking up to the Cardinal's house—in which the current Cardinal wisely refuses to live. I need only find State Street—one block west of the cathedral rectory and the street on which the cathedral itself fronts—and walk north, away, that is, from the downtown skyscrapers.

There is then little chance of my ending up near the projects, which are alleged to be dangerous, though not, I think, for a harmless little priest.

I left at four-thirty, allowing myself a half hour for a twenty-minute walk.

I usually solve the puzzles with which I become involved long before I know that I've solved them. Lavoisier deposited his solution to the oxygen problem on which he was working with the French Academy two years before he was able to come up with the proof. Michael Polyani, the philosopher, calls this "personal knowledge," the kind of implicit, intuitive, insightful recognition of truth which precedes discursive reasoning.

One knows before one knows that one knows.

My experience is of seeing an image of a solution but not being able to recognize it fully.

As if I am waiting for an elevator and one stops at my floor. The door opens and I see what is inside. But before I can identify it and put a name to it, the door closes and the elevator goes up to the next floor.

That experience returned to me as I walked up North State Parkway, from Division Street north one of the most elegant streets in Chicago.

Somehow I had the beginning of a solution lurking in jigsaw pieces scattered around the subbasements of my mind. The facts and suspicions I had devoured in the last couple of days were racing around the disorderly garden of my imagination and trying to come together.

They didn't come together that afternoon. Tragedy would occur before I began to see how the pieces fit.

I did in fact arrive at 1555 North State on time. I found the

Cardinal's house with only a modicum of difficulty, in fact, I had only stumbled a block or two into Lincoln Park when I realized where I was and reversed my path to return to the mansion.

The vast Victorian monstrosity was built at the turn of the century by Archbishop William Feehan on ground owned by the Sisters of Mercy (the *West Side* Mercys because in those happy days there were two Mercy orders in Chicago), the provincial of which was his sister, one Sister Mary Something-or-the-Other. Hence the house, with twenty-six chimneys, was known in ages past as the House of William and Mary.

Despite repeated remodeling it reminds me of a huge funeral home, with many different parlors. Every time I go into a different room, I expect to see a casket and a corpse.

I found the committee assembling in the main parlor, and in the absence of the expected corpse, I joined them. Gene Renahan was pouring the drinks—soda water, tonic with a twist of lime, diet cola, Pelegrino, even Balleygowan Water. Mrs. Leyden was sipping some very dry white wine.

Heavy, heavy drinkers, you see.

I greeted the troops and folded into the scenery and pretended that I had no idea what they were talking about. I am the most inoffensive-seeming person you can imagine. You could pass me on a stairway and not even notice I was there—the little man who wasn't there again today. Or, to return to the elevator metaphor and change its referent, you could get on the elevator and not even notice I was already on it.

I have been compared on occasion to G. K. Chesterton's Father Brown, though only by those who have not read the stories. Some say I deliberately imitate that zealous if somewhat anonymous priest. (Was his sister a Freudian psychiatrist? Did he have a sister?) Others, most notably my womanly siblings, insist that I was born with the persona and developed the personality to fit.

In any event, it is easy for me to become part of the scenery; and sometimes very useful.

Thus I was able to determine that the three men and one woman who presided over the Catholic School Fund were intelligent, able, and creative. They had made superb investments for the fund, were sensitive to the needs of different schools and neighborhoods, and innocent of self-importance.

How I wonder did a quiet, twenty-four-year-old medical student fit into this group? Did she blend into the scenery as I did?

Could the lovely archduchess Terry Scanlan described to me fold herself into the environment?

Not very likely.

Promptly at five-thirty a recess was called and we adjourned to the dining room, presided over by pictures of several Popes, some of whom might even be construed as heterosexuals. We were served a shrimp salad and Evian water.

Sean Cronin wasn't losing much money on entertainment for this group.

Mrs. J. John (Teresa) Leyden engaged me in a conversation about the alleged apparitions of the Mother of Jesus at the Croatian town of Medjugorie.

"How many times have you been there, Bishop?"

"I haven't been able to get there yet," I admitted. "I'm afraid that my family is not much given to traveling. Anything farther than South Bend, Indiana, or Grand Rapids, Michigan, is an excessive strain on our organisms."

"Oh, you really must go there, Bishop. It's so wonderful. I'm sure Our Blessed Lady is speaking to the whole world there, calling us to repentance for our sins."

"Indeed."

"If we listen to her and give up all our bad habits, I'm sure she'll persuade her son to postpone the end of the world."

My own personal observation is that we have a long way to go before we approach what Father Teilhard called *le point Omega*. However, I kept this position to myself.

"I go there every year, sometimes twice a year. Those dear young people talk to the Blessed Mother every afternoon."

"So I am told."

"You see my rosary?" She pulled a very expensive set of ivory beads from her purse. "It was silver when I went there and gold when I returned. Isn't that miraculous?"

"Indeed."

Need I say that the links between the ivory beads were still certifiably silver?

Teresa Leyden, a handsome woman in her middle sixties, presided with intelligence and skill over an empire conservatively estimated at a value of four hundred and fifty million dollars. It was said that she was more talented as an administrator that her father-in-law, Old Tim Leyden, who died the week after his grandson Col. J. John Leyden, Jr., was shot down in a raid on Hanoi. Under her tutelage the Leyden interests had prospered. She was passing on to her second son, Young Tim Leyden, the second or third largest family enterprise in the city, inferior in size, it was said, only to the Crowns and the Pritzkers.

Moreover her comments about the investment portfolio of the Catholic School Fund were incisive and insightful.

Yet she could imagine that a slightly tarnished silver rosary had turned gold.

"My wife was there last summer." Marcantonio Rovere sniffed at the Cardinal's salad and smiled. "She found it deeply moving."

"You should go, Marco," Mrs. Leyden insisted. "It would do you good."

Marco, a sleekly good-looking man with razor-cut black hair and a large ring worthy of at least a cardinal on this right hand, threw up his hands expressively. "What can I tell you? My wife does the praying in our family . . . Nice salad, Bishop. I wouldn't hesitate to serve it in my best restaurant."

"I grew it in my own garden."

Four sets of eyes were riveted on me. "My own basil too."

"No basil in the salad!" Casey Piowar laughed. "I've heard about you, Bishop Blackie. You're a great leg puller."

"Pierrot," I said demurely.

"More likely Harlequin."

So he was as cultivated as my Lord Cronin had suggested.

"Sometimes," he continued, "even Il Professore Di Bologna."

"Arguably."

Casey was the most relaxed of the group and the one most likely to joke. It took a while to recognize the terrible sadness in his eyes.

"You've written a couple of philosophy books, haven't you, Father?" Gene Renahan, the oil speculator, was a large, rumpled, balding man with thick glasses. He looked more like a bartender or an unsuccessful funeral director than a fiscal genius. His eyes were also the giveaway—as determined and as invulnerable as one of my Mandelbrot sets on the computer screen.

"Unaccountably they have not made it to the best-seller list."

"I read the one on William James. First rate. I've always like him. James and Kant."

"You're in a very select company," I said. "I hope you didn't read a library copy."

General laughter.

I hoped they were finished with me and would turn to the appropriate subject—Clare Turner.

Gene Renahan was not one for wasting time. "Well, we have fifteen minutes before the coffee. Anyone have any ideas about how we can help Clare?"

"Surely she will get a new trial." Casey Piowar extended his hands, seeking agreement. "That first trial was a farce."

"Some friends of my friends," Marco Rovere said, "tell me that they were willing to settle for involuntary manslaughter, maybe probation. They don't have a case against her."

"Thank God, the Cardinal found her some good lawyers," Renahan added. "Rollins, Parks may be a prestigious firm but murder trials are not their strong point. Diana Lyons Clarke is among the very best."

"Do you understand what we're talking about, Bishop Ryan?" Teresa Leyden asked me.

"Vaguely," I said, endeavoring to look properly uninformed.

"There was a young woman named Clare Turner on our committee. In fact, she still is as far as I'm concerned. Her parents were murdered in their beds last winter. And she was accused of the murder. All of us are sure that she's innocent. She has been very badly treated in the county court system. Unfortunately she did not have enough experience to hire a criminal attorney so she was not well represented in her trial. The case is now on appeal."

"What was the sentence?" I asked.

"Death by lethal injection," Casey Piowar said solemnly. "Absolutely absurd."

"That will never happen," Marco Rovere assured us. "The Illinois Supreme Court never permits the death penalty to be carried out—with a single exception. But she's being held without bond in county jail pending an appeal in the First

District. You know what the jail is like for young women, Bishop—lesbian rape, unless you're very lucky."

"Indeed."

"Her family has been close to our family since just after the war—World War II that is." Teresa Leyden, smiling, acknowledged her age. "My father-in-law and her father were business partners. I was the one who brought her on this committee. I was very proud of her."

"Sweet little kid." Marco shook his head sadly. "Reminds me of my oldest. Quiet but very bright. Lots of depth there. Even mystery."

"She made real contributions to this group." Casey's eyes misted in remembrance of his lost children. "Remember her ideas about PR for the fund. We've followed them right down the line."

"I'm sure it will work out," I said, offering the usual clerical cliché for a difficult and problematic situation.

"One feels so powerless." Teresa Leyden touched her rosary, which was still on the table between the two of us. "I pray for her every night."

"Poor kid." Gene Renahan summed it up. "I guess we did all we could when we got her new lawyers. Too bad we didn't think of that before."

Another view of the mysterious Clare, compatible surely with that of her beloved. I had learned what I had expected to learn, nothing more.

It was time for Bishop Blackie to throw a bomb.

"I had the impression that her problem might have been tied up with her attempt to learn who her natural parents were."

We might have been in the cemetery which used to be in Lincoln Park just across the street for all the sounds that one might have heard in the dining room.

"I didn't know that came up," Marco said slowly.

"I must have heard it somewhere."

"Remember the night she asked the Cardinal about it last year?" Casey Piowar sighed. "I felt so sorry for her."

"It's becoming fashionable these days," Teresa shook her head, disapproving of the fashion, "for adopted children to pursue that question. I don't see what good it can do. Clare was a fine young woman as it was. It's what comes I suppose of spending too much time with a psychiatrist."

Especially a shanty Irish woman shrink from the South Side.

"They have a right to know," Gene Renahan, always the liberal, insisted. "But I agree about Clare. If my kid grows up to be anything like her, I'll be proud." He reached for his wallet to show me the picture. "Well, even prouder than I am."

"Lovely young woman," I agreed. "Clearly Irish."

"No way to get away from that."

The coffee arrived. Decaf, I hardly need add. Time for business.

"We must all pray for her." Teresa summed up and thus dismissed the problem of Clare Turner.

Casey Piowar cornered me as we were leaving 1555.

"You really think the natural parent business is involved in the murder, Bishop?"

"So I was given to understand."

"It was a poignant night here last year when she asked the Cardinal if he could help her. Teresa and I have lost kids. I guess both of us would have been glad to have her as one of ours. Now even more so with both her foster parents gone. I think the Cardinal took a fatherly interest in her too."

"Indeed."

Tell me about it.

"There's nothing we wouldn't do to help, but what can you do?"

"I don't know, alas."

"I'm going to talk to some friends of mine in politics, see what they can do. I'll see if Marco can do the same thing. Some of his friends—the words mean something a little different there as I'm sure you know—have clout too."

He had made the requisite jerk of the head toward Taylor Street.

"That might be helpful."

"You know what." He laughed as we walked into the soft autumn night. "I don't think you're Pierrot at all. Or Harlequin. Or Il Professore Di Bologna."

"Indeed?"

"You're Scaramouche and I don't mean Raphael Sabatini's Scaramouche either."

"Arguably."

"Yeah. Or you know Walter De la Mare's poem about Chesterton."

This man was entirely too literate.

" 'Knight of the Holy Ghost he goes his way, truth his motley, wisdom his loving jest'?"

"Yeah. He lived in an age of miracles and dared to believe in them."

"Wrong number." I laughed and beat a retreat down Wabash Avenue.

At the rectory I made arrangements for a funeral—an aged but beloved grandmother—and talked a young man out of suicide and into counseling. I also scheduled five baptisms and suggested that the parents might want to come to our instruction class for parents, though, permissive type that I am, I don't make attendance compulsory.

"Will Bishop Ryan be conducting the class?" one of them asked on the phone.

"Arguably."

"Is that you, Bishop?"

"I think so."

"Well, then of course we'll come. We like your jokes."

Knight of the Holy Ghost indeed.

In my study, a glass of Bailey's tucked into my hand, I dialed Mike the Cop for the last time that day.

"Ogden Park is up to its eyelids in oil."

"How fortunate for them . . . Two more questions, Mike. Do I understand correctly that the virtuous Teresa Leyden is an aristocrat?"

"Gives a pretty good show, doesn't she? And a nice lady too. Annie likes her. But no, she's the daughter of a butcher from a little town in the Upper Peninsula of Michigan. Met Johnny Leyden when she was a WAAC at the end of the war and he was a hotshot jet pilot. They say Old Tim really adored her from the first meeting. Saw that she could keep the empire together even if her husband was flying around in jets."

"He remained in the service?"

"No, he went back in Korea. Never came home. A lot of us did. Some of us didn't. Eldest son was also a flyer."

"Tragic . . . Now what can you tell me about Gene Renahan's love life before he married?"

"Did he have one?"

"Didn't he?"

"There were rumors of course. Anyone with all that money and no wife could presumably fool around if he wanted to. He certainly didn't live with anyone."

"You will pursue the matter."

"Find out what I can."

"What's your next move?"

"It is time and way past time that I interact with the seemingly ineffable Clare Turner."

24

"I DIDN'T ASK FOR A PRIEST. I DON'T WANT A PRIEST. I won't talk to a priest."

That last thing I would have expected: the legendary Clare Turner was an anticlerical.

"You don't like priests."

"That's right, I don't like priests. I wish they would leave me alone."

My first reaction to Clare Turner was similar to that of Terry Scanlan the morning after the murder. In prison dress, long dark red hair tied behind her head, and rimless glasses on high cheekbones obscuring her round face, she didn't look all that beautiful.

Then I realized that her beauty, like all else about her by reputation, was mysterious. There was not only a touch of the Slavic lands about her, but something even more ancient—Goth, Vandal, Hun, Scythian, perhaps even Mongol. An archduchess from the steppes, a princess of the Golden Horde.

"You only like cardinals."

That stopped her for a moment.

"He's a nice man. He comes to visit me not to pray over me so that I will speak with tongues."

"Charismatic priests?"

"Three of them have been here. And one from the Opus Dei. They all want me to do penance for my sins."

She spoke in the flat, unemotional monotone that Terry had described. Just the same she was angry. I didn't blame her.

"Clare Marie Turner, I'm Father Ryan. I am not a charismatic, I don't speak with tongues, I don't like the Opus Dei, and Sean Cronin sent me."

"Oh," she said softly and blushed. "I'm sorry, Father Ryan. Please sit down."

We were in a windowless room in county jail. There would not be much to see on the outside—the stone walls of the old jail, the red brick addition with two rolls of barbed wire tipped with razor blades on top of the fences around it, the gloomy County Addiction Center (formerly Contagions Disease Hospital), the barren parkway of California Boulevard—not exactly a place like Wormwood Scrubs, but still a depressing if efficient center of criminal justice Chicago style. Not exactly a place to confirm an optimistic image of the human condition.

We were seated on either side of a steel table. A TV camera watched us, though, since I was a priest, the sound had been turned off.

"You're really a bishop, aren't you?"

"By mistake."

"How do people become bishops by mistake?"

"Well, my Lord Cronin, your friend the Cardinal, for reasons of his own which I suspect have to do with access to my liquor cabinet, wanted me as an auxiliary bishop. He knows that Rome does not give American bishops the men they want in this role, but rather men whom they don't want and who make life more difficult for them.

"So our mutual friend sent in a list of three names of

which mine was not one. The people in charge said, 'Hey, thisa Cronin, hesa no list the funnya little priest at the cathedral, eh? Hesa probably had a fight with the sillya little man. So we makea him a bishop, no?'

"So they do. And I can't turna it down or I'll ruina the joke, no? It's quite a disgrace, my nieces and nephews are most embarrassed."

"Disgrace?"

"Because bishops are generally thought to have a very low level of intelligence. They think it reflects on the family."

My imitation of the thug who is our Papal Nuncio is, I assure you, both accurate and hilarious. It earned me a mild lip movement from Clare Turner. But I think her eyes twinkled.

"You're the one they call Blackie, aren't you?"

"Which is short for Blackwood, according to legend because my mother, God be good to her and She better, made a blackwood convention at bridge the night I was conceived."

"What do I call you?" Again there was a mild twitch of her lips. "Bishop Ryan, Bishop Blackie . . . ?"

"Most people revert to Father Blackie."

"I think that's neat." She folded her hands on her lap and looked for all the world like a novice in an old-style religious order for women.

So after considerable effort I was now a man approved.

"Why did the Cardinal send you, Father Blackie?"

"On certain occasions in the past I have been able to resolve some puzzles for him."

"You're his Sherlock Holmes? No." The ends of her lips turned up in the beginnings of a smile. "You're his Father Brown! Father Blackie is Father Brown! How wonderful!"

I think there may actually have been a bit of a laugh in her voice.

"I have a few questions to ask."

"Of course."

"Your wolfhound, the fabled Fiona, did she bark at all the night your parents died?"

She thought for a moment. "No, Father Blackie, she didn't. She sleeps on my bed when I let her, and she didn't make a sound till the phone rang."

"Ms. Kincaid?"

"That terrible sex-starved woman."

"Indeed . . . and then how did Fiona act?"

"She was very nervous because I was nervous. I didn't let her out of the room. She would have gone wild at the smell of blood."

"Did your foster parents know who your real parents were?"

The blank mask returned to her haunting face.

"I think so . . . They were very angry when I asked them a year ago, more angry than they had ever been. They said no good would come of it. I suppose they were right. Funny, I don't care much about that anymore."

"You told many people about your search?"

"No, not at all. Not even Jane Martin, who is my best friend. I told the Cardinal of course because I needed his help."

"Do you have any hints at all?"

"I think they may have been Slavic, don't you? I mean isn't my face kind of Eastern European?" She took off her glasses. "Round and high cheekbones. Maybe a little bit of Tartar even?"

"Not a West of Ireland face, I'll admit."

"But that's just guessing, Father. I don't really know anything."

"I see . . . Now tell me about the McLaughlins."

"Not much to tell. They were very good to my parents and

nice to me when I was around on weekends. I suspect they thought I was ungrateful and maybe I was."

"You trusted them?"

"I didn't distrust them. I mean, they weren't sneaky or anything like that."

"What do you remember of the time you lived with your natural parents?"

She closed her eyes, concentrating on the past. "I've asked myself that many times. Many, many times." She shook her head disconsolately. "All I remember is sunlight and blue sky and a lot of warmth and laughter. But I'm not sure any of that is accurate. Maybe I'm simply trying to recreate something that never really was."

"How long have you known you were adopted by the Turners?"

"As long as I can remember. They never pretended to be my natural parents."

"What were they like?"

She opened her eyes. There were tears in them. "They did their best with me, Father. They were older and set in their ways; and I was a stubborn little girl. From the very beginning. I don't think they ever knew what to make of me. But we got along, more or less. Better than a lot of people do. They were certainly good to me; and supportive in their way. They didn't want me to go to med school, but toward the end I think they were proud that I had done so well."

"Who do you think killed your parents?"

"I didn't, Father Blackie."

"I know that."

"Do you really?"

"Yes, I do really."

"You don't think, like my lawyers, that they don't have a good case against me?"

"I do think they don't have a good case against you *and* I think you didn't kill them."

"I'm so glad to hear that, Father. Most people don't believe me. The Cardinal believes and a certain boy, ah, young man . . . Did he send you too, Father? I mean he and the Cardinal?"

"Arguably."

Then she smiled, actually smiled. It wasn't one of your total earthshaking smiles, but it was not bad, at all, at all, as the Irish would say.

One might walk across several miles of desert to see that smile.

"He *is* a nice boy, isn't he, Father Blackie?"

"Arguably."

"I mean, I'm not fooling myself about him, am I? He's *really* nice, isn't he?"

"Yes, Clare Marie Turner, he is *really* nice. You've been very fortunate and that's what you'll remember in years to come."

"I'm so happy whenever I think of him." She sighed. "Just thinking about him keeps me going in this terrible place."

"Did you ever have any sense of, ah, psychic manifestations at your home in Lakewood?"

"You mean those ghost things that Daddy took pictures of?"

"You have seen the pictures?"

"Daddy was into the paranormal. He thought it was a mechanics phenomenon that we did not understand."

"And you did not credit those manifestations?"

She shrugged her admirable shoulders. "I thought they were kind of weird, but I didn't feel that the house was haunted . . . Do you think it is?"

"Not exactly. But with your permission I'd like to poke around inside it."

"*My* permission?"

"It's your house now."

"I guess it is. I don't think I could ever stay in it overnight again. But, sure, Father Blackie, poke around in it as much as you want."

"Excellent." I rose to leave. As charming as she was once she had discovered that I was not about to pray over her, there was work to be done.

"May I have your blessing, Father?" She knelt on the floor.

"A noncharistmatic blessing?"

"Definitely."

"May almighty God bless you, Clare, and set you free to begin the rest of your life, Father, Son, and Holy Spirit."

"Am I really going to get out of here?"

"Yes, Clare Marie Turner," I helped her off the floor, "you are going to get out of here, and in the words of Blessed Juliana of Norwich, all manner of things will be well."

As time would demonstrate that was a presumptuous and premature prediction. Seldom have I been so wrong.

I left the jail, as forboding and unhappy a place as exists in Chicago—a giant walled block of evil and suffering—and drove down California Avenue to the Congress, still touched by Clare Turner's young love, which brought however briefly spring sunlight to the dank ugliness of her environment.

Several times in that drive I caught a glimpse of the solution, but each time I missed it, though just barely.

In fact I had then all the elements of a solution. Certain pieces needed to be fit into the puzzle to confirm that solution, but they were details. Alas for all concerned, save the killers, it would require more time before I grasped even the outline.

Terry Scanlan was waiting for me in my first-floor office. I invited him upstairs to my rooms.

"Did you see her, Father Blackie?" he blurted as we climbed the stairs—as a matter of unshakable principle I do not use the elevator which yet another one of my predecessors of glorious memory had installed.

"Indeed."

"How was she? What did you think of her? Isn't she wonderful? Can we get her out soon?"

"As to the first, she seems to be resolute, as to the second, she is impressive, as to the third, who am I to dispute your judgment on that matter, and as to the fourth, the sooner the better."

"The defense has entered its motion to restore bail. We have responded with what is essentially an agreement. First District is taking it under advisement. I have the impression they're going to hand down a ruling on her appeal in the next couple of days, which could moot the motion. We may have to wait till then."

"You assume she will win the appeal?"

"I don't see how they can avoid overturning the trial verdict. B. Michael made a farce out of the trial."

"Yet the illustrious Judge Block . . ." It was after lunch, so it was all right for me to remove the precious bottle of Black Bush and pour us both a few drops.

"Thanks, Father . . . Even he couldn't vote against reversal."

"To freedom for Clare Turner." I toasted him.

"Amen to that." He inclined his Waterford tumbler in my direction. "Isn't she wonderful, Father?"

It was a question he had asked before, and it deserved a more detailed response than I had given him.

"She is a remarkable young woman, Terry, possessed of great resiliency and resourcefulness. Your taste is to be commended, however late it may have asserted itself over other instincts."

"I knew you'd like her." He grinned happily.

"You will have to deal with her directly and candidly for the rest of your life. The indirection which we Irish, including the Italo-Irish, love so much will not be functional in that quarter."

"I suppose I can learn that."

Like all loves theirs would have its ups and downs in the years ahead. Its flames, however much they might dim on occasion, would never go out. Two fortunate young people. But first we must remove his mysterious archduchess from Cook County Jail.

"I have some more information for you." He put aside his empty tumbler. "In my excitement about Clare I forgot it. The case is really breaking open. We have to go in for a new trial even if the First District does turn us down."

"Indeed!"

"April Kincaid broke down completely this morning. Poor woman. I guess I don't know much about them, Father. First Clare, then April."

"Ah?"

"Her husband is kind of pompous, but he does love her and he stands by her no matter what. She's getting psychiatric help, lots of it, and they both agree it's a long-term need."

"She credits you with saving her life?"

"Yeah. I figured it would be too complicated to bring you into the picture."

"Indeed yes."

"She admits now that she went to the Turner house in the early afternoon."

"Indeed!"

"She wanted assurance from Jack Turner that he would not tell her husband about her escapades. She used the protest at the railroad station the next morning as an excuse. She said that she wanted to talk to Mary Turner about the demonstration."

"Fascinating."

"The front door of the house was open and the McLaughlins were not around. Just as she was going in, Dick Martin emerged with a large package of computer printout."

"So!"

"She walked into the house and back to the workshop."

"Going up the stairs to the bedroom floor?"

Terry hesitated. "I presume so. There's no other way, unless she went down to the garage."

"No other way of which we know."

"That's right. Mary Turner, according to April, had gone to the store with Moire McLaughlin. Dermot McLaughlin had driven them to the Lakewood Springs shopping plaza."

"That's hardly compatible with the story we have heard of the Turners' total dedication to their project."

"Maybe poor Mary wanted a chance to breathe some fresh air. Anyway, April went into the workshop and begged John not to tell her husband. He was busy at his computer and hardly spoke to her. But, if only to get rid of her, he promised that he would not carry out the threats he had made."

"No sexual games?"

"She denies that there were, and I suspect that the CRT was more compelling for Jack Turner than any woman."

"Arguably."

"On her way out, whom does she encounter driving up in a Budget rental car?"

"Fred Turner?"

"Precisely."

"A lot of traffic into the Turner house that day, wasn't there?"

"Let's see," Terry ticked them off on his fingers, "Dick Martin, April Kincaid, Fred Turner, Clare . . . and the McLaughlins and Mary Turner driving to the plaza and returning."

"And the plumbers. Were you ever able to track them down?"

"They were not from Lakewood. The McLaughlins had never seen them before."

"And the Garda reported to you that those latter worthies were not always in domestic service?"

"I don't know how you figure all these things out, Father Blackie. No, they were unsuccessful actors. There was no secret about that, however. It turns out that they were involved in some amateur theater up in Lake Bluff."

"Indeed."

"You've noticed that the workshop seems to have been open at least for a time that afternoon."

"But one still has the problem, does one not, of the fact that at least Mary Turner was alive at seven-thirty—unless the penitent April has changed her story on that."

"No, she hasn't. And her husband told me that he was in the room when she talked to Mary Turner on the phone."

"Fascinating."

"Indeed."

"You will ask your friend on the Tucson police force to speak with Fred Turner, hinting that there might be a request for extradition?"

"I sure will."

"I may have a word with Dick Martin." I sighed. Once again we had too many suspects. "You will check with the McLaughlins about the shopping expedition of which as I recall they made no mention. Also find out whether the door to the workshop was routinely left open."

"Can do."

"I have the amiable archduchess's permission to poke around her house. I think I'll devote tomorrow morning to that effort."

"Good." He bounced out of his chair. "At last we're making some progress."

"Possibly."

When he left, I called Mike Casey.

"I've got some information about the Turner converter for you, Blackie."

"Indeed!"

"It's ambiguous. The research people at Turner Electronics think that by and large it's crazy. It could reduce gasoline consumption marginally but wouldn't save enough money over the life of a car to justify the cost of manufacture and installation."

"Ah."

"However, one or two of the brightest of their people think the old man may have been on to something. They're trying to figure out what it was, so they can continue his project."

"In deepest secret?"

"You can understand that. They're trying to keep the oil companies at bay."

"If they can develop the project further, the worth of the firm increases dramatically, does it not?"

"It sure does, either as a target for big oil or as the source of an automotive revolution. Lots of money."

"Much of which will accrue to the Catholic Bishop of Chicago, a Corporation Sole."

"You said that, I didn't."

"Nonetheless I must report this possibility to the Lord Cardinal."

I secured two dishes of chocolate chocolate chip ice cream, doused them in raspberry sauce, and bore them to the Cardinal's room.

"Still doing the work of the devil, I see." He removed his glasses and shoved aside the pile of papers he had been signing.

"I've come to offer a progress report."

"Get her out of jail," he said.

"We progress."

I told him, in digested format, what we knew.

"Sounds like the brother to me."

"Arguably."

"And I don't believe this stuff about the magic converter."

"But we will accept such income as might accrue to us?"

"Is the Pope Polish? . . . What do you do next?"

"Visit the Turner house."

"And commune with the spirits? . . . You know I don't like that stuff, Blackwood. I don't want it in my Archdiocese."

"So I understand."

"Be careful. It's a seller's market for auxiliary bishops."

25

"**Y**OU DID NOT TELL ANYONE THAT YOU HAD VISITED THE Turner house the day of the murder," I said bluntly to Dick Martin.

"I didn't deny it either," he said blandly. "No one asked."

"You removed several reams of computer output."

"That crazy woman next door who was always hanging around their house saw me. I figured she would tell the police and they'd come talk to me. I guess she didn't say anything till now."

"So you remained silent?"

We were sitting in his rather small and obsessively neat office at Turner Electronics—on either side of which there were two massive windows, one looking out on the clean and quiet assembly lines of the factory, the other on the grim autumn skies. In front of his beige computer work station, in rolled-up shirtsleeves and suspenders with the plastic pen protector in his shirt pocket, Dick Martin looked like a middle-aged nerd as corporate president.

Which is exactly what he was.

"Sure. Why get involved in a murder investigation if you don't have to? Anyway I had nothing to tell them. If I did have something to contribute to the investigation, I would have come forward, especially to help Clare."

"Why did you visit Jack Turner that early Saturday afternoon?"

"He called me the day before and asked me to pick up some of the specifications he had developed for the converter. Periodically he'd feed his results to our R and D department for their reactions."

"I thought he was very secretive."

"Up to a point he was. But he liked the R and D kids and valued their reactions—which were usually pretty honest."

"Could not he have sent the materials over with his chauffeur?"

"Not Jack Turner. Trust no one but the most trusted employees . . . I had dropped my son Brian off for a hockey game at the Lakewood Rink, so I had time to stop by and pick up his output."

"You spoke with him at some length?"

"Hardly a word. He was deeply involved in his work. That's the way he was sometimes."

"The door was open to the workshop, was it not?"

"That didn't surprise me. He said Mary had gone shopping. He'd leave the door open when she left so he wouldn't have to be distracted when she came back in."

"Despite all his precautions, he was lax in security measures?"

"Who's consistent?" Dick Martin threw up his hands. "Anyway, an outsider would have a hell of a time making sense out of what he was doing. We knew, more or less, but even our brightest young R and D people were usually mystified. To be candid I had begun to think he was round the bend."

If my questions were bothering Dick Martin, he did not show his concern.

"Not so far round the bend that you didn't remove all his notes and models after the funeral."

"You'd better believe it. Chances were that he was going nowhere with his new converter. But what if he was on to something? Can you imagine the revolution it would have caused? No way we'd take the risk of losing that."

"And you've discovered?"

He threw up his hands. "It's ambiguous. The model in its present form looks to be worthless, or more precisely it would improve gasoline mileage only marginally. But one of our kids thinks the old man was on to something. It's hard to know what he was up to because his style of work wasn't like anyone else's. All the machinery was just a tool for his intuition."

Martin's story was not substantially different from the report I had heard from Mike the Cop. However, he might be attempting to overwhelm me with truth.

"I should think the oil companies would offer notable inducements to terminate this project."

"You'd better believe it. If we sold out, I'd be a rich man, I mean really rich, without ever doing a day's work for the rest of my life."

"You've resisted the temptation?"

"Hell," he threw up his hands again, "what's money? Anyway, if this thing should actually work, it will be a gold mine."

"Not necessarily for management. After all, you own no stock."

He shrugged. "I'd probably get a big raise and a nice benefits package. I don't need anything more. Besides I don't like oil companies."

"The Leydens would want to sell?"

"Probably. Unlike Old Tim, the present crowd goes for the immediate buck rather than for the long term. But they don't own the company; Jack did and now the Endowment does."

"And the Endowment is Clare?"

"And the Archdiocese."

"Which in its present manifestation doesn't much like Big Oil either."

"So I hear." He smiled benignly. "Just the same I want that poor kid out of jail and sitting at the board meetings. It'll bring a lot of stability back to this place."

"Did Jack Turner say anything about his brother?"

"Fred? That jerk. No, he didn't mention him. Why?"

"One hears that Fred visited him later in the afternoon."

"To borrow money, I suppose. Usually in six figures. Jack would always refuse and then the next day send him a check. Like I told you he had a soft heart. Loved to be generous. He was mightily upset when Clare wanted to pay her own medical school tuition."

"It all would come from the same pocket, would it not?"

"Not the way he saw it. Her allowance was hers. The medical school check came from his account."

"Would you see Fred Turner as a murder suspect?"

"I'd like to say that he might have killed Jack because that might help Clare. But, seriously, I don't think he'd have the balls for that sort of thing. Fred is a loser, a weakling, a phony, maybe even a cheat. But a killer? I doubt it."

"Indeed."

"I suppose he lied about seeing Jack the day of the murders."

"It would seem so."

"Does that help Clare?"

"Not necessarily with the First District Appellate Court, whose ruling is expected almost immediately. But it could give the defense the opportunity to ask for a new trial independently of the Appellate decision, especially if the state's attorney should agree."

"Is there enough evidence to ask for a new trial?"

"It would appear so."

"I really want her out of jail, Father. She's a good kid. Everyone in our family is fond of her. But this damn company needs her too."

Many people wanted and needed Clare Turner free and alive. But, I was now convinced more than ever, someone with great resourcefulness and ingenuity wanted her out of the way.

Alas as I drove up the Edens to Lakewood, I did not draw the proper conclusion from that premise.

My next stop was the house on Sylvan Lane.

The thick curtains of rain which were sweeping in from the lake made it a perfect day for visiting a haunted house.

Arguably haunted.

There were, however, no vibrations when I opened the door and entered.

The house was as Terry had described it. Elegant and tasteful in an automatic and mechanical way, but too large in its whole and its component parts to seem either warm or comfortable.

A layer of dust had settled on the interior. Clare would either have to sell everything or have someone come in and put covers on all the furniture.

She had other things on her mind just now, however.

I inspected the kitchen and the garage, in which the relatively new Lincoln town car and the battered old Porsche also displayed a layer of dust.

How like a young person—you drive a car whose name says that you're rich, but choose a version which is a couple of decades old and which needs constant service.

The door to the apartment once used by the McLaughlins

was locked. It had probably been thoroughly cleaned out before they left for Florida.

I turned back to Clare's Porsche. What a clumsy plant to put the book bag in the front seat. The plotter was ingenious and resourceful, but the agents were clumsy. Not full professionals.

I saw an avenue for exploring the implications of that insight.

I wandered back into the house and up to the second floor. Still no vibrations.

I paused at Clare's room. Terry had accurately described it—she had left no impression of character or personality on her physical environment. Hiding and protecting herself even here. I pondered what kind of environment a liberated archduchess might create for herself.

I looked through the drawers of the desk on which her Apple Macintosh had been gathering dust. After all, she had given me permission to poke around, had she not?

I found a folder on which a neat label had been printed: "Natural Parents."

Inside there were a few articles clipped from the feature sections of newspapers about the pros and cons of searching for natural parents—arguments carefully emphasized with transparent yellow markers.

She had also printed out a neat list of archdioceses and dioceses in the West.

Nothing more. Clare Turner was apparently not the journal-keeping type. Not yet anyway.

I replaced the folder in her desk and turned to leave the room.

At that moment the vibrations assailed me with almost overwhelming intensity. They wanted me to do something or more likely find something. They drew me around the corner and down the stairs to the entrance of the workroom.

The lock had been removed from the door, leaving two large holes—one where the lock had been and the other where Dermot McLaughlin had cut the hole to gain entrance the night of the murder.

How convenient.

I pushed the door open. The workshop, drapes drawn at all the windows, was dark and chill. I found a light switch on the wall by the door and flicked it. Powerful floodlights on the glass ceiling illumined the whole place with TV studio intensity.

I blinked more than I usually do.

The computer banks were still intact. I know enough about such wonders to know that there was a small fortune in equipment in the room. Someone ought to take care of the machines. But Clare Turner had other problems.

The vibrations insisted that I approach the open safe.

"All right, all right," I said. "I was going there anyway."

Did I think that there were actual beings in the workshop with me? Was the uncanny experience an actual contact with the dead?

Perhaps. I don't know. But I rather doubt it. More likely I was encountering memories for which my own interest was acting as a receptor.

Anyway I went into the large standing safe, just as the vibrations insisted that I should.

It was lined with shelves, some of which contained carefully constructed models of what I took to be parts of automobile engines. But most of the shelves were piled with computer output—graphs, charts, and unintelligible (to me) numbers.

The vibrations, impatient with my slow and methodical poking, insisted that I go to the very back of the safe and inspect the top shelf.

Alas, they reckoned without what we may call my modest

stature. I had to leave the safe and find a chair to stand on. The vibrations became angry and demanded that I return.

Angry, but not hostile, much less malign.

"Already, all right," I insisted.

I placed the chair at the rear of the safe, noting that it was none too stable, and climbed up on it. Even with such an addition to my stature I could barely see the top shelf.

The vibrations insisted that I move my hand to the back of the shelf. There I encountered a cardboard box which I coaxed forward.

It tipped off the edge of the shelf and tumbled toward the floor. With my usual quick responses, I grabbed for it; and with my usual athletic skills I tumbled to the floor after it.

I was not—and I wish to insist on this point—knocked totally unconscious. I was merely dazed.

The vibrations gave me little sympathy. They continued to insist that I explore the contents of the shoe box which I had crushed beneath me.

Though I ached in a number of places, I seemed to be able to move everything. I untangled my legs from the chair and with some difficulty stood up. I righted the chair, eased my battered body into it, gathered the few papers which had fallen to the floor, put them in the shoe box, and placed the box on my lap.

An old-fashioned shoe box in the midst of all the modern technology! How appropriate.

It contained what one might have expected—baptismal certificates for John Turner and Mary Clausen, an old photostat (white on black) of a wedding license, report cards on the performance of Clare Turner—always exemplary— some honor certificates for the same young woman.

A picture of a pretty girl child of perhaps two years, grinning at the camera. On either side of her were a set of legs, one in trousers, the other in women's stockings.

Yes, yes, keep going, the vibrations demanded.

Then I found what it and I were looking for: a faded letter dated in March of 1968 from a Father Rory O'Kelley at St. Eustace's Church in Camarillo, California. It was written in a large, elaborate, and obscure scrawl.

Dear Mr. and Mrs. Turner,

I'm very grateful for your generous contribution to our building fund and even more for your generosity in taking into the bosom of your family the poor little orphan tyke. She is so pretty and so bright that I'm sure she'll bring you as much happiness as you bring her.

Cordially yours in Our Lord,

I held up the letter in triumph. Now I had a parish and the name of a priest.

There were no more vibrations.

As soon as I turned over the ignition key in my car, the phone rang, a phone which my siblings had insisted on installing—despite my protest that it was inappropriate for a Bel Air from the 1950s. I used it rarely because I could never ascertain how it worked, much less actually work it while the car was in motion.

No one had actually called me on the line before.

Tentatively I lifted the phone.

"Father Ryan."

"I've been trying to get you for an hour, Bishop."

"Yes, Melissa?"

"Mr. Scanlan called. He said to tell you that Clare is in Presbyterian–St. Luke Hospital. She's been stabbed. They think she's dying."

26

An anxious threesome awaited me outside the ICU at Rush-Presbyterian–St. Luke's Hospital, to give it the proper ecumenical name (no name so Catholic as Little Company of Mary would have fit): Terry Scanlan, a blond young woman who I assumed was Peg Burke, and a handsome matron with gold-and-silver hair who, unless I was quite mistaken, was my sibling the illustrious Dr. Mary Kathleen Ryan Murphy.

"Bishop Ryan," Terry said, his face drawn and parchment pale, "this is Dr. Murphy and my associate Peggy Burke."

"Hi, Punk." Mary Kate bussed me on the cheek. "I figured you'd be messed up in this."

"You know each other?" Peg Burke seem surprised.

"What happened?" I demanded.

"She was attacked by a group of four women during a recreation period. It was well organized. It looked like a conspiracy."

"Of course it was a conspiracy," I said impatiently.

"She gave a good account of herself . . ."

"Broke the arms on two of them," Peg said with sisterly pride.

269

"But one of them managed to jab a razor-sharp piece of coat-hanger wire into her side."

"It 'nicked' a blood vessel," Mary Kate continued, "to use the term the surgeons here favor. Another tiny fraction of an inch and she would have bled to death on the spot. As it is she lost a lot of blood. It took the authorities at the jail an unconscionable amount of time to call for the helicopter from here."

"Indeed."

"They didn't have time to open her up." Terry seemed stunned and disoriented. "They're using one of those balloon procedures, what do they call it, Dr. Murphy?"

"Laser catheterization."

"They hope to cauterize the wound as they say, at least to stop the bleeding so they can build up her strength and her blood supply in case they have to operate again."

"Prognosis?"

"Guarded at best." My sibling shrugged. "The surgeon is first rate. You bring your oils? I don't think she's been anointed yet."

To my surprise I had remembered. I flipped my small stole around my neck. It slipped to the floor. Mary Kate replaced it carefully so that it would not fall again.

Ritual in one hand and my oil stock in the other, I entered the ICU as I usually enter any place, so unobtrusively that the doctors and nurses and technicians didn't know I was there.

Yet when I started to pray, oddly enough, they responded, a young black woman more loudly by a factor of two than all the rest.

So too did my three companions, who had straggled in after me.

I stood next to the bed. Clare Turner, her dark red hair arrayed loosely on her hospital gown, looked frail and vulnerable—and incredibly lovely.

"Father, you raised your son's cross as the sign of victory and life. May all who share in his suffering find in these sacraments a source of fresh courage and healing. We ask this through Jesus the Lord."

"Amen."

"God of compassion, you take every family under your care and know our physical and spiritual needs. Transform our weakness by the strength of your grace and confirm us in your covenant so that we may grow in faith and love. We ask this in the name of Jesus the Lord."

"Amen."

"Let us pray to God for our sister Clare and for all those who devote themselves to caring for her.

"Bless Clare and fill her with new hope and strength, Lord have mercy."

"Lord have mercy."

"Relieve her pain, Lord have mercy."

"Lord have mercy."

"Sustain all the sick with your power, Lord have mercy."

"Lord have mercy."

"Assist all who care for the sick, Lord have mercy."

"Lord have mercy."

"Give life to Clare, on whom we lay our hands in your name, Lord have mercy."

I traced the sign of the cross in the oil of the sick on her chill forehead.

"Through this holy anointing may the Lord in his love and mercy help you with the grace of the Holy Spirit."

"Amen."

And then on her pale hands.

"May the Lord who frees you from sin save you and raise you up."

Her hands moved in response to my touch; her fingers closed briefly on mine.

"Amen."

"Let us pray. Father in heaven through this holy anointing, grant our sister Clare comfort in her suffering. When she is afraid, give her courage; when afflicted, give her patience; when dejected, give her hope; and when alone, assure her of the support of your holy people. We ask this through Christ our Lord."

"Amen."

Behind me now there was audible weeping.

"Lord Jesus Christ, our Redeemer, by the grace of your Holy Spirit, cure the weakness of your servant Clare. Heal her sickness and forgive her sins, mercifully restore her to full health and enable her to resume her former duties in the service of others who are ill. We ask this in your name."

"Amen."

We withdrew so as not to be in the way of the ICU personnel.

"I know," my sibling sniffled, "that she's too heavily sedated to realize what's happening. But she did just the same."

"Indeed."

We waited.

"Maybe we should say some prayers, Punk."

I reached in my pocket for the rosary which is there some of the time. Mary Kate pressed one into my hands. Then, oblivious to the steady procession of doctors, nurses, aides, orderlies, and visitors, we knelt on the floor outside the ICU and began the rosary.

Halfway through the second decade, I stopped.

"There are no cops in evidence!"

"No." Terry glanced up in surprise. "I don't think anyone is worried about her escaping."

"I didn't mean that! They have struck and they will strike again! Peggy, call whoever is appropriate and get us a twenty-four-hour guard! Immediately! Terry, get out your prosecutor's warrant and check everyone who goes into that unit!" I struggled to my feet. "I have a phone call to make."

Mary Kate thoughtfully pressed a quarter into my hand.

I rushed down the corridor to a public phone.

"Annie, let me talk to Mike. It's an emergency!"

"We just heard it on the radio," she said.

"I've got people on the way over," Mike said as he picked up the line. "And I'm leaving myself. See you soon."

Oh, the Ryans were swarming all right.

Peg and I arrived at the entrance to the ICU together.

"There's some officers coming over right away . . . and, Ter, I have some bad news. First District rejected the appeal and directed that no bail be granted."

"Damn!" His shoulders slumped. "We keep losing."

"Her defense is seeking immediate relief from the Illinois Supreme Court. They'll certainly order a new trial."

"Terry, Peggy," I said, "listen to me and listen to me carefully. This young woman's life is in grave danger and will be in grave danger for some time." I almost saw the picture, the image in the elevator. Then the door slammed shut. "Under no circumstances until we finally prevail is she ever to be left unguarded. And under absolutely no circumstance is she to be remanded to Cook County Jail. If she is to be held at all it must be at a safe place like the county jails in Will or Kane or Lake County, is that clear?"

They both nodded solemnly.

"If the State of Illinois is unable to protect her, then I assure you that the Roman Catholic Archdiocese of Chicago is prepared to give her sanctuary—and indeed to spirit her away from state authorities if that be necessary. Do I make myself clear?"

They gulped but nodded again.

Did I mean what I was saying?

Oh, yes, I meant it all right.

"Giving orders, Punk?"

"Ah, the prize-winning columnist arrives. That is all on the record, Red."

Red Kane hugged his sister-in-law and shook hands with me. Mary Kate introduced him to Peg and Terry without informing them of the relationship.

Just then a young doctor with curly blond hair and dark blue eyes came to the door of the ICU and motioned us inside.

"Dr. Murphy," he extended his hand, "Kevin Phelan. It's a pleasure to meet you."

He sounded as if he meant it.

"My brother Bishop Ryan, my brother-in-law, Mr. Kane. Ms. Burke, Mr. Scanlan from the State's Attorney . . . How is she doing?"

He extended his hands out, palms down, and smiled. "Ms. Turner is doing pretty well. Vital signs are strong. She's accepting blood transfusions nicely. Our seal seems to be holding. Still critical, but if something doesn't go wrong in the next twenty-four hours, we probably won't have to operate again. Keep your fingers crossed—and pray."

"And if something does go wrong?"

"Then we'll operate immediately. I'm confident that we can save her. It's a blessing that the guards at the jail remembered to leave the weapon in her. If they had pulled it out, there's no telling how much blood she would have lost."

"Doctor," I said, sounding like the crisp, confident leader whose role I was then playing, "this attack is part of a monstrous conspiracy which we will defeat. However, until then Ms. Turner will require twenty-four-hour protection from both police and from a private agency we are providing. I trust you will inform the proper authorities in this institution."

"Of course, Bishop." The young man was very solemn. I mean how else do you react if you're an Irish Catholic and a bishop begins to give orders?

The job has its advantages.

"She didn't look like a killer to me," he added. "I'm glad to hear she's not."

"Indeed," I agreed.

"Is she under your care, Dr. Murphy?"

"Mary Kate . . . Yes she is."

"Then I presume you will want to visit her while she's recuperating."

"I will indeed."

"Good. I will make the proper arrangements. It'll be forty-eight hours."

"Fine job, Kevin," I heard her say, a crack in her voice. "Fine job."

"Thank you, Mary Kate. Our work is easy compared to yours."

When we returned to the corridor, Mike Casey was talking to two uniformed patrol officers, a man and a woman. Two of his own well-dressed and efficient "associates"— also of both genders—were with him. They were all addressing him respectfully as "Commissioner."

It can safely be assumed that when he is present, all police officers, no matter what rank, take their orders from him.

"We want at least one person outside, and one in the room with her," he was saying. "Can that be arranged, Nurse?" He turned to a competent-looking woman who was clearly the head nurse.

"If you say so, Commissioner."

"Are you all related?" Peg Burke's big blue eyes were bigger than ever.

"Kind of." Mary Kate pointed at me. "He's my kid brother, he's my sister's husband, and he's our cousin."

"Wow!"

"When we tend to swarm, we swarm," I added. "The virtuous doctor is of course the matriarch."

"Judge Kane's husband?" Peg asked Red with reverence.

"The green-eyed one, you mean? As of this morning anyway, yes . . . By the way, the First District's appeal, who wrote it?"

"Burns with Block concurring."

"Myra Dawson dissenting?"

"Right."

Red grinned. "Figures."

I knew without reading it that Red's column on the morrow would sing the praises of Dr. Kevin Phelan and flay the State's Attorney's Office for permitting this tragedy to happen. He also would continue his long-standing vendetta against Judge Burns, of whom he had once written that he never saw an injustice that he didn't like.

Suddenly I felt very tired. It had been a taxing day, I still ached from my lamentable fall in the Turner safe, and I had absorbed enough data for several days. It was time to return to the rectory, make sure that my young associates had not burned it down, and soothe my nerves with a tiny sip of Black Bush. Perhaps in a more relaxed state, the elevator door would open long enough for me to see what was happening inside.

Clare Turner was well protected for the moment, the enemy was at bay, and if all manner of things were not yet well, at least nothing disastrous was likely to happen that night.

I could not have been more wrong.

27

THE RAIN HAD FINALLY CLEARED AWAY, THOUGH ITS SMELL still hung on the air, heavy and enticing. Rush hour traffic had cleared away when I entered the Congress Expressway at Ashland.

I could not quite understand why the other side had moved so quickly. They surely knew what the ruling of the First District would be, so there could have been no fear that Clare Turner would be released from county jail. Perhaps they feared that she would indeed be transferred to the William Campbell Metropolitan Correctional Center—a modernistic concrete fortress at the south end of the Loop—or to a jail in another county where it would be more difficult to stage an accident. Eventually an accident of this sort would have to occur, because they could have no reasonable hope that the Illinois Supreme Court would not toss the case back to the Cook County Circuit like a catcher throwing the ball back to a pitcher after a third strike.

Ideally, Clare Turner should have died in an accident at the Dwight Prison for Women, some time after the case had vanished from the media. But with the possibility of a new trial, she might get off scot-free. They must have cursed the stupidity of Boyle Michael O'Malley. Yet to strike at the same time as an appellate ruling they knew was theirs was curious. They could not have expected the Supreme Court to act the next day.

Puzzling over this oddity, I turned from the Congress to the JFK, and shortly thereafter, having skillfully maneuvered my classic Bel Air to the right side of the Kennedy, I eased over to the Ohio off ramp.

Then I knew why they had struck when they did.

I also knew who else's life was in danger.

Mine.

I sat up straight and jumped at the thought.

My overworked guardian angel earned a bonus that night. My quick movement caused me to swerve the Bel Air to the far right lane on the off ramp, just as a very large black van, a creature out of a Stephen King film, endeavored to shove me into the retaining wall. Instead of hitting me broadside, the truck struck a glancing blow.

With more skill than I had ever dreamed that I had, I regained control of my trusty steed and leaped ahead of the van. The driver gunned his engine, but he did not have, as my nephews say, eight big ones under the hood. I sped away from him.

Unfortunately, a cab, trying to escape the onrushing van, cut in front of me, slowing my progress. I slammed on the brakes, permitted the van to surge ahead of me, and then cut over to my left, where I was almost demolished by yet another cab. I swerved back to the right, speeded up, and tried to run right by the van driver, who I assume by now was thoroughly befuddled by my evasive actions.

Almost as befuddled as I was.

But another cab cut in front of me, doubtless racing toward some Near North hotel with an executive in a rush.

I was, as they say, a sitting duck for the van. He nudged me, but I refused to yield. He nudged again, harder.

As a last move to escape him, I deliberately swung off the roadway and onto the shoulder. He roared on, unable to slow down. I had escaped him.

Nonetheless my blue-and-white classic hit the wall and climbed up the side of the embankment. Fortunately, its original condition had been modified, to honor the laws of the state, by the addition of seatbelts. Thus when the car finally came to a stop, its nose pointing almost directly toward the sky, I was still safely inside, bruised perhaps, but conscious and still able to move my arms and legs.

Someone, it must have been said angel, suggested that I call the police on the car phone. With unearthly calm, I dialed 911.

"Good even, Officer," I said to the young woman (black to judge by her voice) dispatcher. "This is Bishop Ryan. There's just been an attempt on my life. I am on the Ohio Street off ramp, about a quarter mile west of the river. I'd appreciate it if you could call out the reserves."

Note how skillfully I used my ecclesiastical position. I believe that ability comes with the oils of ordination.

"What kind of a car, Bishop?"

"A 1955 Chevy Bel Air, turquoise and white, Officer, with its nose pointing directly at the Big Dipper."

I was exhilarated, riding along on a wave of excitement and confidence. It did not occur to me that there would be a letdown. Had I not routed the enemy?

"Goodness me, Bishop. I'll send out the Seventh Cavalry right away."

"And the Black Horse Troop should it be still around."

I then punched the number of the Reilly Gallery.

No answer.

I called the Casey apartment at the Hancock Center. Annie answered the phone.

"Anne, would you do me the great good favor of hunting

down your husband and telling him that I am currently on the Ohio Street off ramp, or rather more precisely on the embankment next to it, alive and more or less well, but with a badly damaged classic automobile."

"An accident?" She gasped.

"No indeed. Someone did it deliberately."

"Did you call 911?"

"Indeed. The patrol officer promised the Seventh Cavalry, the Black Horse Troop, and a substantial contingent of the United States Marines."

I must note that while I shivered as I described the incident, I felt little fear at the time. Only anger at the van driver and a perhaps sinful pride that I could beat him.

Which in a way, I suppose, I did.

Almost at once, a whirling blue light appeared next to me and behind it a red light—Chicago and Illinois State cops.

"Are you up there, Bishop?" someone yelled.

"It would appear so."

"Don't try to come down."

"I have no intention of doing so."

"We'll come up and get you."

"Capital."

I returned to the insight, furnished as I believe by a hardworking angel, which had come just before the crash. Oh, yes, I knew why they had tried to kill Clare and why they were after me.

And I had a pretty good idea who they were.

And who Clare Turner really was.

I was removed from the car with considerable care and caution—having been warned several times that I should not loosen my seatbelt, lest by falling backward (toward the ground) I should shift the weight in the car sufficiently to cause it to slide backward on the expressway.

I needed little urging on the matter. The letdown had

come. Try as I might I could not stop the shaking that ran through my body. However, nothing if not skillful at pretending, I emerged from the car with all possible aplomb—a diminutive raja being freed from a recalcitrant elephant.

They deposited me in front of "Commissioner" Casey.

"You all right, Blackie?"

"It would appear so. I would, however, be much better if I were in my room at the cathedral with a glass of Black Bush in my hands. Then arguably my body might stop shaking."

I was greeted at 720 North Wabash by Anne Reilly, the Cardinal, and my senior associate, a child of twenty-nine summers.

"What the hell is this all about, Blackwood?" the Cardinal declaimed. "I told you not to take any chances!"

"An accident?" asked the young priest.

"In the words of Captain Nemo when asked the same question, no, an incident."

I delivered myself, under my own power, to my study. The Cardinal with his own hands poured me the required drink. Then, the young priest having returned to the office downstairs, I explained to Mike and Annie and my Lord Cronin why I thought they had tried to kill both Clare and me, who they were, and who Clare really was.

They listened carefully.

I passed around the letter from Father Rory O'Kelley.

The Cardinal whistled. "It fits perfectly, Blackwood."

"Oh, yes, it does that."

"It's incredible, but it fits." He paused. "And maybe not so incredible after all."

"You'll have to put together some of the pieces," Mike said, studying the letter, "check out a few things."

"Two visits will be necessary," I said, "no, three."

"To whom?" Annie asked—a University of Chicago graduate she always put her pronouns in the proper form.

"To Taylor Street, to Camarillo, California, and to Clare Turner."

"Why to Taylor Street?" the Cardinal demanded.

"To see that the contract is terminated—and if possible who the ones are who are in charge of it."

"And Clare?" Anne asked.

"She has the right to say what is to be done about some of it."

"Indeed she does."

I sipped my drink appreciatively. Among the Cardinal's many virtues is that he has what the Irish would call the heavy hand.

"It's going to create a gosh-awful scandal," the Cardinal said, "not that it should be covered up."

"Can you make it stick, Blackie?" Mike Casey asked.

"There are certain people who played a crucial role," I said, astonished at how much of the Black Bush had disappeared, "who are weak links. When they break, the whole plot will collapse."

"Might they go after these people?"

"Only if they suspect that I have outsmarted them. I think the one in charge is too arrogant to think that. There are, however, other techniques that could be used. Oh, yes, we'll get them, most if not all of them."

"Be careful," the Cardinal and Ms. Reilly said in unison.

"I'll have him under surveillance every minute," Mike assured the others.

"It might be proper to put out the word that Bishop Ryan was slightly injured by a hit-and-run driver on the Ohio Street off ramp this evening and will be confined to the cathedral rectory for the next several days."

"Sipping Black Bush all day long." Mike laughed.

"And drinking apple cinnamon tea," Anne added.

"And devouring chocolate ice cream." The Cardinal finished the litany.

"Hopefully with raspberry sauce," I responded with my most monumental sigh.

It was necessary to phone my siblings and assure them all that, whatever they might hear on the radio, I was fine. "I'm going to be grounded for a couple of days," I assured Packy.

I told the matriarch the whole truth.

"Get the assholes, Punk," she insisted.

"I will indeed."

Nonetheless shortly before noon the next day, aching in virtually every part of my body, despite the fact that the clan had turned my rooms into a massive floral display, I was transported in a nondescript Ford Victoria motorcar to a certain restaurant on Taylor Street where I was to eat pasta with a certain friend of mine who will be nameless, save to say that both his first and last names end in a vowel—though not the same vowel.

Taylor Street is the name of an east-west street on the near West Side of Chicago and, by extension, of the whole neighborhood. It is at the heart of the First Ward, which has always been reputed to be the center of criminal activities in the city. At one time, with different boundaries, the ward was the domain of the famous "Lords of the Levee," aldermen (we had two per ward in those days) "Bathhouse John" Coughlin and "Hinky Dink" Kenna and their business associates, the Everleigh sisters. More recently Taylor Street has become the Old Neighborhood for the Outfit. And most recently, under the impact of the University of Illinois at Chicago and the vast West Side medical center, Taylor Street has gone yuppie—with boutiques, bistros, and bannered lampposts. It has even been renamed—by real estate folk—as "University Village."

The mob, it is said, is bemused by the change. They hate

to see the Old Neighborhood go, but they can, as business-men, savor the appreciating property values.

The street itself, I thought as we rolled down it, had taken on the "artsy-craftsy" look that marks any university area, a mini Ann Arbor or Hyde Park.

Old-fashioned Chicagoan that I am, I liked it better when it was Taylor Street.

It would be inaccurate to say that my luncheon companion was not "connected." However, to be fair one must quickly add that he is "strictly legitimate."

I do not suggest that Outfit money did not go into his busi-ness. I'm sure it did. I am saying rather that, like many oth-ers, "on the West Side," he does not break the law. Indeed those in charge would not let him break the law because he is too useful to them as someone that is legitimate. His particu-lar role is to be a communication link between the "big guys" and the particular part of the business community in which he works.

He will refer to them as "friends of my friends," which is accurate enough, because I doubt that he has ever done more than say "hello" to the Big Tuna or the Lackey at a wedding or a first communion or some other religious rite which the Outfit considers important enough to demand attendance.

I report on his culture. I do not approve of it. Moreover if I were his confessor I would advise him that his behavior was if not dangerous (and it is probably not) at least arguably immoral and he should not do it.

But I'm not his confessor.

Moreover, don't misunderstand me: unlike those who produce films about the Outfit, I think they are evil people, a blight on society.

However, they do have internal rules of their own, the en-forcement of which can redound to the general welfare of so-ciety.

Got it?

Anyway we ate lunch at this certain restaurant on Taylor Street. I will not describe the place were we ate, save to say that it is always very dark, or my friend, save to say that he looks like what he is—a very prosperous businessman.

"Jeez, Father, I heard on the radio you were in an accident. You OK? You look kinda beat up."

"I'll survive."

"Yeah, well glad to hear it. Can't lose a new bishop, can we?"

"There's a problem between you and me," I said, using the language of their culture. "I'd like to work it out. That's why I wanted this sit down."

"Jeez, Father, that's pretty heavy. What did I ever do to you?"

"Some friends of yours tried to put a hit on me."

"Nah, Father, my friends wouldn't do that, I mean the friends of my friends. They wouldn't put a hit on a priest or a bishop. Not in this country, anyway. No way."

I continued to eat my pasta, which was excellent by the way.

"They also tried to kill that girl over at county jail yesterday."

"Hey, Father, they're not into that sort of thing. They have enough trouble as it is, with all these buggings and trials and competition from the foreigners, Mexicans and Colombians and Orientals. These are tough times for the friends of my friends. You read the papers, you know that."

"Then why do they let people mess around with things that are none of their business? Why put out a contract on that kid and on me?"

"Nothing like that goes down in this city unless the friends of my friends know about it."

"That's why there's a problem between them and me."

"Jeez, Father, I don't know what to say."

"And fixing trials, all the way up to the First District, why do they let that happen?"

"Look, Father, I'm not defending it, see, but sometimes people are really innocent even though there's evidence against them, so, you know, it's like fixing a traffic ticket. Get me?"

"No big fix goes down in this city that the friends of your friends don't know about—or take a cut from."

"No one would dare put in the fix without them knowing."

"And fixing it so that an innocent person looks guilty, bribing a judge, a jury foreman, and an appellate judge to convict an innocent person?"

"That's immoral, Father. The friends of my friends, they wouldn't stand for it."

"My point is that they did."

I told him the story the way I thought it went down.

He stared at me, speechless. Then he spoke cautiously. "You sure, Father, you're sure it all went down that way?"

"I don't see how it could be otherwise."

"Jeez! Wow! I mean the friends of my friends won't like that at all. I mean, you read the papers, you know the trouble we have with these court corruption cases. There are some really important people, made guys, if you know what I mean, that are going to have to do time. My friends' friends don't need any more hassle."

"That's what I would have thought."

"I mean it's gotta be some punks who have no respect, that's the trouble, Father, they don't respect men of respect. What can you do!"

"You can stop them."

"Yeah, sure, Father, count on that. The friends of my friends are conservative people. They won't like it when they hear about this at all. They'll find out who did it before the day is over. The guys are punks, I guarantee you that, punks with their brains in their ass."

"They're amateurs," I agreed. "They left too many trails. We're going to break some of them down as it is. But this is a personal thing for me. They ruined my classic car. They tried to kill me. I want it stopped."

His friends' friends would understand about the classic car all right. Actually the insurance company would have to restore it.

"I can guarantee that it will be stopped. The punks responsible . . . well, we'll take care of them. Absolutely."

"No you won't. I want them."

"You want them?"

"I want the cops to arrest them for murder. We need them to clear the kid."

"Oh, yeah, I get you. Sure, that'll go down all right. You can count on it, Father."

"I certainly hope so."

"I'll be back to you first thing in the morning. You can count on it. Absolutely."

"I'll hold you to that promise."

So, feeling like Robert De Niro or Al Pacino, I finished the pasta and ate some spumoni. I then complimented the owner and the chef and left the restaurant to be picked up by my plain black car.

My host promised me at least a dozen more times that I could count on him. Absolutely.

"You feel like Al Pacino?" Mike asked as I got into the car.

"Or Robert De Niro," I admitted. "Or maybe like Special Agent Dale Cooper. Absolutely."

"How did it go?"

"Pretty much as I figured. Some rogue soldiers thought

they could pull a fast one. Now they'll take the heat. Either they do time or they end up in a car trunk someplace. We'll be told who they are, we pick them up and bring them in, they don't admit anything, but we'll have other evidence on them."

"From whom?"

"That depends."

I explained to him how it depended.

"Up to Clare?"

"Doesn't it have to be?"

"You talked to her; Blackie, which way will she choose?"

I thought about it. "The second way, obviously. But that's enough for our purposes. We don't get everyone, but we get enough of them."

28

"I GUESS I WAS PRETTY LUCKY, HUH, FATHER BLACKIE?"
Clare Turner was still immobilized, but conscious and able to talk a little.

"Very lucky. Your guardian angel did a good job."

"Dr. Phelan is cute, isn't he?"

"As cute as Terry?"

"No way . . . and he's married anyway. But he is cute."

"I think, young woman, that the medication is destroying your inhibitions. Be good to Terry."

"Oh, Father, how could I ever be anything else?"

It was not time yet to tell her about Camarillo, California, and the choice she would soon face. That would await my return from California.

In Mike's car again, I had another idea.

I punched in Terry Scanlan's office number, astonished at how skilled I had become with the machine.

"I just saw herself."

"Hey, I thought you were hurt."

"Reports were premature."

"Was it a hit?"

"You bet."

"Why?"

"Tell you later."

"How was she?"

"Dazed from drugs. She still thinks you're a hero."

"Isn't she wonderful?"

"I believe she addressed the same rhetorical question to me about you . . . Your friends in Tucson going to bring in Fred Turner this afternoon?"

"Right. Do you think he'll talk?"

"He'll babble. And they'll send us the videotape, Federal Express, today?"

"They guarantee it."

"Good. Now here's a question to add to the ones they're going to ask."

I told him the question.

"That's a long shot, isn't it?"

"As long as they come, but it's worth asking."

"You've got it figured out, Father Blackie?"

"I'm close."

"Close!" said Mike the Cop, after I had turned off the phone. "That's an understatement."

"There's no point in burdening him with too much information too soon. He's still technically committed to the proposition that Clare is guilty of murder. Besides, only you and Annie and the Cardinal know the whole story. I want to keep it secret till I've filled in some of the blanks. This afternoon I want to check over some old newspaper clippings and a will."

"I'll pick them up for you and bring them to the rectory."

Despite my convalescent condition, I was able to consume a malted milk brought to me by Melissa from the Ice Cream Studio, an emporium just down the street from the cathedral, which makes the best malts in the city.

Then Mike Casey returned with the materials I had requested.

"You'll like them, Blackie," he said. "Just what you thought. Sometimes you scare even me."

I grabbed at the materials and shouted for joy.

"We have them, Mike."

"And there'll be hell to pay."

I sobered instantly. "There sure will. We must protect whomever we can, but it won't be easy."

After Mass the next morning, I was summoned from my breakfast (pancakes with maple syrup, bacon, raspberries, orange juice, and tea) by an urgent phone call.

My friend from the West Side.

"It's all set, Father. The contracts are cancelled. You and the young lady are safe. You can take my word for it. Absolutely."

"I'm happy to hear that."

But I was not about to cancel our protection.

"And you don't have to worry about the trial or anything like that. The friends of my friends are really humiliated by that. They feel disgraced. The punk that organized it all won't be doing anything for a long, long time."

"I'm happy to hear that too."

"And let us have a few more days to clean everything up, and we'll let you have the guys that did the killings. Those are the ones you want?"

"With evidence."

"I'm told that will take care of itself. Absolutely."

Either they had kept all the jewels, I assumed, or the jewels would mysteriously return just before they were arrested.

"I'll be waiting patiently," I said and hung up.

Some progress. We could for the moment do without the go-between, but to clear Clare we absolutely had to have the killers. The evidence I would collect on my flight to California the next day would leave no doubt in anyone's mind who was behind the plot, even if we couldn't prove it in a court of law.

I returned to my breakfast.

The newspapers continued their fight about Clare. The columnist who had been attacking her was now denouncing the county for spending taxpayers' money to keep her in a private hospital. If she were poor and black, he said, she wouldn't be recovering in the lap of luxury.

Red Kane had replied that Clare was paying her own hospital bills and that a number of black prisoners had received the same treatment when they were injured in the jail.

The state's attorney temporized: nothing would be done until the doctors said that it was safe to move Ms. Turner.

I sighed loudly as I ordered more pancakes. Under the influence of my matriarchal sib, "the doctors" would undoubtedly keep her in the hospital for a long time.

Despite the phone conversation with my friend from Taylor Street, the guards would continue in her hospital room.

Then Terry Scanlan appeared in the cathedral dining room with a videotape cassette. "I picked it up at the Fed Ex terminal at O'Hare."

There would be no chance, none at all, for a second round of pancakes.

"I haven't played it yet," he said as we adjourned to my study. "I talked to them last night. They were very happy with the interview."

"Capital."

I am quite incapable of making a VCR work. Normally I summon one of my associates to make mine function. The young priest is always amused that the pastor is an electronic illiterate—I get no points for being able to work a computer because, as it is explained to me, even an infant can do that. In this particular instance, however, I let Terry take charge.

Fred Turner, suntanned and prosperous in a beige sports

jacket and bolo tie, looked relaxed and confident on the screen. I assumed that, although we couldn't see them, he was wearing cowboy boots.

"You understand, Mr. Turner, that this interview is being conducted at the request of the Cook County State's Attorney's Office?"

"I do."

"You also understand that you have the right to refuse to participate in this interview?"

"Yes."

"You further understand that you may refuse to answer any of my questions and you have the right also to demand that your lawyer be present?"

"Sure."

"Finally you understand that in the absence of this interview, Cook County authorities might seek your extradition to answer questions in connection with a murder?"

"I have nothing to hide."

"Fine. Now my first question: did you visit your late brother the afternoon he was murdered?"

"I did." Fred squirmed. "I did not admit this to the Lakewood police because, first of all, they didn't ask me, and second of all, I understand that my brother died after seven-thirty. Thus my presence in his home three or four hours prior to that time seemed to be irrelevant."

"Why are you willing to discuss it now?"

"Because the Chicago cops have been told, apparently by the lovely lady next door, that she saw me enter my brother's house. I can't imagine why that matters almost a year later, especially since there has been a jury verdict in the case."

"Did you go to Chicago specifically to visit John Turner?"

"Well, not specifically, I did have an interview with a banker about some loans and I did meet with him. But I took an early plane because I was going to use the occasion to visit Jack."

"Also to seek a loan?"

"Well," he frowned, "as a matter of fact yes."

"Can you describe your visit?"

"The door to the house was open. I would later learn that Mary, my late sister-in-law, and the servants were shopping in the Lakewood Mall."

"So?"

"So I went in and climbed upstairs and then down again to my brother's workshop."

"Was he glad to see you?"

"Jack was never pleased at an interruption. He was civil, however. He explained to me that he was working on a gimmick which would enable drivers to get seventy-five miles a gallon."

"How did you react to that?"

"I guess I laughed. My brother is . . . was a genius. I thought the idea was crazy, but I admitted to him that if anyone could do it, he would be the person."

"Than you asked him for a loan?"

"More like a cash advance."

"For how much?"

Fred waved his hand dismissively. "A couple hundred thou. Short-term till I could resolve my cash flow problem."

"And he declined?"

"That was Jack's way—God be good to him—he'd bluntly refuse one day and denounce my spendthrift ways. I'd tell him that I had always paid him back eventually. And he would say that made no difference, he didn't approve of my ventures and he would not be part of them."

"It was a brief meeting then."

"Not too brief, a half hour or so. We did not argue or quarrel; that wasn't our way. Finally I said good-bye and left the workshop. I did tell him that I'd stop back on the morrow.

"I wanted to talk to Mary and also to give my greetings to the child, Karen is it?"

"You would ask for the money again on your return?"

"Naturally. That's how it always happened. He'd agree to give me a cash advance."

"So you were not angry when you left the Turner house?"

"No, not angry. I will confess that I did not enjoy the ritual of asking twice. But it was his money, after all, and he could advance it any way he wanted."

"Interest free?"

"Oh yes. But when other projects of mine were successful, projects in which he had invested some of his money, I'd pay him interest anyway. He would thank me courteously, but I don't think the interest payment made any difference to him."

"How much did you owe him at that time?"

"Oh, let me see, not much. Six, maybe seven, big ones. I've paid most of it back since then—into the estate. Karen might need something when she finally gets out of jail."

"You mean Clare Turner?"

"That's right, Clare. Poor kid, it must have been a dull place for a bright girl. Jack and Mary were nice people and generous too. But stodgy, know what I mean?"

"So you went back to O'Hare at what time?"

"Perhaps four o'clock. I bumped into Mary coming in the house with her groceries. She wanted me to stay for supper. I told her I had to go back to O'Hare for a meeting, but, weather permitting, I'd stop in again the next day."

"Your meeting had already occurred?"

"Oh, no, I met with the banker back at the Westin."

"On Saturday?"

"It was kind of an emergency meeting. But the Lakewood

police have checked that out. They have testimony that I really was at a meeting, before supper."

"You thought it wiser to ask again the following day, rather than making your second request after you had a cup of coffee with your sister-in-law?"

"That's exactly right. John always needed to sleep on it before making a cash advance."

"And you returned the next morning to find him dead? Wasn't the news already on the radio?"

"I don't like to listen to news broadcasts when I'm driving."

"You did receive a substantial legacy from your brother, did you not?"

"I'd say a modest bequest, given his wealth. Of course I haven't seen a penny of it yet."

"But you were able to borrow on expectations of that inheritance."

"Right. It turned things around for me. Now I'm in great shape, better than ever."

"You did not kill your brother and his wife?"

"Oh my goodness no. I wouldn't be able to do something like that. I can't stand the sight of blood."

"Yet you have no alibi for that night."

"I'm afraid not. If I were the killer I would have made sure that someone in the hotel remembered me, would I not?"

"Perhaps . . . Was there anyone coming in the house when you left?"

"Only a plumbing truck which had just pulled up. Mary said that there was a leak in one of the pipes."

"Did you by any chance note the license number?"

"As a matter of fact, I did. It was rather unusual, one of those vanity plates with letters PALUMB on it. It struck me at the time that they didn't need the letter *A*."

"That's all." Terry pushed a reverse button. "I'll call for the license."

I busied myself with the essential task of making mid-morning tea—Earl Grey at that time of day of course.

"The license," Terry looked up from a piece of notepaper, "has been issued to a seemingly legitimate plumbing company in Highwood. Palumbo Brothers—hence the extra *A*. Should we bring them in?"

"Not for the moment. I think you'd want to have a word or two, as they say in English mysteries, with the McLaughlins. They didn't tell us about all the traffic that afternoon."

"Right. They're in Florida. If necessary I'll go down there and interrogate them."

"First, make sure they're there. You might also want to interview Ladd Crane, or is it Crane Ladd? Mike Casey tells me that he has made substantial sums of money this year—in cash."

"The jury was bribed?"

"That seems obvious, bribed for a conviction not for an acquittal, which is usually the case."

"Wow!"

"It is possible that Mr. Crane or Mr. Ladd, whichever is correct, will want to tell you who gave him the money."

"Bribes have always gone the other way."

"So now you have an exception. I'm sure that Judge O'Malley and Judge Block have made recent deposits, most likely offshore, sometime this year."

"So that explains it. I thought Boyle Michael was stupid. I didn't think he had been bought."

"Arguably both. If he had been more restrained he would have served his masters better."

"And his masters are?"

"That remains to be seen . . . The distinguished Dan Hills knows of your current activity?"

"Sure. And he approves."

"He will find the information about the two judges interesting, no doubt."

"He sure will . . . Are you going to be able to figure out who the mastermind is?"

"I already know. I must collect some evidence first. I'm planning a little trip tomorrow for that purpose . . . How's Clare?"

"Much, much better, Father Blackie. She remembers you praying over her."

"Remarkable. I note that the district attorney is ignoring media demand that she be moved to County Hospital."

"The protests outside his home finally got to him. To say nothing of Red Kane."

"Indeed."

"I'm glad the Ryans are on my side."

"On certain occasions we are useful . . . What does one hear of the plans of the Illinois Supreme Court?"

"Clare's attorneys are seeking immediate relief. They argue that the First District's delay was unconscionable. We're not opposing quick action. My guess is that they'll order her release on bail almost at once and consider the appeal in a more leisurely fashion. Can't tell for sure. They may be embarrassed by the behavior of the lower courts and act quickly."

"To order a new trial."

"Right. And it will take us a couple of weeks to make up our minds whether a new trial is justified."

"More than enough time," I murmured. "I may be able to clear this problem up by the beginning of next week."

After Terry had floated out of the rectory on his fluffy cloud of love, I made a chart for the events at the Turner house the previous winter.

Noon–1:00—John and Mary Turner come out of the

workshop. Mary drives to the Lakewood Mall with the McLaughlins. John walks over to visit April Kincaid.

1:30—John returns to his home.

2:00—Dick Martin arrives at the Turner house, allegedly to pick up computer output.

2:30—Martin leaves; April Kincaid arrives.

3:00—April leaves; Fred Turner arrives.

3:30—Mary Turner comes home, with the McLaughlins in tow (presumably); Fred Turner leaves, just as the Palumbo van appears.

5:30—Clare returns home, with Fiona.

7:30—Mary Turner talks to April Kincaid on the phone. Snow begins to fall.*

9:00—April tries to call the Turners in their workshop and fails.*

I added an * after the last two times:

* Mr. Kincaid confirms calls.

The outline was consistent with my theory. Now I had to find the proof to make my theory stick.

29

"**MY PEOPLE WILL FOLLOW YOU ALL THE WAY,**" MIKE Casey assured me as we sped toward O'Hare. "We're taking no chances that your friend from the West Side isn't telling you the whole truth."

"Capital."

"You won't see them, so don't bother looking. But if you sense you are being followed, the reason will be that you are being followed."

"Indeed."

We were driving in his plain black Ford Victoria toward O'Hare International Airport.

"You'll be coming back early on Saturday?"

"A day to get there, a day at Camarillo, and a day to return."

"Time to visit Lisa Malone and her family."

"Naturally."

Lisa had been my grammar school sweetheart—after a fashion.*

The car phone rang. "Commissioner, this is Terry Scanlan. Is himself in the car with you?"

"He is."

*See *Happy Are the Clean of Heart.*

"We can't find the McLaughlins."

"What!"

"They've disappeared from their job in Florida."

"Find them, Terry, it is absolutely essential that you find them. And extradite them to Chicago. No video interviews with them."

"We'll try."

"Trying isn't good enough. It is imperative that you get them. Now. Today. At once."

"I'm not sure that I'd want to work for you." Mike the Cop chuckled. "I never gave an order like that when I was commissioner."

"Good for you."

"Grumpy this morning."

"Angry."

"At what?"

"Evil."

"That's reasonable."

The legend is that Blackie Ryan does not get grumpy, save when he hasn't had a chance to eat his breakfast. My young associates might want to dispute that, however.

The truth, I suspect, is that I never become grumpy with women, a fact which on the whole gains me much merit.

Early the next morning, satisfied with breakfast, but exhausted from the harrowing ordeal of flying from Chicago to Los Angeles (if God had meant us to travel in such fashion She would have given us feathers or aluminum bodies), I arrived at St. Eustace's Church in Camarillo. The good Eustace, you will recall, is the patron of hunters; in Rome antlers replace the cross above the facade of the church. In California, however, he is honored with the typical pseudo Spanish Mission architecture.

The parish "plant"—church, rectory, convent, school, and gym—was surrounded by expensive homes. If Father

O'Kelley had needed money for his building fund twenty-two years before, his successor apparently had no such worries.

The successor turned out to be a man of my age with a long blond beard and the build of a linebacker. He was dressed in gray slacks and a sport shirt.

"Happy to meet you, Bishop Ryan." He extended a huge paw. "Most bishops that come around here stay up on the hill in the seminary."

"I don't think I'd fit up there."

"That would do you credit." He laughed genially. "Come on into my office. How can I help?"

I passed the faded letter across the desk to him.

"The old man again. He was a crafty FBI—Foreign Born Irishman—if there ever was one."

"Did he keep records on this sort of matter?"

"Oddly enough he did. He kept records on everything which involved money. There wasn't much up here then. They retired him from the seminary because he was too liberal. He was determined to show them how to run a parish. He did, that's for sure."

"You inherited these records?"

"I did. I glanced at them and sealed them up. Someone might think his annual Christmas appeal to those folks was a form of blackmail. I've thought of burning them, but I hesitate to do that."

"The name is Turner."

"I can see that . . . I'm reluctant to betray confidences, Bishop."

"That does you credit, Father. However, in this instance a young woman's freedom and arguably her life are at stake."

He considered me carefully. "Is there something that you can tell me that I'll find in his file which will confirm the need?"

I removed a piece of notepaper from his desk, wrote two names on it, folded the paper, and put it in front of him on the desk.

"Remove the Turner file from your archives, Father, and then look at the names I've written on this paper."

"Fair enough." He grinned and bounced out of his chair. "Give me a minute to plow through his stuff. He never kept it in any order."

While he was gone, I made a credit card call on the rectory phone.

"Did you find the McLaughlins?"

"Still looking. We have a few leads."

"Find them. It's imperative."

I hung up and waited for the return of the pastor.

"OK, I have the file. They did send a check every year while he was alive. Are they still alive?"

"No, they died this past winter."

He picked up the notepaper with my two names on it, glanced at the names, and then considered the file.

"You got it, Father. I'm impressed."

He handed the file over to me. Sure enough, marriage certificate, baptismal certificate, funeral certificate, even a picture of a happy, grinning little girl child, the same picture as the one I had found at the Turner house. I placed the picture on the desk, reached into my wallet, and matched it with its twin.

"You're the detective, aren't you?" the priest said. "The one they call Blackie?"

"Arguably."

"I didn't realize they made you a bishop."

"I do my best not to realize it either."

"Well, you've done a good job on this one, all right. Is she still called Laura?"

"No, her name is Clare now."

"Another pretty name . . . You want copies of these?"

"Indeed."

"Only take a minute."

This time I called my Lord Cronin.

"Got it."

"What you expected?"

"All of it."

"Astonishing, Blackwood."

"Elementary . . . Inform Mike the Cop if you will."

"As soon as you hang up . . . A lot is up to her now, isn't it?"

"She must decide whether she is Clare or Laura."

"When will you see her?"

"On the way in from the airport."

30

"CLARE, FATHER BLACKIE," SHE SAID FIRMLY. "I'LL ALways be Clare. That's final. I don't want to be Laura."

"Your natural parents loved you very much, Clare."

"How do you know that?"

"Because you are who you are. I'm sure your shrink will confirm that."

"That's what she keeps saying, but can't I be Clare and still love them and be grateful for their love?"

"Surely."

"That's what I'll do then."

I had shown her the materials from the safe in Lakewood and from St. Eustace's parish, even the picture of the legs of her natural parents. The documents told her who she was. She realized immediately who was trying to kill her and why.

She had listened to my narration with an impassive face and no hint of tears in her eyes.

"They were so young, Father. My real mom, I guess I should say my natural mom, was six years younger when she brought me into the world than I am now."

"Young and innocent in a youthful and innocent age, the last moments of it."

"The pain for the other person must have been terrible. Only terrible pain can make you do that sort of thing."

"You're very generous, Clare Turner."

"Am I? I don't think so, Father Blackie. I merely know who I am and I intend to continue to be that."

"A wise decision. I presume you will share it with that nice boy of yours."

She smiled as she had when we discussed the boy at county jail. "I'm sure he'll agree. I'm a very fortunate woman to have him loving me."

"One could make the case that he is fortunate too."

Back at the rectory there was a message from my Taylor Street friend. I called him before I took my coat off.

"I got the names for you, Father."

"Palumbo, Highwood. Specialists with knives, I believe, but not all that bright."

"Jeez, Father! How did you figure that out?"

"A couple of good clues."

"Well, the friends of my friends, like I say, really feel disgraced. These guys are punks, and not such young punks either. It was a big contract too. Lots of big ones. They thought they could pull it off without telling any of the friends of my friends. If these friends knew, they would have forbidden it."

Or at least demanded a cut.

"I'm glad to hear that."

"We can't let you have the broker, but he's in big trouble anyway. It'll be a long time before he does anything like this again. If ever."

"I understand."

"And, Father, the dummies still have the stuff. They've kept it in their place up in Highwood ever since. Too greedy to give it to a fence. I don't understand what's getting into people these days, know what I mean?"

"Indeed."

I then phoned Terry Scanlan. "Two things, Ter, I've just explained to the fair Clare who she really is. She's taken it well, but you probably should get over there and talk to her."

"Right away."

"Hold it for a minute. What about the McLaughlins?"

"We know where they are. I think we can have them picked up tomorrow."

"Capital. Bring in the Palumbos too. And check out their shop and homes. I have reason to believe you'll find all the evidence you need there."

"After we get the McLaughlins."

"Precisely. Right after."

"You know who the mastermind is?"

"I do. I'll handle that tomorrow morning myself and be back to you."

I then paid my respects to the Lord Cardinal.

He was packing his crimson robes for a confirmation that night.

"Well done, Blackwood." The hoods pulled back from his eyes and the light of victory shone for a couple of seconds. "Well done."

"There remains the one behind it all."

"You will take care of that?"

"Tomorrow morning. I don't want to approach the subject without a good night's sleep."

"What do you think will happen?"

"I have no idea."

"Can you prove involvement?"

"Maybe. Maybe not. I may not have to. When the exemplary Dan Hills finds out about it, he will surely want to indict."

"It'll be a mess."

"Indeed."

"And Clare?"

"Elects to remain Clare."

"That's terribly generous."

"Happy are the merciful," I said.

The Cardinal nodded. "For they shall obtain mercy."

"I will report before noon tomorrow."

"Be careful, Blackwood. That one is very dangerous."

"I'll have Mike and one of his stalwarts waiting downstairs."

31

THE PERSON IN QUESTION WAS NOT HAPPY TO SEE ME.
We were sitting in the parlor of the two-story coopera-
tive apartment, looking out on North Lake Shore Drive and
the lake. It was a gray autumn day with the smell of yet another rainstorm in the air. The lake was a flat, dull gray, the
same color as the sky, without a horizon line—appropriate
background for the conversation.

The other person seemed sick, wasted, exhausted—at
least ten years older than the last time we'd met.

"My first point is that a number of other people have the
same materials that I do. Hence there is no point in repeating
the attempt on my life for which you were responsible the
other night."

"I don't know what you're talking about."

"Yes you do. Moreover, we know everything that you've
done, all the way back to setting up the McLaughlins to spy
on John and Mary Turner. You arranged to have them working in that Irish castle when the Turners were in Ireland.
They preyed on the Turners' generosity."

"You're drunk."

"Hardly. We know about the Palumbos, about Ladd
Crane, about Judges O'Malley and Block, and about the at-

309

tempted murders last week. In point of fact we know everything that there is to know."

"You must be mad. Please leave at once or I shall summon
security."

"Your worst mistake was to order that I be killed the same
day that Clare was stabbed. It occurred to me immediately
that only those who supped with me at the Cardinal's that
night were aware I was pursuing the question of Clare Turner's origins. I knew enough about your family to have a
pretty good idea why. After that it was easy."

"I am ringing for security." She rose with difficulty from
her chair.

"Most important of all, we have Laura Wrobleski's baptismal certificate, the marriage certificate of Lance Corporal
Thomas Wrobleski and Mary Diane Leyden, and the certificate of their burial in the Catholic cemetery in Camarillo,
California." I laid copies of these items on the coffee table in
front of her. "We have correspondence between the pastor of
St. Eustace's parish and the Turners and a picture of Laura as
a little girl from both the pastor's files and from the Turners'
files."

Teresa Leyden sat down again. She began to finger her allegedly golden rosary.

"We have the little item in the *Tribune* about the
Wrobleskis' death in an auto accident, only a month after her
brother was killed in a battle over Hanoi, May of 1968. You
managed to keep out of the paper the fact that they had a little daughter."

She glared at me with implacable hatred.

"And with good reason. Your father-in-law had designed
his will in such a way that the inheritance would be passed
down to eldest children and to their eldest children. Your son
John died in combat. A week later your father-in-law died.

Mary Diane was therefore the rightful heiress to the Leyden family wealth.

"You may have had her killed, I'm not certain about that, but you're capable of it."

"No!" she screamed.

"In any event, when Tom and Mary Diane died, their infant daughter became the heiress. You feared that Tom's parents, ignorant Polish immigrants that they were in your opinion, might win control of the Leyden fortune—if they ever found out about the will. So you spirited Laura away and gave her to the Turners, who wanted a child to adopt. That way you could keep an eye on her and make sure she would never find out who she really was. I can't understand why you didn't have her snuffed out when she was an infant."

"I thought of it. She was my granddaughter. I didn't have the heart to kill her."

"Until you learned that she was searching for her natural parents—the night she spoke to the Cardinal about it in your presence. Moreover, you were afraid that the Turners might guess who she was. Perhaps she looked something like Mary Diane."

"The same hair . . . They were suspicious; I could tell that. He would have taken everything away from us, everything."

"You were determined that all the work you'd done for forty years to build up and protect the Leyden family fortune would be passed on to the one whom you considered to be the rightful heir, your son Tim, born while your husband was flying in Korea, and possibly Old Tim's son rather than your husband's."

"You're the devil incarnate."

"No, however ineptly, I am on the other side. So you decided that it was necessary to do away with both the Turners and Laura/Clare. You hired an Outfit thug to arrange it.

Through him you corrupted judges and ordered the attack on Clare and later that day on me. It was a brilliant, ruthless scheme, and it failed because Judge O'Malley is a fool and because you overreached."

"You'll never be able to prove any of that."

"The major weakness in your plot was the locked room. There was no possibility of blaming Clare for the murder as long as there wasn't a second key. The McLaughlins were too dumb to figure that out and so were the Palumbos. It was the puzzle that saved Clare."

"Mary Diane," she closed her eyes, "was a provoking child from the day she was born. I sent her to the University of San Diego so she would receive a good solid, conservative Catholic education. Instead she married that Polish marine . . . Do you know what the Poles did in my hometown, Bishop? They cleaned up the slop at the packing house. Do you think I was going to let them take away the family fortune for which I had worked so hard? They are inferior and degraded human beings. They would spend it, waste it, squander it!"

"Casey Piowar is a degraded human being?"

"A vulgar little man with absurd pretensions . . ." She twisted the rosary in her fingers. "The money is mine not that stupid child's. It belongs to me and to my loyal son, to Young Tim. If I had to kill two hundred men and women to protect what is rightfully ours, I would gladly do so and without the slightest touch of guilt."

"You say that murder is not immoral?"

"I am confident that God approves of what I did." She opened her eyes wide and stared at me with burning hatred. "I'm only sorry that we didn't kill you. You're a depraved little wart. You don't deserve to live."

"Arguably."

Grief, anger, hatred, suffering, loneliness, pain had

twisted the personality of the bright young WAAC who had come home from the war with John Leyden. All that was left now was a single-minded dedication to preserving the money for her son, the last remnant of her dreams. She was pathetic, but still dangerous.

"And don't think you're going to send me to jail for what I did. I'll be dead before you can bring me to court. I'm entering the hospital tomorrow. You'll never see me alive again."

"So be it," I said, realizing that she was telling the truth. I rose to leave. There was little more to be said.

"At least I will not have to live to see that little Polish frump taking over everything that is rightfully mine."

At the door I turned to face her. "In your last days on this earth, Mrs. Leyden, you might want to ponder the fact that your plot and your murders were unnecessary."

"What do you mean?"

"Clare is her mother's daughter, as strong-willed and as independent as Mary Diane. She will make no claim on the Leyden estate. Indeed she authorized me to tell you that she would not accept a penny of Leyden money even if offered on a golden platter."

"I don't believe you," she stammered.

"Suit yourself." I shrugged. "Nonetheless, Young Tim's inheritance is not in danger and never was."

"Impossible." She steadied herself against a chair.

"Think of how happy your last years might have been if you had been willing to trust her."

I walked out of the apartment and closed the door.

32

IN THE NEXT TWO WEEKS A NUMBER OF EVENTS, SEEMINGLY unconnected, occurred.

The Illinois Supreme Court, in the strongest possible terms, reversed the conviction of Clare Turner and ordered a new trial.

On leaving the hospital a free woman, Clare Turner announced that she would use her inheritance to found three chairs at Loyola in honor of her parents. The trust fund, she legally could not touch, because it was her father's wish she use it for her own life and "for the college education of my children, if I ever have any." What was left over would go to charities of various sorts, including, she said, Holy Name Cathedral, which was now her parish.

Asked by reporters if she would sue the State for its prosecution of her, she replied, "Certainly not. If it had not been for the work of Mr. Scanlan and Ms. Burke I would still be in jail. They're excellent lawyers. I much prefer having them on my side."

Jane Martin greeted her at the entrance of the hospital in the company of a large canine who seemed beside herself with joy.

You say that she seemed to ignore the contribution made

by the Most Reverend John Blackwood Ryan, D.D. (*honoris causa*), Ph.D.? Who was now in fact arguably due the respect she owed to her pastor?

Only because that hierarch warned her of the most solemn excommunication if she mentioned his name.

The Palumbo brothers were arrested and accused of the murder of John and Mary Turner. The missing jewelry was found in the garage where they stored their van.

The McLaughlins were extradited from Florida. Dermot blamed his wife for cooperating in the murder of the Turners. They admitted their guilt, identified the Palumbos, and turned State's evidence.

Judge B. Michael O'Malley retired from the Circuit Court of Cook County.

Judge Conrad Block left the First District Appellate Court to return to private practice.

Crane Ladd made substantial donations to charity.

Terry Scanlan left the State's Attorney's Office to become deputy corporation counsel.

Clare Turner was elected chairman of the Turner Endowment and chairman of the board of Turner Electronics.

Joseph Seritella, a middle-level soldier in the mob, was found dead in the trunk of his own car on a side road in Northern Indiana.

Teresa Leyden entered Passavant Hospital in the terminal stages of inoperable cancer of the liver.

"You know that Mrs. Leyden who's dying over at Passavant?" one of my young priests asked me.

"I've heard of her, yes."

"There's a gorgeous, and I mean gorgeous, young woman in there with her every day. The old woman clings to her hand all day long."

"Indeed?"

"I think it's that Clare Turner you got out of jail."

"Ah?"

"You know how to pick them, Boss."

"I try."

The Cardinal said Mrs. Leyden's funeral Mass and preached. I was deputed to preside over the ceremony at All Saints Cemetery on the boundary between Chicago and Evanston.

Next to Tim Leyden and his wife and kids, clad in mourning black, stood Clare Turner.

"You think I'm really weird, don't you, Father Blackie?"

"Rather I think of the words of the Founder—'Happy are the merciful for they shall obtain mercy.' "

"She was my grandmother, after all."

"Indeed."

"Maybe Jesus should have said those happy ones who obtain mercy will be merciful."

"Arguably."

Later that week, at a highly secret meeting between Clare Turner and her lawyer (who was also a deputy corporation counsel) and Tim Leyden and his lawyer, Ms. Turner signed a quit claim to all Leyden family properties.

"Can I do anything in return, Clare?" he said awkwardly.

"Nothing" was her crisp response.

"I hope we can be friends."

"Cousins," she said with a quick movement of her lips which her own attorney had learned to interpret with a smile.

"The past can be forgotten?"

"It must be forgotten."

"Suppose that, as a gesture of, ah, renewal, we turn over our share of Turner Electronics to the Endowment—for the benefit of Catholic schools."

"That's very generous, Tim," she said in some confusion. "It's not necessary, however."

"It's what I want to do."

"I . . ."

"My client," said Terry Scanlan, "will take it and run." That was that.

So Clare completed her medical education and, with a few waivers from the school, was told she could graduate in January. She was also accepted into a residency program in psychiatry at Northwestern University Hospital.

Thus it fell out that I was entertaining Clare and her faithful attorney at lunch in the Chicago Yacht Club. It was a gray day, and the lake had been converted once more into an ice palace, an impression softened by the pre-Christmas lights in the club.

"You must," I insisted as we browsed around the salad table, "save room for at least three desserts. I favor the raspberry tart, the white chocolate mousse with raspberry sauce, and the flourless chocolate cake."

"I'd say the priest has an addiction, wouldn't you, Doctor?" suggested Terry Scanlan.

"Harmless addiction and harmless priest," I pleaded.

They both chortled with what I thought was a conspicuous lack of respect.

Back at our table, Clare began the conversation. "It's all over now, Father Blackie, and all's well that ends well, I guess."

"More or less."

"But I don't understand the locked room puzzle. How do you explain that?"

"It was imperative that the room be locked so that only you could get into it. Otherwise any one of a number of other people might have been suspects. But the other side of the coin was that if it were locked, you couldn't get in. I'm afraid the Palumbos couldn't cope mentally with just one key."

"But how did they do it?"

"As I told your companion here it was the phenomenon of Fiona not barking at night. If she slept the sleep of the good dog, the murder had already been committed before you came home from school. If that were true, it meant that the call to Ms. Kincaid was a fake. Who would fake such a call, obviously Moire McLaughlin. Hence my guess that she was an actress. The blizzard was unanticipated good luck for them, because it provided two locked rooms—but locked in both cases not before the murder as everyone thought but after."

"Everyone but you." Terry speared a piece of smoked salmon.

"I saw the matter differently because I began with the presumption that the virtuous and exemplary Clare was the victim rather than the victimizer. I asked who would want to arrange it so that she would be charged with murder and how such a person might go about plotting that outcome. It would, incidentally, have been much more difficult to prove you innocent if the Palumbos had followed instructions and left all the jewels in your car and put them in the trunk instead of the front seat."

"So it was finished before I came home from school?"

"Absolutely."

"But how did they do it?"

"I presume your parents told Moire they would take a nap before supper. Characteristically they left the door unlocked as they had done all day. Moire told the plumbers that now was the time. They did their work quickly. Then they discovered the problem of the unlocked door. I would imagine they departed hastily, leaving the problem to the McLaughlins. These latter worthies then took turns staying in the death room and locking it from the inside until you rang their quarters in the early morning."

"How ghastly."

"Indeed but there was an enormous amount of money riding on success—hundreds of thousands of dollars at a minimum—and the crime had already been committed. Remember that you never saw them together until the next morning."

"What if Ms. Kincaid had not called?"

"I'm sure that was not part of their plan. They probably had another method for awakening you."

"So when I called Dermot, Moire was hiding in the workshop?"

"Behind the curtains I would imagine. You ran out of the workshop to make your phone calls to priest, cop, and doctor. She then scurried through the door and back to their quarters, whence she would emerge in a few minutes to console you."

"But what if I had called from the workshop?"

"Then Dermot would have escorted you away from the grisly scene and upstairs and thence out to the front of the house. Moire would have followed the same procedure as I've just described. It required courage and acting skill, but as I've said they expected a substantial payoff from the unfortunate Mr. Seritella of happy memory."

My two guests were silent for a moment.

"If I say amazing," Terry Scanlan said as we rose to assault the main course buffet, "will you say elementary?"

"Doubtless."

"Amazing."

"Elementary."

As we consumed our desserts (they did follow my advice, and under the principle of "waste not, want not," chose three desserts), Terry turned to his beloved. "You've been incredibly generous, Clare. I'm proud of you."

"Not really. They were all things that should have been done."

"What I don't understand, however, is what you get out of it."

I knew the answer, but the good priest knows when to keep his mouth shut.

She pointed at him. "You!"

Then she smiled, this time a complete and total smile.

For a moment, just a moment, all the lights in Chicago seemed to go out.

ROBERT B. PARKER'S
NATIONWIDE BESTSELLERS!